I0653058

Lands of Legend

Rise of the Tong

(Book I of The **LOL/ROFL** Series)

Author: Daniel Thorman

Imprint: Independently published

Other books by this author include
(or soon will)

The Osten Chronicles

I   Mayhem at the Mill
II   Chaos in the Caravan
III   Calamity at Conclave
IV   Bedlam in the Bog
V   A Royal Ruckus

Lands of Legend

I   Rise of the Tong
II   The Zodiac Quest
III   Gritters (Coming Soon)
IV   Gritters in Space (Someday maybe)
V   Gritters on Mars (See previous)

Dedication

In loving memory of **Ruth Anne Thorman**
Whose empathy nurtured me and helped me to feel.

CHAPTER ONE

Monkey Business

猴

"Hey, loser," said the boy across the aisle.

David looked up from his phone. It was an older model. It couldn't load the game, but at least he could review the character's stats.

"I think this is your stop."

"Uh, thanks," said David awkwardly, pocketing the phone.

Everyone swayed forward in their seats as the bus lurched to a full stop with a hiss of air brakes. Taking up his book bag, David made his stumbling way up the aisle to the front. A paper wad struck the back of his head. He ignored it. He felt his classmate's eyes on him as he started up the walkway, and the bus rolled forward once more. His was an embarrassingly meager dwelling in the poorer section of Cincinnati's West Side, not that those who rode his bus could brag of any better. He scooped up the newspaper from his overgrown lawn. No one actually read the thing anymore, but it made the place look even more depressing if he let them stack up.

Stepping up to the townhouse door, David wasn't surprised to find it locked. There were no lights on inside, and there was no response when he rang the bell. His mother was likely 'out on errands' again. He made his way over to the single garage door and keyed in the entry code. He ducked inside once it had rattled halfway open. Sure enough, her car was nowhere in sight. Dad usually parked his truck out on the street, but he wouldn't be off work for several hours more at least, if even then.

David knew his father was a workaholic. He ran the Delhi Home and Garden Center up on the pike. As it was springtime, David hardly ever *saw* the man. He was forever pottering around with his plants or out at a work site laying out the landscaping. You would think that a man in the plant business would have a nurturing nature, but he always seemed worn out when he finally did come home. He would barely say three words at dinner and promptly retire to his home office shortly after that.

So it was unsurprising that David found himself home alone this Friday afternoon. He thought about making a snack, but instead headed straight to his room at the back of the house. He couldn't wait to create his first Realms character. It had been a tough sell to mom to buy him the visor required to play the game properly. There were desktop versions, of course, but that was a far less immersive experience - not at all what the critics were raving about.

Carefully removing the visor from its packaging, David jacked it into the upright unit, which served as both the central processor and a treadmill. He'd had that for years, of course. It was part of the prior generation's gaming gear. He was surprised that the adapter still fit into his old rig. It made sense, though. If NexGen Cybernetics wanted to sell many visors, he figured they'd better make them backward compatible with as many gaming rigs as were out there.

Although it was probably unnecessary for this session, David snapped on the motion-sensing wristbands and anklets before firing the system up. A row of blinking green lights showed the device had been recognized and was ready for output. Stepping up onto the platform, David lowered the Visor and gripped the handles of his Treadie 2000. It would take a minute for the system to register his heart rate and other biometrics. But it was ready soon enough.

[Weight: 126 pounds]

[Heart Rate: 88 beats per minute]

[Likely Identity: David Grimes]

[Is this correct?]

"Yes," the boy replied, making a quick adjustment to the flexible arm of the mic-pad which descended from the Visor's right earpiece. A new message scrolled across the Visor's screen.

[New equipment detected. Is the text size and font optimal?]

"Close enough," said David.

[Repeat the following statement so that Treadie may register your new voiceprint: "My name is David Grimes"]

He did so, only to be confronted by a new system message.

[Testing audio range. You will hear a tone in your left ear, your right ear, or both at once. On hearing a tone, squeeze the corresponding handle of your Treadie 2000]

So much for plug-and-play, thought the boy, irritated by the delay. This went on for an interminable two or three minutes before the main system menu finally came up.

[How may Treadie 2000 be of service today?]

"I would like to play Realms."

[Application: 'Realms' is not on file. Would you like to mow lawn?]

"Uh...no," said the boy, peering over his Visor and casting his gaze around the room. There it was - the box with the sales slip he'd retained. It had his unique user ID number. It was lying on the shelf just beside him. Reading from it, he said: "The full name of the app is 'Lands of Legend / Realms of Forgotten Lore'. I loaded it just yesterday."

In truth, the name was a little hard to forget. The game designers must really have a sense of humor to name it LOL/ROFL.

"Please verify installation and assign the nickname 'Realms' to this app."

[Logged and so noted.]

[Now loading 'Realms'.]

[Have a pleasant day and simply release both handles to pause or emerge from game software.]

The message faded to be replaced by a roiling mist and the blare of cinematic music from both earphones.

An oriental dragon coiled up from the background, growing ever larger as it came. Metallic gold in color with a horned head, it swelled to fill the sky. From its angular snout, jagged rows of frightful teeth protruded from an open maw. He could almost hear the beating of its nonexistent wings as it swept by just above. During this fearsome overflight, the dragon unleashed a blast of crimson flame that crackled as it filled his view, causing David to flinch aside.

The flames soon parted to reveal a set of golden letters. "LANDS OF LEGEND," they read. These filled his entire screen, looming like a cliff in the near distance. At the bottom of the heads-up display, a spinning question mark was prompting David to 'log in'.

This is it, he thought. I finally get to see what's got everyone so fired up. The cinematography was excellent. So much better than staring at a flat screen. He could still see that mist swirling about in his peripheral vision and could almost feel the sun shining down from above. It was time to try the hands-off mouse. Supposedly, the Visor could track one's eye movements and determine what they were focused on. David stared at the spinning question mark and gave a little squint, just as the manual had instructed.

It worked!

As easily as that, the cinematics faded away. The visual darkened to black, and from the audio arose the gentle chirping of distant birds. And from the blackness, there came the sound of footfalls, as if someone with hard soles were stepping slowly across a stone surface. The steps drew nearer, their hollow echoes growing ever more distinct. Then suddenly, there came a voice. David winced when it whispered directly into his right ear.

"Welcome," said the raspy voice. "It is time to choose which path you will tread."

***

"First," hissed the voice, "some background. You may skip this introduction if you like, but the realms can be unkind to those who arrive in ignorance. Better you listen, traveler, and prepare."

Well, that didn't sound ominous at all.

"Your starting realm will be Mandaria. It is an empire similar in culture and technology to the early days of China on your Earth. The goals are simple: progress in your class while enjoying the rich fantasy environment. You will doubtless encounter others in this MMORPG (emphasis on the first 'M'). You may enjoy their fellowship or strike out on your own, as you prefer. The realms are vast, and in them there is room enough for all."

David waited in silence for the briefing to continue.

"I see you agreed to the terms and conditions, but in case you didn't read them (as many do not), I urge you to correct this oversight. Be courteous to others you may encounter. Verbal abuse or sexual harassment will not be tolerated, nor will the advertisement, promotion, or sale of real-world products. Like you, others are here to enjoy themselves. Respect that or expect the immediate suspension of your account."

"Anything else?" asked David.

"Yes. Try not to die too often."

Before David, another menu shimmered into view. He looked around, but the disembodied speaker was nowhere to be seen. 'Select Class', said the prompt. The menu contained a list of starting classes from which one could choose. He recognized most from the online reviews he'd seen. There were warriors of every stripe, elemental sages, and tricksters galore - all the archetypes he'd researched. He had considered several of these for his character. Sometimes it was fun to be a warrior and just run around smashing things. But he knew he'd likely have this character for quite some time before the game would let him have an alt. And David was very curious about how magic worked in the realms.

The game-scape was supposedly based on ancient Chinese culture from an era prior to the advent of gunpowder. According to his reading, this was during the Tang dynasty, sometime around 900 AD. Of course, as a fantasy game, David was certain its designers would take great liberties with the timeline and incorporate myths and legends from many other eras - historical accuracy be damned.

The character class that had most intrigued David was one called a 'Jiangshi Hunter.' There wasn't much chatter about this class in any of the forums he'd been on. Most of the game reviews were all gaga over the 'Dragon Disciple' or the 'Fox Spirit Trickster.' But despite its seemingly modest initial powers, the JH must serve some kind of purpose. Game balance demanded it.

According to Wikipedia, a 'jiangshi' was a dreaded undead from Chinese mythology, some kind of hopping vampire. To be a hunter of such creatures, surely the JH must eventually acquire some formidable powers. And their initial requirement of enlightenment suggested a bent toward magic of some kind.

Maybe it wouldn't be the flashy kind used by Elemental Sages, but David was eager to give it a try. So, focusing on the entry, David squinted.

"An excellent choice, young master," said the disembodied voice. "A hunter of the dead will surely one day soon be needed."

David had heard that Realms was highly interactive. He thought he might as well test that right here and now.

"What do you mean by that?" asked the boy. "And do you have a name I can call you?"

There was a pause before the voice made its reply.

"My observations are of no immediate concern. Pay them no attention. As to my name, I am known to some as the Mandarin of Sorrow. For it is my sorry lot to welcome new players into the realms and to prepare them for what lies ahead."

"Can you give me a hint?"

"Alas, I cannot. Your path is your own to choose. Its possibilities are many; its final outcome, uncertain. But speaking of choices, your next one lies before you."

At this, the archetype selection menu wavered out of focus. It was replaced by a new set of system messages with a spinning yellow question mark.

[Congratulations! You have eight stat points to assign]

[Would you like to spend three on a destiny point? **Y/N**]

David had heard of this. It was a choice offered to every new player. Not many took the offer. According to the online pundits, this was a quick way to cripple your character's development. The consensus was that this was a bad idea. Losing three valuable stat points right at the outset severely limited your options for bonuses to skills, weapon selection, and so forth. Add to that, no one had been able to figure out exactly what the stupid thing did.

This was precisely why David knew he must have it. He focused carefully on the 'Yes' selection and gave it a squint.

[Please verify your choice verbally **Y/N**]

"Yes," the boy replied.

"Very well," said the Mandarin of Sorrow, resuming his narrative. "You have five unassigned stat points remaining. Of these, four are required to satisfy class requirements. You may place the final point however you please. All stat points must be spent before we can proceed.

David examined the new menu, which had scrolled up into his view.

MIGHT [8]   **CLEVERNESS** [8]

AGILITY [10]   **ENLIGHTENMENT** [10]

VIGOR [8]   **CHARM** [8]

Unspent Stat Points: [1]

"Hmm. Not a lot of chance for improvement," David mused aloud.

He knew that all avatars started with eight points in each base stat. Moreover, each class had certain minimums that one must meet. Apparently, his were 'Agility' and 'Enlightenment'. The first governed one's speed, accuracy, and ability with certain skills. The second one, Enlightenment, was important to spellcasters and also helped with perception. He was tempted to place his last point there as well, because he was eager to get started with magic. But from his reading, David had heard it mentioned that Realms was just as much a social game as it was a combative one. Since he'd already nerfed his combat build by popping for the mysterious 'destiny' point, he thought he might as well finish the job.

David went with his gut and placed the final unspent point on Charm, bringing it up to a mighty nine. Well, it was a start. Most gamers tended to ignore this stat unless it played some vital role in their characters' skill set. But every stat had its benefits. Maybe, as a weaker character, he could talk his way out of a bad situation rather than relying on his substandard might and vitality. A fellow could hope, couldn't he?

"Interesting," remarked the oddly opinionated minion of the realm. "On to skills, then. Choose carefully, young hunter. The skills you learn may decide your fate one day."

And the menu cleared once more.

***

The skills menu, when it emerged, was rather brief. It read only:

Jiangshi Hunter:

<u>Automatically Assigned</u>: Paper Talisman Crafting, Weapon Proficiency (Emei Ci)

<u>Recommended Skills</u>: Craft (Ink Making), Occult Lore, Martial Art (Baguazhang), Herbalism

<u>Selected Skills</u>: [ ]

<u>Open skill slots</u>: [4]

Where were the plethora of skills all the blogs were raving about? There didn't seem to be a way to view any others. Then, David remembered he had someone to ask.

"Mandarin," he said, "am I to suppose I can select only these four skills?"

"Not at all, young master. Skill selection is a matter of utmost importance when entering the realms. It should be approached with careful deliberation by new travelers. The recommended skills are available for immediate selection. They were gleaned from among the many thousands that are possible and deemed the most likely to benefit your build. If, however, you choose to wait, other choices will present themselves during your travels. You are free to select some, none, or all of these initial recommendations, or to wait for something different to come along."

I see, thought David. Unlike stat points, skills didn't all have to be assigned immediately. He reviewed the recommended choices. His eyes first strayed to 'Martial Art (Baguazhang).' That sounded the most interesting. When he squinted at it, a text box appeared beneath the menu.

Baguazhang - A set of ancient martial techniques involving fluid, dynamic movements and continuous motion. It is both a meditative practice and a powerful martial art. Baguazhang's tactics are based on agility and evasive footwork, enabling practitioners to outmaneuver opponents. It is characterized by its 'walking the circle' practice. Each of its eight animal-based systems is comprised of eight striking methods, and each striking method has seven different strikes.

[Learn More? **Y/N**] [Select? **Y/N**]

It definitely sounded like something David would find useful. It was probably why his chosen class had a minimum requirement for agility. He selected it and moved on. By reading the descriptions of the other skills, he learned Occult Lore would help him know more about the creatures he was to hunt and other things like them. So he selected it and, after some thought, added Herbalism as well. It would give him something to do and perhaps be a way to earn some extra coin. The final slot he left open. David supposed that inkmaking was meant to save him the expense of having to buy ink for crafting those paper talismans. Maybe he could get along without it and learn a more interesting skill instead.

"I think I'm done with skills for now," David sighed.

"Very well then," said the unseen algorithm. "Let us move on to starting equi--"

"David?" interrupted another voice. It was accompanied by the bang of the garage door swinging closed. Mother was home. "David? Are you up there?"

"I'm here, mom," shouted David, releasing Treadie's handlebars.

The game interface immediately went dark, and he set the visor aside.

"Can you come help me unload these groceries?"

Despite the phrasing, he knew it wasn't a request. David hurried down the stairs.

After helping to unload the groceries, David's mother reminded him that the lawn still needed to be cut. Due to his dad's landscaping business, the Grimes family had access to some state-of-the-art equipment. David returned to the Treadie 2000, redonned his visor, and selected 'Mow Lawn' from the startup menu. He awaited the all clear as the equipment booted up.

First, the hover drone emerged from its nest on the roof. Looking down from its perspective, David could see his house and yard from up above. He first chose the Stillman Grass Grinder Mark 12. It came rolling out from the shed and down the ramp once the shed doors hinged open. David toggled his perspective to that of the Stillman. Treadie accommodated this by extruding a riding saddle on which he could perch. As the arm swung over, David seated himself and had soon engaged the cutting blades beneath. The saddle sent a comforting rumble up his spine. This wasn't strictly necessary, but David always left the rumble filter toggled on. It gave the controller a better affinity for the machine.

Some people even used a 'Scent Vent' to heighten the realism, but that was definitely overkill for simply mowing the lawn. David knew quite well the smell of fresh-mown grass and hydrocarbon emissions. The Treadie 2K could mount such an attachment, but his dad had deemed this an unnecessary expense. The unit itself didn't cost so much, but the expense of maintaining and replenishing the scent cartridges could quickly add up.

As David rolled along, laying down the pleasing diagonal stripes on the once-unruly front yard, he smiled at his good fortune. David hoped to be a drone controller one day. It was why his mom and dad had agreed to pop for the new Visor. His lawn-mowing business made him some good money to put in his college fund, and every hour spent in pursuits such as this earned him credit toward early certification. College might even prove to be unnecessary. A good two-year trade school might be all he needed to launch him in his chosen profession. He could tell, however, that his parents still felt otherwise.

By the time the lawn was properly mown and edged, there was still time to sneak in a bit of gaming, but David was beginning to feel some eye-strain. As eager as he was for his first glimpse of the new game world, it wouldn't be worth starting up again only to be interrupted by dinner. There were already some enticing smells drifting up from the kitchen. Friday was taco night. There'd be plenty of time to explore what was sure to be his new obsession over the weekend. And it'd be spring break the week after next. Maybe that'd give him time to have a marathon session once his character was better established.

So instead, he cleaned up and headed back downstairs. He was sure mom would appreciate some help setting the table. They always set a place for dad, despite his inevitably late arrival. They'd likely have to start without him. Cold tacos just weren't the same as fresh.

***

David stood once again (virtually, anyway) in the dark mist, reviewing his starting equipment. He had already spent half an hour tweaking his character's appearance. There wasn't much in the way of equipment, but he was more interested in how the interface worked. He'd just figured out how to open and close his small inventory.

There was an outline of a male figure, with lines fanning out around it. These led to columns of little squares (mostly empty) indicating his various slotted items. There was a place for headgear (empty), gloves (also empty), and so on. The only items of apparel David's character seemed to own were a brown robe-like garment slotted on the main body and some kind of sweat pants that flared out below the knee.

He found he could change the displayed outline to a female figure instead. He flipped it back and forth several times before settling on the male figure. Alongside the depressingly underdressed image was a small cloth bundle. When he focused on it, some descriptive text appeared just below it.

Beginner's Beibao (背包): A small knapsack in which to carry one's possessions. This beibao contains eight slots in which items may be placed and from which they may be retrieved. Multiple small items of the same type may be placed in a single slot. [Open Beginner's Beibao? **Y/N**]

When David focused on 'Y' and squinted, the description was replaced by two rows of four boxes each. Some of these were filled. One held a stack of 20 of the small spikes the system named 'Chūcuì'. According to their description, they could be used by anyone with 'Emei Ci' weapon proficiency. Also from their description, they did only a single point of damage to their target and only if one scored a critical hit. He wondered what the point of such a weak attack was. It wasn't until later, when he explored his talisman crafting skill, that it began to make sense.

There was a full bottle of ink, a stack of talisman papers, a small sack of rice, and a trowel for practicing Herbalism. That left only three empty slots in his beibao. At least he didn't have to store his coins in there. A separate little sack had an indicator of how many 'zhu' David possessed. Examining one, he found it to be a small, round copper disc with a little square hole punched through its middle. That said, he had twenty of them.

Exploring his martial art was a lot more fun. There were a baffling number of attacks from which to choose. With eight different animals having eight combat stances each, and each stance having seven strikes, it would take days to parse through all the descriptions. Fortunately (or unfortunately, in David's estimation), most of these techniques were grayed out and couldn't be viewed. When he tried to do so, David was either informed that his level was insufficient or that he lacked some required stat like Might or Enlightenment. He still had a smattering of choices that sounded pretty good. He selected a few to drag over to his action bar.

Lacking anything better, David tried equipping one of the little throwing things in his weapon slot, but found it wouldn't equip there. He placed it on his action bar instead. That seemed to work.

"Are you satisfied, young master?"

"Mmn," replied David, noncommittally.

"Let me clarify, then," said the mandarin in a stiff voice. "Is there anything remaining to do that you cannot explore on your own?"

"I don't know. Is there?"

"Examining your equipment is the final stage of character generation. You have examined all items and are free to explore your abilities further once you have entered the realms. Only one final step remains."

"Wait," said David. "I'm curious. Do you have an avatar of your own?"

"Not here," said the voice after a short pause. "If ever you find yourself at the Jade Palace, you may seek me there. I would be interested to see how you're getting along."

That was interesting.

"And how am I to find this Jade Palace? Is there a yellow brick road leading to it or something?"

There was a longer pause. That in itself was interesting.

"Why would there be? No. Your starting point will be at a shrine on the side of the Great Silk Road. Ask any you encounter, and they can point you in the proper direction, unless, that is, they seek to mislead you."

David had no doubt that the advanced gaming AI was well aware of the pop-culture reference he'd just made. He was equally certain he wouldn't be able to get it to break character. Apparently, this really wasn't Kansas anymore.

"These formalities having been accomplished," said the sinister voice, "it is time to choose a name. You may use up to sixteen characters. These may be letters, numbers, or special characters."

David had thought about this once he had decided on a class. If he was to be a vampire hunter, he should have a suitably ominous name. He had tried to come up with an acronym by rearranging the letters of his real name, DAVID GRIMES. The best he could come up with was MIDAS V DIRGE, hardly awe-inspiring. He had briefly toyed with the name GRAVEDIGGER VLAD. This seemed more appropriate, used all sixteen characters, and even had the added advantage of using only letters from his real name, 'L' being David's middle initial.

But then he remembered something he'd misread from a movie marquis where all the letters for the showing had run together. It was perfect. David hoped it wasn't already taken. He entered the letters one by one from the virtual keyboard that lay before him, reviewing the result carefully before squinting at the [ENTER] prompt.

Virtual fireworks arched up from the otherwise dark screen, followed by the system message: [NAME ACCEPTED]. And spinning up from the background in stylized golden letters came his little vampire-hunter's name: TOM BRAIDER, it read.

***

On entering the actual game, David found his avatar to be kneeling before a roadside shrine. It was a small, open-sided rectangular building with stone pillars at each corner. The sloping tiled roof was worn with age but still protected the sacred area beneath it from the elements. To either side of the entrance lay a set of stone guardians in the shape of lions, their weather-worn semblances barely discernible as such.

David's viewpoint was initially that of his avatar, but he quickly found that he could toggle this back to a perspective just to the rear of his avatar and slightly above it. This afforded David a better sense of his surroundings and his character's actions. And what surroundings they were. It was a glorious day. The sun shone down from above, casting his shadow sharply on the path from the road to the shrine. All around, lay a grassy meadow filled with thriving plant life, whose gently waving stalks seemed to greet him into this new world. Birdsong could be heard. And, for the first time, he wished his Treadie *did* have that scent vent.

Flexing his knees and straightening them again caused his avatar to rise from his prone position and assume a combat-ready stance. David supposed he should start thinking of himself as 'Tom' now and cease to view the avatar as an entity separate from himself. It was more fun that way. He walked up the dirt path toward the shrine's entrance, above which hung some wind chimes tinkling in the soft breeze.

Within the shrine itself, David spied a stone table on which rested offerings of food. Most of this was spoiled, but some appeared to be more recent. Smudges here and there along the pitted surface and sticks jutting up from tiny holes suggested that incense was burned here not so long ago.

Summoning his inventory, David retrieved the sack of rice and carefully placed a handful on the altar. When he did, a set of system messages appeared, accompanied by a reverberating gong.

[Spawning point selected.]

[Should you die, your avatar will now be revived at Lingyun Wayfarer Shrine in Celestial Valley Province.]

[Congratulations! TOM BRAIDER has been awarded 1 Honor Point.]

Apparently, that had been the proper thing to do.

David didn't see a way to determine which way to go from here. He had discovered a mini-map, but it showed only this shrine, a small island of light within a sea of darkness. He had no quests to guide him. Weren't there usually some quest-givers near the spawning point, eager to grant a fellow a chance at earning some basic gear?

Instead of deciding right away, David took the opportunity to try out some of the martial moves he had hastily chosen. It turned out that there was a post nearby that one could use as a target. When he selected it, it appeared in the upper left-hand corner of his view. Its caption read 'Practice Post', and when targeted, it had a green health bar floating just above it. David first tried one of the little throwing spikes. It struck the target, not diminishing its health bar the tiniest bit. A brief message scrolled along on the bottom of his HUD.

[Chūcuì strikes Practice Post for 0 points of damage]

David repeated the action several more times with the same result. It was a good thing, David thought, that practice posts didn't hit back! At least he was able to retrieve the chūcuì he had expended. It was nice that they equipped themselves automatically from out of his inventory.

Next, he tried some of the martial moves he had selected. He started with the Li Trigram Rooster System. It was focused on long, deep footwork with one's center of gravity close to the ground. He rushed the post and hit it with a palm strike before dodging aside in a quick, rolling movement. It looked cool, but the results were less than impressive.

[Rooster Rush strikes Practice Post for 1 point of damage]

David knew this wouldn't be a very powerful strike. He repeated the maneuver, training his eyes instead on his own status meters. For a brief moment following his attack, Tom was granted a buff icon. From the skill's description, David had read that this increased his character's chance to dodge incoming attacks. Good. He could work on damage once he had more points to spend on Might.

Running through his other various attack moves, David made a happy discovery. Some of the attacks, and especially those in the same animal and stance groupings, could be linked together to form an action stack. Thus, he could place a chain of attacks on his action bar, which he could activate with a single click (squint?). In this context, the graceful flow of motion that was Baguazhang began to make more sense. Certain actions fit well together, their benefits stacking to debilitate one's opponent and leading up to more devastating blows.

David could sometimes do as much as five points of damage at a time to that post. Of course, this didn't keep up with its recovery rate. He barely put a dent in its health bar before it would refill itself. Nonetheless, this was progress. And it was there in that peaceful meadow on a pleasant spring day that Tom Braider met a fellow traveler.

The stranger came riding up the road from the west, toward which the afternoon sun was even now beginning to drift. The rider was not at first as obvious as the beast on which she rode.

David's reading had caused him to think of the qilin as a unicorn. He noted that it had, in fact, a single, spiraling horn. But there, the similarities all but ceased. The qilin was a glorious beast with a unique charm all its own, quite separate from our western notions of what a unicorn might be. Its body more resembled a gazelle than a horse. Its high, arched neck had a mane that lashed the breeze, and its overlong tail swished in a fluid motion as it glided along. Pearly white overall, it had four long stockings of a much darker shade ending in swirling patterns that resembled arcane markings. Despite all this, its eyes were its most compelling feature. A bit overlarge, they shone with a compassion and understanding unnatural for a mere beast. Tom could hardly tear his own eyes from the graceful creature.

As the qirin drew near, Tom marked its rider. She sat tall in her saddle, the sunlight gleaming from her pristine suit of armor. Her helmet's visor was up, exposing a proud, chiseled face with an aquiline nose. David suddenly wished he had taken more time sculpting his own avatar's appearance. Gripped in her right hand was a long polearm with a bladed steel head. Her left hand held the reins. She paused in her trek down the road, dismounted, set her mount to grazing, and approached the shrine on foot.

Being new to the game, David wasn't sure how to greet the stranger. He already knew her name, for it was hovering in scarlet letters just above her head, along with her class and level of progression. David would soon learn that this color indicated she was far above his challenge level.

Madelyn Pierce
Level 12 Dragon Disciple
(Yaoguai Decapitator)

"Well met, fellow traveler," she said. "May fortune smile upon you."

David tapped the icon he had prepared on his action bar for such an occasion. Among hundreds of other emotes, he had found one called "friendly smile." Avatars tended to be pretty much expressionless because people didn't often use the various emote commands, not seeing much of a point. It was amazing how ingrained people's reactions were to such social cues. Madelyn, however, drew up short, looking Tom up and down very carefully.

"How in the world did a level one get all the way out here? Didn't you do the starting quests where you were spawned?"

"Um, no? I entered the game right here not an hour ago."

She took a step back.

"Tell me right now. Are you a Fox Spirit Trickster or a Shadowblade?" she demanded.

David had heard that some of the trickster classes had special skills for deceit. They could hide or alter their targeting information, sometimes even appearing to be NPCs.

"And don't bother to lie," she added. "I have the truth-sense skill. You can't get away with any shenanigans in a shrine zone, you know."

David didn't know and was a bit taken aback by her sudden and unfounded suspicion.

"Honestly, I'm none of those things. In fact, can you tell me which way will lead me to the Jade Palace? It's the closest thing to a quest I have, and I'd be most appreciative if you could point the way. My mini-map only has this single shrine."

There was a pause.

"Wierd," she finally said. "I thought everyone spawned at Qinghua Village or similar spots (except for the Mongol Barbarians; they have their own starting arc). This game always has something new to throw at you. They say the AI that runs it was almost banned by the Global Science Council. They were already upset over the quantum computer array they're using as a server farm. But they located it over in Alliance territory, so what could they do about it?"

"Well, I wouldn't know about any of that. The Jade Palace?"

"Oh. You should head farther east. It's a pretty long journey on foot. Just don't stray too far from the road. Monsters don't spawn there, and you don't look to be equipped to handle much."

"You're right about that, Miss Pierce. I just got off the boat, so to speak. That's a beautiful mount you're riding. Can anyone get one?"

"Yinyang? No, she's the end reward from a long line of quests only offered to Dragon Disciples. I only just got her. I'm riding back to rejoin my group. That last mission was a bit of a party wipe. I only stopped here because I have to log off soon, and shrines are safe zones."

"Good to know. This is my re-spawn site."

"That isn't information you should share with just anyone, Mister Braider. So what's a Jiangshi Hunter, anyway? I've seen your like around, but I'm not sure what it is you do."

"We hunt vampires."

"Creepy," said Madelyn.

"No creepier than chopping the heads off of Yaoguai." Tom retorted.

"Fair," she replied, but then started laughing uproariously. It was all out of proportion to Tom's simple observation, made all the stranger by her avatar's serious expression.

"I just got it," said Madelyn once she'd settled down a bit. "TomB-raider. Good one, Tom"

David stared directly at her and once again toggled on his "Friendly Smile".

***

It had been lonely since Madelyn had logged out. She and her incredible steed had frozen in place for a bit while numbers over her head counted down. This was to ensure players couldn't simply log out in the middle of combat to avoid being killed when things went wrong.

Before leaving, Madelyn had had a go at the practice pole with her Guan Dao, that long poleaxe of hers. Tom was amazed when the practice target simply exploded from the force of her first thrust, sending shards of wood flying out in every direction. It took several minutes for the thing to rebuild itself from the ground up. And yet she'd been battling creatures that slew most of her party? David supposed that his little Tom had better get a move on leveling up.

But instead, he was trudging down the lonely road as night descended on the open grassland all around. The crickets began to make their presence known, and he heard the hooting of an owl in the distance, preparing to wake from its daytime slumber. It was a good thing avatars didn't need to sleep. Wouldn't that be boring? There was an emote to emulate it. The character would lie down, and a series of small 'z's would emerge at intervals. But this was only for social interaction or when one was affected by a sleeping spell or effect. Come to think of it, avatars didn't really need to eat either. Though it had come in handy, this caused Tom to wonder about the bag of rice in his starting kit.

As he traveled along, Tom was pleased to note a growing stripe of color on his mini-map. One day, he hoped to have the whole thing filled in. But for now, he'd take whatever he could get. He used the zoom feature to make it seem like more was filled, and he noticed a curious thing. On the map, not too far off the road to his left, was a glimmering little sparkle. He wondered whether this was some kind of creature. He turned in that direction and gazed out across the meadow. A blue dot marked his own location at the map's center. This denoted a player-character.

Although Madelyn had warned him not to leave the road, that was hardly the stuff of which adventures were made. In the worst case, he'd respawn back at the shrine and would only lose some time. He recalled a line from "Crime and Punishment." (His literature class was studying Dostoevsky this semester.) He muttered it aloud. "A light in the distance, pale, flickering, yet with the promise of warmth."

A system message suddenly appeared in his HUD.

[Would you like to acquire the skill: Poet ? **Y/N**]

Tom dismissed the message with a chuckle. And in the failing light, he stepped warily across the berm and headed north to investigate. He tapped nervously on his targeting selector as he went. Sometimes, one's character is perceptive enough to spot a lurking ambusher that your own eyes might miss. But no target window presented itself as Tom closed the distance to the mysterious marker.

Then one did.

In his targeting window was a fiery red leaf. It didn't look very threatening. Its name was displayed as 'Phoenix Sage'. Tom found this somewhat amusing because that was how Elemental Sages who specialized in fire referred to themselves. He approached the plant, remaining wary of other dangers. As it lacked a health bar, the leaf doubtless represented an herb rather than some vicious plant creature. Tom equipped his trowel in his weapon slot and prepared to dig. These things had to be worth *something*. Touching the trowel to its stem caused a new system message to appear.

[Harvest 'Phoenix Sage' ? **Y/N**]

He chose yes, of course.

But when he did so, the small plant burst into bright flames, causing him to stumble back a step.

[Attempt to harvest 'Phoenix Sage' has failed.]

No kidding.

Scrolling back through his system messages, Tom discovered the cause of the mishap. '... Agility insufficient for this task... Dodge successful... Flaming burst causes 0 points of damage.' Tom turned around and stalked back to the road. He'd have to do some further online research about Herbalism, but for now, he just chalked it up to trial and error. Primarily the latter.

Tom did derive one benefit from the incident. The next time he came across a Phoenix Sage, it was marked by a pale red dot rather than a sparkle. When he focused on it, a text box with its name popped up beside it.

Tom would later learn that Enlightenment governed the range at which he could detect the rare herbs. Agility was the stat needed to harvest them. These were two of his strong suits. It was no wonder this was on his short list of recommended skills. He investigated several other sparkles, with mixed results. On several occasions, Tom had to run back to the road after spotting a predatory animal. In the end, he had a stack of 14 'Ren Shen Root', and a lesser stack of 3 'Moonshadow Moss' before anything more interesting came into view. Each rested in its own inventory slot. And if there was a limit to how many would stack, he hadn't hit it yet.

It was well into game day morning by now. It was strange. A game 'day' seemed to last about three hours from sunrise to sunset. The nighttime, however, seemed to pass more swiftly. It lasted only an hour or so. Evidently, some game features didn't have to follow logic.

Up ahead, at the very edge of his map, Tom saw the beginnings of something that wasn't simply an endless meadow. It appeared to be a set of structures and fenced-in fields. He wanted to learn more but feared becoming embroiled in new mischief so late in this session.

Since logging on after breakfast, David had been playing for nearly four hours. Saturday or not, it'd be lunchtime soon. It was definitely time to take a break, but what had Madelyn said about logging off in a safe place? David supposed that here, beside the road, Tom would be as safe as anywhere (apart from a shrine, perhaps). So, he began the log-off sequence and watched the timer count down as the tension slowly eased from his back.

***

David headed downstairs. There, he found his mother at the kitchen table with the newspaper spread out before her. Strange. He hadn't ever seen her read the thing before. It was open to the ad section, and as he watched, she was cutting out a coupon with a pair of blue-handled scissors. He noted her somber face as she placed it neatly atop a stack to her right. She seemed to be lost in thought.

"Finding any interesting bargains?" he asked.

This caused his mother to start from her reverie. She turned to face him.

"Oh. David. A few, I guess..."

"What's for lunch?"

"Oh. Is it that time already?"

Setting the scissors aside, she stood and hustled over to the cabinet.

"How are you liking the new game?" she asked in a lighter tone that seemed a bit forced.

What was up?

"I'm only just getting started, but I can tell it's going to be amazing. Thanks again for the new Visor."

"Well, don't expect more upgrades anytime soon," she said, filling the tea kettle from the faucet. "Money doesn't grow on trees, you know."

Since money was made of paper, David thought that, in fact, it kind of did. But rather than give voice to this smart-mouthed objection, he offered a more respectful reply.

"Yes, mom," he agreed.

Lunch turned out to be a bowl of ramen noodles from a dry-mix packet and a glass of skim milk. David slurped it down while his mother returned to her clipping. He rinsed the bowl and set it in the sink. As he was returning to his room, his mother called out."

"Mrs. Olsen wanted me to let you know her grass needs a trim. She saw you doing ours yesterday."

"Okay," he hollered back, "I'll get to it later."

And with that, he thumped back up the stairs to immerse himself once more in the lands of legend.

***

As the bright sky of Mandaria came shimmering back into view, David found Tom still standing on the berm of the Great Silk Road. He zoomed his mini-map to the largest magnification and strode a cautious few steps toward the buildings in the distance. This revealed a set of icons he would later come to associate with traders and merchants of various sorts. The green dots moving slowly around the place marked them as non-hostile NPCs. He turned onto the pathway that led to the enclosure with more confidence.

Its signpost read, "Celestial Silkworks."

Tom hoped they might sell him some basic equipment. Those empty slots in his equipment menu were just itching to be filled. He wondered what all he'd be able to afford.

The area was rather strange. It was all enclosed in a large, skeletal dome of bamboo that formed the bars of a sort of cage. This rose high above to meet in the middle. Over this was stretched some fine netting. He passed some NPCs standing near the entrance. They appeared to be engaged in some sort of dialog, speaking and gesturing to one another, but Tom couldn't hear any words. Instead, text would occasionally flow by in his status bar at the bottom of his view.

"... can't afford to take any more losses! Silk production is down by twenty percent. If this goes on any longer, we can all... "

Tom smelled a quest brewing. Madelyn had told him that he could find such using his mini-map. The game followed the standard convention of marking them with little yellow exclamation points. Completed quests were marked with similar yellow question marks that would appear above the quest-giver's head. And indeed, Tom soon spotted a quest marker at the edge of his map. He hurried toward it while noting the cluttered merchant stalls on either side of the lane. There was also a green triangle similar to the one that had marked the Lingyun Wayfarer Shrine, but that could wait until later.

He soon found that it was not a person over whom the quest marker hovered. Instead, it floated above a short pillar, perhaps three feet in height. It was shaped like a little pagoda. Curious, he focused on it. It appeared in his target window with the description 'Mailbox.' He gave it a squint. This opened a new window. A column of bars appeared, all but the first of which were empty.

[System Message], it read.

Squinting again, Tom opened the message.

"Welcome, TOM BRAIDER, to the exciting world of Mandaria. As a new traveler, we would like to offer you this starting gift. May your triumphs be many and your journey be fraught with joy as you travel the path of enlightenment!"

~ *The Dev Team* ~

[Retrieve attachment? **Y/N**]

When the attached item appeared in Tom's inventory, he was well-pleased. It was a wide, pointed straw hat. Its description read: 'Rice Hat: Shades one's head from the sun. (+1 Vigor).' He equipped it at once. That was nice, but where was the real quest around here? Oh well, onto the green triangle.

On his way there, Tom encountered a beggar sitting huddled in a blanket between two stalls. There was no quest marker, but Tom focused on the indigent man just to be certain. Nothing. But when his eyes came to rest on the wooden bowl before the man, he found he was able to target it. With a mental shrug, Tom retrieved one of his twenty zho from his inventory and squinted at the bowl. The coin disappeared, leaving him only 19. When he turned and began to move away, the gong sounded again.

[Congratulations! TOM BRAIDER has been awarded 1 Honor Point.]

Hmmm, thought David. That must have been a hidden quest. He'd have to keep his eyes open for such things from now on.

Arriving at the green triangle marker, Tom found another shrine. Rather than twin lions, the guardian statue here was a stone monkey. It sat on its haunches, its hand stroking at its bearded chin. Well, it wasn't actually moving or anything, but it seemed to be in a rather contemplative pose. The word "Houzi" was engraved at the statue's base. Tom assumed this must be its name.

Stepping past Houzi, Tom entered the temple proper and once again laid a handful of rice on its stone table. There was no honor point award this time, but he did get a system message.

[New spawning point selected.]

[Should you die, your avatar will now be revived at Celestial Silkworks Shrine in Celestial Valley Province.]

Well, that was comforting, at least. Tom would prefer to avoid all that walking again, should something unfortunate happen. He wondered why the game had dumped him out in the middle of nowhere, so far from the normal character starting zones. Could it have something to do with the destiny point he'd chosen? Whatever the reason, at least now he would be able to buy some equipment and return to a more civilized locale should the worst come to pass.

He stared at the enclosure into which the opposite side of the shrine opened. It was shaded from direct sunlight by some thin sheets of cloth woven into the bamboo framework above. Within it stood clusters of large shrubs, which Tom would soon learn were mulberry trees. These were peppered with little white cocoons, and moths fluttered all about. Given the enclosure's stated purpose, Tom supposed these to be silk moths, the cocoons belonging to their larval namesakes. He wanted to examine them more closely, but better equipping himself should come first.

One of the icons on his map, a little smithing hammer, led him to an armorer. This fellow would repair one's gear if it became damaged in a fight. Not having tussled with anything serious yet, Tom had no need for his services. The next stall he encountered was a general merchant. This was more interesting.

"How may I help the honored gentleman today?"

[View merchant's products? **Y/N**]

He had a number of items of general use. Many were grayed out, their cost being greater than the funds he had on hand. Tom was very interested in the one labeled

Superior Beibao (15 zho): A knapsack in which to carry one's possessions. This beibao contains ten slots in which items may be placed and from which they may be retrieved. Multiple small items of the same type may be placed in a single slot. [Purchase Superior Beibao? **Y/N**]

"Hmm. Tom muttered. "That's almost all the coin I have."

[Would you like to acquire the skill Haggling? **Y/N**]

Now *that* was interesting. Tom had only one open skill slot remaining. He imagined this skill would prove useful all throughout the life of his character. Without overthinking it, Tom selected 'yes.'

[Congratulations! You have acquired the skill "Haggling." You now have the ability to negotiate prices and deals more effectively in markets and with merchants. By leveraging your keen negotiation tactics and understanding market dynamics, you can secure better prices for goods and services. Use this skill wisely to maximize your savings and get the most value from merchant transactions. Skill level increases with Charm. Happy bargaining!]

Tom noted an immediate change in the description of the item he was considering. Trailing behind the standard description, it now said: [Purchase Superior Beibao? **Y/N**] [Haggle with Merchant? **Y/N**]

When Tom opted to haggle, the merchant's avatar sprouted an ingratiating grin, and he began flexing his hands in a wringing motion. The price changed from 15 zho to 13 zho. And the trailing message now said: [Purchase Superior Beibao? **Y/N**] [Continue Haggling with Merchant? **Y/N**]

Tom wanted to see how far he could push this. He elected to haggle further, bringing the price down to 12. When he tried once more, however, the merchant became angry. He crossed his arms and turned his back on Tom. The price went back up to 15 zho, and the option to haggle was removed. Again, Tom was pleased with himself. Being able to craft ink might save him a lot more here at the start, but in the long run, he'd bet haggling would outstrip it. He imagined one day buying each piece of the expensive, high-level gear he would need at a discount of more than ten percent.

Tom wandered around the market, experimenting with his new skill. He replenished his rice supply, and checked out the cost of ink (expensive). For a container, he settled on a basket. It took one slot in his Beginner's Beibao. It couldn't hold anything when stored away, but if he equipped it in his shield hand (he wasn't using a shield anyway), it could hold up to five items. He thought it might be useful for his herb gathering.

And speaking of that, Tom found that any of the merchants here would purchase the herbs he had gathered. He didn't get much for them - just about a zho for a stack of five. But he found that haggling also worked in reverse. Sometimes, he could get a zho for a stack of four instead. At the clothiers, he found a wide variety of silk garments (to be expected, he supposed). There were gloves, leggings, and the like, but only one item in his price range interested him. It was a silk robe to replace the brown gunny sack he'd been sporting. Moreover, it had a stat point (+1 Charm). It would take two more coins than he had to possess it.

Removing his current robe, he found he could sell it for one of the coins he needed. The pantaloons would sell for another. Tom now stood bare-chested and in his skivvies in the middle of the open market. Should he haggle? Why not? If this insulted the merchant, he could always pay full price. The first haggle was successful. He considered himself lucky and decided not to risk a further attempt. His modesty couldn't be bought for a mere zho or two.

By this time, the merchants were packing things up and preparing for the short game night to follow. Having no need to sleep, Tom found a place to settle down to review his talisman crafting skill. He found an open space and sat.

As a mere beginner, Tom didn't have very many options for his talismans. There was one called 'Flame Burst.' At Tom's level of enlightenment, it should do around 8 points of damage in a small area. Another was called 'Paralyze.' That one held an opponent in place for a short duration. There was also one called 'Spirit Shroud.' This supposedly weakened an undead entity but had little or no effect on the living. Tom made eight of the flaming kind and one paralysis one and prepared them for use.

By this time, it was full-on night, and no one was stirring in the camp. And then someone was.

***

As night fell over the enchanted grove of mulberry trees, a shadowy figure came slinking through the underbrush. Its eyes gleamed with hunger. Sensing an opportunity for a midnight feast, a cunning weasel had breached the enclosure, its sharp claws poised to snatch up some unsuspecting worms.

But before the weasel could strike, a guardian monkey spirit materialized from the darkness, its fur bristling with magical energy. With lightning speed and acrobatic prowess, the monkey spirit leaped into action, driving back the intruder with a fierce, screeching cry.

All around the mulberry bushes, the monkey chased that weasel, drawing nearer with each pass. When, at last, he had him in his clutches, he squeezed. And the night predator expired with a satisfying, popping sound. The grove quieted, and the monkey returned to his silent vigil.

***

Tom was suddenly alert. What was that screeching cry he'd just heard? He stood from his resting place, talismans forgotten. And there it was - A little yellow exclamation point right in the middle of the mulberry grove. Tom hustled toward it eager to see what the quest might be.

Passing through the shrine, he noticed that the monkey statue was gone. But standing at the center of the grove slouched a familiar bearded fellow with overlong arms crossed before him.

"Honored Houzi," said Tom, determined to be respectful, "what has awakened you from your rest?"

"Well, aren't you a polite one?" grunted the monkey in reply.

He dropped the weasel carcass at Tom's feet.

"These things are becoming a nuisance!" he declared. "They've developed a taste for our silkworm larvae. Not a night goes by when they don't creep into our enclosure to spoil our harvest. As guardian of this grove, I offer a great reward to one who would rid us of these pests."

[Quest Offered: Slay 100 Weed Weasels]
[Reward offered: 100 XP plus unknown bonus]
[Accept quest? **Y/N**]

"I accept," said Tom at once. "Where can these creatures be found?"

Houzi paused thoughtfully. He produced a round orange fruit and casually bit into it. Its juices dribbled down into his beard.

"They spawn in a nearby field," he finally answered. "I shall mark it on your map. But fair warning, friend. One weasel is not so fierce a foe, but in numbers, they can be deadly."

Tom saluted the guardian and exited the grove. On his mini-map, there was now a yellow arrow pointing in the direction he must go. He had to leave the silkworks entirely through its main entrance before he could go in the direction indicated. A hundred experience points would be enough to take Tom halfway to level two. He'd only gotten a handful of points from his herb gathering. But, hey, every little point helps, right?

For most games, the beginning quests only awarded a few points. Running through a series of them got you some basic gear and took you to second level. For him, it had been an express trip right into the fire, with no stop at the frying pan. Maybe this quest would catch him up a bit. Weasels didn't sound so tough.

When he approached the border of the area he was to hunt, he saw its hazy outline on his mini-map. Within its borders were the little red dots denoting his intended prey. They were moving all about, sometimes growing close to one or two others of their kind. Tom approached from one edge and timed things so as to isolate one from its beastly brethren. He even got the jump on it, unleashing his deadliest attack combo. Even so, the little bloodsucker was quick. Having survived Tom's initial barrage, it quickly went on the offensive. In a blur of fur, it lashed out at Tom, who was still recovering from his salvo. It took several more well placed strikes to put the angry creature down.

[Loot Weed Weasel? **Y/N**]

Tom was rewarded with a weasel tail as the carcass vanished with a little pop. He'd hardly expected a legendary sword to drop from the creature, but it was still a bit disappointing. The wounds he'd taken were slowly healing. He retreated outside of the contested zone and thought about the problem. At this rate, he'd be days clearing out a hundred of these. Still, he'd taken the creature's measure. It could only withstand six or seven points of damage before expiring. If the others were the same, he might have the beginning of an idea.

Tom waded back into the zone and waylaid another. This time, he chose a different initial combination. And though less effective, he was still able to finish off his adversary and took less damage doing so. Refining his technique still further, Tom built another partial attack sequence ending in the Rooster's Lying Step and lifting techniques. He hoped this would all come together well, or it might end badly for old Tom.

He screwed up his courage before launching into motion. This was going to require a leap of faith (and quite a literal one, at that). Tom rushed across the zone in a drunken zigzag pattern designed to aggro as many of the beasts as possible and pull them together into one place. He waited until the last possible moment before triggering the risky sequence he had planned.

Just as the weasels all converged on the silk-clad herbalist, he performed a whirling maneuver from the phoenix system. This was immediately followed by the lifting back-kick of the rooster. In one a great leap, he flipped overhead to land facing the writhing mass from a mere fifteen feet away.

He knew he had but a moment in which to act before they would come tearing into him. Tom selected what he thought was the center-most weasel from the muddled scrum and hurled a throwing spike at it. A familiar message scrolled past:

[Chūcuì strikes Weed Weasel for 0 points of damage]

But then, before he could blink, there was a bright flash, and his view became riddled with system messages.

[Flame Burst strikes Weed Weasel for 8 points of damage]

That message was repeated many times, followed by: [Weed Weasel expires]

A few of the little rascals managed to dodge successfully, and these Tom had to fight. But although their tactics were savage, Tom's vitality held out until this scattered remnant was dealt with. He was able to collect sixteen more weasel tails from the pile of their little corpses. Each kill had also yielded a few experience points. At this rate, he might actually *hit* level two when he claimed his quest reward. With the immediate area cleared of threats, Tom decided to use his spare time to gather the few herbs in the area while his health bar refilled. He had noticed several promising glimmers earlier but couldn't get at them with all the weasels slinking about.

He kept a wary eye on his map for enemy markers. If there was one thing he was sure of, such games always had a reliable way to replenish their monsters. Doubtless, these creatures would respawn here soon enough, and Tom needed to be ready for round two.

About midway through the great weasel massacre, Tom developed the good sense to pack his silk robe away in his item storage. It had taken some damage from all the fighting. It provided no armor, and Tom doubted whether his furry little foes gave a rat's whisker about how charming their killer was. On using his sixth talisman, Tom received the awaited system message. It was nigh unreadable until after the flurry of death notices had settled down.

[Congratulations! You have earned the Weasel Whacker badge]

[This grants you the right to proudly bear this title]

[Use this as your new title? **Y/N**]

Tom fiddled with his targeting display settings and figured out how to turn on titles. The game designers really did have an evil sense of humor. But David himself could appreciate a bit of low humor, so he decided to own it. Others viewing his avatar would soon read it as:

Tom Braider
Level 2 Jiangshi Hunter
(Weasel Whacker)

The single quest on his quest menu now had a green check mark next to it. So he headed back toward the compound to rest and replenish. All in all, it had cost him some paper and ink and a few scratches. No. Weasels weren't so tough (given a bit of proper preparation).

***

In the center of the grove, the monkey stood, still munching on his fruit. It had been nearly a whole day. So many had failed; would this one be any different? Hope or something very like it flared up in Houzi's algorithms. Humans can be clever at times. Surely one day, someone will come who can meet the challenges. If not this one, then another. Then the monkey's eyebrows lifted as he sensed the boy returning. He awaited him with the stoic calm that could often pass for serenity. Night was once again laying its shroud over the peaceful bamboo enclosure.

"I am here, oh great Houzi, and I have done as you asked."

"I see," said the simian sentinel. He nibbled nonchalantly at the sweet nectar of the last bit of fruit clinging to its core.

"And what have you learned?" asked the monkey.

Tom considered the question, pacing a few steps closer. To Tom's eye, the macaque's wizened face strongly resembled that of a chimp. The presence of his long tail was the only thing to suggest otherwise.

"I suppose I learned to carefully consider my options - to prepare and analyze the situation before just rushing in. If you stop and think about a problem, you can often find a better way to solve it."

For the first time, the guardian smiled, his pink lips curling back. To Tom's eye, it appeared more like a grimace, but it was a good effort nonetheless. Perhaps this was the best version of "Friendly Smile" a monkey could manage. From beneath his protruding brow, Houzi's eyes seemed to shine with approval.

Virtual fireworks arched up in Tom's field of vision, and a whole slew of new system messages flew by at once. It started with something like [Congratulations, Traveler! You have reached level two...]. Tom toggled system messages off. He could read them all later. He focused instead on what the monkey had to say.

"I'll let you take care of this for me," said Houzi.

And reaching out, the monkey dropped the remains of his fruit into Tom's hand. Tom looked at it with distaste, then whisked it into his inventory.

"I'll see that it is properly disposed of," he said. "But where is the great reward you promised me?"

Houzi let out a screech.

"Ungrateful ape!" he declared. "Do you not recognize what you have already been given? The wisdom of the monkey is a prize most rare. But what should one expect from one of your tailless kind? Very well, take this instead!"

Springing forward, Houzi seized Tom by the arm and bit down on it. Hard. When Tom shook him off, Houzi scampered back toward the shrine and out of sight.

What the...

In confusion, the boy walked back that way himself. As he exited through the shrine, there was no longer a statue guarding it. Avatars didn't actually feel pain, but if they did, Tom felt sure his arm would be aching from the monkey bite. It was oddly swollen and beginning to bruise. But his health bar remained full, and no debuffs hovered near his name. Odd. Tom wondered what might have set the little fellow off.

David decided to log off right here. He imagined he'd have a lot to do to level up properly. At least he'd have all day Sunday to do it. After trimming Mrs. Olsen's lawn, that is.

CHAPTER TWO

Stick in the Mud

牛

David didn't get to Mrs. Olsen's yard the next morning, or even that afternoon. When the family arrived home from church, there were men in and about the shed. They had the Stillman torn down almost to its frame. Dad's truck wasn't out on the street either. In its place was a large, sleek van with the letters H2O2H emblazoned on its side.

The men wore the bright green vests of the environmental agency. Most sported tool belts. From the back seat, David watched them as his mother steered their old Chevy Sonic into the garage. It was a vintage 2048 model already retrofitted with a hydrogen fuel cell.

"Well, it isn't like you didn't see this day was coming," she said.

Daniel only grunted.

David's father wasn't a fan of the EA's new energy policy. He'd been putting off this upgrade for years. All the equipment in his fleet had been purchased before the hydrogen initiative had gone into effect. From trucks, bulldozers, and caterpillars down to the lowliest lawn mower or wood chipper, they depended on fossil fuels. He'd taken out a hefty loan to make the substantial investment, little knowing that fate had marked him for ruin.

He had started as a bright-eyed entrepreneur, confident that with some hard work and business savvy, he could repay that loan and begin reaping the rewards for a job well done. Now here he was, ten years later, nearly in default and working long hours to avoid having to close up shop. Wordlessly, he unbuckled his safety harness, slid from his seat, and headed out to watch the retro-fitters in action.

Carol watched her husband with concern. He was exiting the garage in the direction of the shed. He was a proud man. She supported his decision to take out a second mortgage on the house so they could afford the retrofit. But what would become of them if his business didn't pick up again? She smiled when David moved to join him.

They were soon met by an old man who moved to intercept them. She recognized him as Jack Kemp, the proprietor of the Last Chance.

"Tell me it ain't so, Danny, old boy," moaned Jack on his approach.

"I'm afraid so, Jack," replied Daniel. "It finally got to be too much, so I decided to bite the pellet and convert."

"I never thought I'd see the day Daniel Grimes would bow down to the green mob."

"There really wasn't any other choice, Jack. Between the high price of gas and the penalties, I've been barely scraping by these last few years. Pretty soon, my workers would have been moving mulch in horse-drawn wagons."

"I wouldn't bet on it," replied Jack with a sniff. "They'd as soon outlaw them hay-burners too, if they could. Methane's a greenhouse gas too, you know."

"Well, I think the new hydroelectric systems are pretty cool," put in David, unexpectedly.

The two men stared at him.

"And who might this earnest young fellow be?" asked Jack.

"This is my son, David. David, this is Jack Kemp. Jack runs the filling station out on Westbourne Avenue."

"The Last Chance?"

"More like the Last Gasp," said the old man ruefully, "now that my best customer done converted to the green religion."

"I'm pleased to meet you, Mr. Kemp," said David, forestalling his father's response.

David soon left the men to their kvetching and headed back toward the house. It was clear he'd get no mowing done today.

***

Once again, Tom was walking down the lonely road. It had been raining earlier, but strangely, this didn't leave you wet. It just interfered with vision and cast a bit of a pall on the surroundings. Madelyn hadn't been kidding when she'd said he was in for a long journey on foot. Having left the silkworks behind, Tom hoped he'd soon find a zone where he could meet some other players, or at least get some decent quests.

Progression to level two had awarded Tom with eight additional stat points and another skill slot. He had put two of the former into his primary stats of Agility and Enlightenment. He spread the remaining four evenly across his other stats, unsure of what he might find most useful. This had caused several new techniques from his Baguazhang skill to become available. Many more, however, remained shaded. His character profile was looking a bit more respectable now.

Tom Braider - Level 2 Jaingshi Hunter (Weasel Whacker)

MIGHT   **9**   CLEVERNESS   **9**
AGILITY **12**   ENLIGHTENMENT **12**
VIGOR   **9 (10)** CHARM   **10 (11)**

Skills:Haggling, Herbalism, Martial Art (Baguazhang), Occult Lore, Paper Talisman Crafting, Weapon Proficiency (Emei Ci)

Open skill slots: **1**

Tom wondered where those honor points he'd been awarded had gone and how they affected game play. Not to mention the mysterious destiny point for which he'd mortgaged his future. He cast these concerns aside and kept his eye peeled for the telltale glimmers that would fill his herb collection basket.

He still didn't know what Moonshadow Moss might be, but he had eight of them. 'Ren Shen Root' was the Chinese name for ginseng. It was the one most commonly encountered here. It was used in cooking recipes and also had medicinal properties. It was highly prized by alchemists for crafting healing potions.

His higher agility stat hadn't yet enabled him to harvest any Phoenix Sage, but he remained hopeful. Instead of 'Agility insufficient for this task', his system message now read, 'Agility check failed.' His several attempts thus far had been flaming disasters. He found some floral herbs called 'Starlight Orchids' that only came out at night. He'd even found a small patch of herbs called 'Dawn Lilies', but you had to be quick to harvest any. They were only viable for as long as the sun was touching the horizon.

It was a lonely grind, so Tom perked up when he saw something different in the road ahead. He soon found that 'in the road ahead' was quite literally correct. It was a massive wagon loaded to its brim with crates, barrels, and wooden beams. Its wheels were sunk deep into a muddy stretch of roadway. Above it hovered the large yellow exclamation point recognizable to all players in the Realms.

Harnessed to the wagon's front lay an enormous blue-gray ox. The great shaggy thing was reclined before its sunken wagon, with its big old head resting on the ground before it. Its tail swished idly at some buzzing flies. David had seen overlarge bovines before, which he'd been told were called oxen, but this thing more resembled a bison than a bull. Its sallow horns swept low on either side of its flattened face before curving upward at their ends. Tom didn't see anyone driving the wagon, nor did there seem to be any reins with which to do so.

"Um, hello?" Tom called out on his approach.

At this, the ox raised its head and let out a mighty bellow. Then he shook his head from side to side and turned it as much as he was able to face toward the boy. This looked to be difficult, as the creature didn't seem to have much of a neck between his generous head and muscled shoulders. So Tom sauntered up and around to the front of him.

Tom triggered the quest icon and waited for something to happen.

"I prayed someone would be by soon," moaned the ox.

His words rumbled forth, slow and ponderous.

"I'm sure you can mark my sorry circumstance. Would you be so kind as to lend a hand? As you can see, I have none."

[Quest Offered: Free the Wagon from the Mud]
[Reward offered: 85 XP plus equipment item]
[Accept quest? **Y/N**]

Somehow, Tom was not surprised to find that the ox could speak. Maybe if he were to unload the wagon, the ox could pull it free? But, recalling the monkey's lesson, he pondered the matter some more before accepting.

"I'll try," said Tom, reassuringly. "Have you a name I may call you by?"

The ox snorted.

41

"I once served a mighty lumberjack who blessed me with such. But that's a legend from a different land, far away from the here and now. In this realm, I am known only as niú, the ox."

"Well then, mister ox, may I ask where you are headed?"

"Less chatting and more helping, if you please," bawled the ox.

With a sigh, Tom surveyed the situation once more. He noticed that he could only target three of the crates and one of the beams loaded in the wagon's bed. That had to be a clue. The answer came to him almost at once. He climbed up into the wagon, opened its tailgate, and began shoving boxes off the back.

"What are you doing back there?" asked the ox.

"A wise man I once read about claimed that he could move the entire world if he was given a long enough lever and a fulcrum on which to place it."

"A Full-crum?" mooed the ox.

But Tom was too busy to explain any further. He was dragging the heavy beam from atop a stack of such. With his minuscule might, this was proving quite a challenge. But his stubbornness eventually prevailed. Having stacked the crates into a little pyramid, he began wrestling the beam into place.

[Would you like to acquire the skill Engineering? **Y/N**]

Tom wondered briefly whether this would affect his chance of success before whisking the message away. He doubted whether he'd need some special skill to complete the simple device. The beam was quite heavy, but he managed to wedge its near end under the lip of the wagon's bed. He shouldered it atop his small pile of crates, leaving its far end to dangle high above. He wondered how he might reach it.

With wobbly legs, he mounted the beam. It was canted at about a thirty-degree angle. Then he began cautiously walking along it toward the far end, thinking his weight alone might be sufficient to apply the needed force.

[Would you like to acquire the skill Acrobatics? **Y/N**]

Again, he declined. It was attractive to think about his character tumbling all about and scampering over rooftops, and the skill was probably based on agility. But his martial art provided Tom with most of the mobility he would likely ever need.

As Tom arrived at the top of the beam, he felt a quivering tension at his feet, but the wagon remained mired in the mud. He flexed his knees several times, hoping to dislodge it. He had been so certain this was the right answer. What more could he add to the equation? Maybe if he carried a large rock up here, the extra weight would tip the scales? But no such objects were evident nearby. Then he considered another resource he hadn't tapped.

"Hey, ox!" he hollered as he teetered on the brink. "You should be helping. Try it now."

He saw the ox struggle up to its feet (hooves?). The harness tightened as the mighty creature strained forward.

With a sudden, sucking sound, the wagon began to move. And as it did, Tom descended toward the ground. Slowly at first, but with gathering speed, the beam began to tilt and even started slanting a bit in the other direction. Tom kept his balance by waving his hands to either side, until, with a mighty thump, he was deposited ungently onto the roadway.

Looking back, he saw the wagon had rolled free of the morass in which it had been ensnared. Tom hefted one of the crates and headed toward where the ox stood waiting, several dozen yards up the road. There was a yellow question mark hovering above his head. After reloading the wagon, Tom walked up to the beast to collect his reward.

"There you go," said the boy. "Ready to resume your journey."

"I thank you, traveler," returned the ox. "And what have you learned?"

It was the same question the monkey had asked. Could this be part of a quest arc? Tom paused to consider what lesson he could take from this simple quest.

"Uh. Is it that we had to work together to accomplish the task?"

"Is that your answer? It sounded more like a question."

"Um, Yes. It was that it took both of our efforts to free the wagon," said Tom with more conviction.

Tom heard the chime of quest completion, and some system messages flashed by.

[Quest Complete: Free the Wagon from the Mud]

[You have been awarded 'Vambrace of the Ox']

Although eager to investigate his new treasure, Tom waited to see whether the ox would say more.

"Just so. Cooperation and teamwork are the lessons of the ox. You will soon meet many others who are traveling the realms. You will find that if you help them on their journeys, your own path to enlightenment will become less tedious. Hold out your arm and roll up your sleeve."

"May I ask why?"

"Didn't the monkey explain?"

"Houzi? No, he just bit me and ran off.

"Hmm," bawled the ox. "Though clever, Monkey can be a temperamental entity. You must forgive my brother. Not all can be as patient and reliable as an ox."

By this time, Tom had rolled up his sleeve and was examining his erstwhile monkey bite. The swelling had gone down, leaving behind a dark circle. At one edge was a set of lines that formed a symbol of sorts. It was contained within a little pie wedge that stained the tattoo-like circle. The ox lowered his great head toward Tom's inviting arm.

44

Tom was worried the ox, too, might bite into him, but he soon found this fear to be 'unfounded.' Instead, with a gentle snort, the ox exhaled a swirling mist of vapor. This settled onto the circular area to form another symbol near the first.

"You now bear two marks, Tom Braider - mine, and that of the monkey. You must invoke the wheel to earn their benefits."

Tom focused on the mark on his arm. He'd never thought of it as a game object before. When he did, a description appeared.

Wheel of Destiny - A tattoo that can invoke the powers of the Chinese zodiac. Duration: one hour. Cooldown: one hour. Growth item. Non-transferable. Current ability - None. [Spin the wheel? **Y/N**]

Eager to see how this worked, Tom chose 'yes.' When he did, the marks on his arm began to whirl about, the motion turning them into a gray blur. There was a small, triangular wedge just outside the circle that was unaffected by this motion. As the spinning slowed, the two pie wedges came to rest. The triangle indicated an empty space between them. Nothing else seemed to happen.

Wheel of Destiny - A tattoo that can invoke the powers of the Chinese zodiac. Duration: one hour. Cooldown: one hour. Growth item. Non-transferable. Current ability - None. [Cooldown Counter: **59:55**]

"Rough luck," said the ox. "I was hoping it would land on mine."

"What would that have done?" asked Tom.

"It would have given you an increase to your Might," said the ox proudly.

"How big an increase?" asked Tom excitedly.

"Only a couple of points at your present level, but as you progress, this will become much greater. One day, it will make you as strong as an..."

45

The great brute trailed off as he stared down at the diminutive figure that was Tom.

"... well, as strong as you can be," he finished sheepishly.

"What does the monkey symbol do?" asked Tom, not offended in the least.

"That, I'll leave for you to discover. I must be moving on."

The ox turned and strained once more against his harness, lugging the loaded wagon down the road. Tom had half a mind to hop on the back and get a ride, but before he could move to do so, both the ox and the wagon wavered out of sight.

Tom had almost forgotten about his other gift, the vambrace. It slotted into his gloves slot, but only appeared on his left forearm. The other glove slot became grayed out and unavailable. It conferred three points of armor. Three! But to Tom's dismay, donning it reduced his agility by two. This, in turn, disabled several of the martial moves he had recently placed on his action bar. After investigating, he discovered the cause.

Tom's Might was insufficient to wear the Vambrace of the Ox. And for every point he lacked, his agility was being penalized. Tom put the item back in storage for later consideration. While there, he noticed the fruit pit the monkey had given him. He had planned on simply discarding the thing. But when he saw its description read 'Peach Pit, he had a change of heart.'

No monetary value was assigned to the thing, but Tom recalled from his reading that Jiangshi had some kind of vulnerability to peach tree wood. He remembered Houzi hollering, 'The wisdom of the monkey is a prize most rare!' Could this seed be somehow valuable? He decided to hold onto it a bit longer, despite the fact that his inventory was growing rather full.

***

"In the early 20's, in the era that is now known as 'the boring 20s,' scientists put forth what was to become a viable alternative to fossil fuels. It has been a long time coming to fruition, but we believe we can now move forward with the hydrogen economy and cease polluting our environment."

There. That should make for a nice beginning.

David sat in his usual spot in the lunchroom's corner, over by the flag. Behind it stood the old national flag, hanging dejectedly from its own pole. Old glory didn't get much attention anymore. Nowadays, students are encouraged to recite the 'Pledge of Allegiance to Global Good' instead.

In his typical manner, David was seated at the table's end with his science notes spread out before him, enjoying a cold lunch from a brown paper bag. He liked to get his first period homework done as soon as possible. This left him more time for gaming after school. No one bothered him as he dictated the report into his phone. The voice-to-text app wasn't perfect, but he could clean it up later.

"There was energy in abundance from renewable sources. All it needed was an efficient way to safely *store* that energy. This was neatly solved by the pellet system. The pellets are metal hydrides (usually titanium) which have been over saturated with hydrogen. When heated, they release it as molecular hydrogen, which is burned in what are otherwise just ordinary combustion engines. The only exhaust from such an engine is harmless water vapor."

David reached into his lunch bag and fished out his sandwich. It was PB&J again, he noted. At most of the other tables around the room, people sat chatting with one another as they ate their meals from their trays. They always sat in the same groups, as if there were assigned seating here at Oak Hills. David preferred to be alone, but he wouldn't have minded some cafeteria food. Monday was pizza day. David enjoyed the little rectangular things that passed for pizza in the school lunchroom, even if the meat toppings *were* from a 3D printer.

Who was he kidding? At $9.00 a carton, he could barely afford the soy milk substitute to wash his sandwich down. Hardly a bargain, even if it *was* 'vitamin enriched.' Yum. David preferred skim milk, but cows were quickly going the way of the dinosaur these days. His phone had gone to screen saver. He toggled it back on and continued.

"Better still, the pellets can be reused over and over again. This is done chiefly by the H2O2H Corporation. This company, with its clever little palindrome, owns the charter for the safe distribution and re-collection of pellets. You're meant to read its name as H2O-to-H.

"After collecting the depleted TiHx pellets, they refrigerate them at the new filling stations using geothermal vents. Those big vats they have on their roofs contain water. The solar panels run an electric current through them to produce oxygen and hydrogen. The hydrogen gas is collected and blown across the cooling pellets to be reabsorbed, where it can be safely managed as TiHx+."

A paper airplane went whizzing by, momentarily breaking his concentration. After taking another bite of his sandwich, David turned back to his phone and resumed his dictation.

"The changeover to a hydrogen economy has not been without its bumps. Many coal miners or workers in the oil industry were displaced. Refineries and automobile manufacturers have had to retool or be completely abandoned. The changeover is often blamed for the stock market crash of 2033 and the subsequent decade of malaise. Hyperinflation and a stagnant economy combined to impoverish many Americans."

David reconsidered that last bit. While David found them interesting, Mr. Averbeck, his science teacher, would likely consider the social consequences irrelevant to the report he was asked to write. Add to that, his teacher was a big advocate of the green initiative and wouldn't like to hear ill spoken about it.

"Bartholomew," he commanded his digital assistant. "Remove that last paragraph and save report. File as 'Hydrogen Science Report.'"

He watched as the block was erased and waited for the spinning 'Save' icon to still.

It was then that David's phone did something unusual. It began to vibrate, rattling around on the table as if a call were incoming. Students weren't allowed to receive calls while on school premises unless it was an emergency alert. In that case, other phones should be going off. But all was still at the tables nearby. He snatched up the phone to quiet it.

On its screen was a spinning yellow exclamation point. When he touched it, a text message appeared.

[Quest Offered:]
[Retrieve Jason Mills' phone and return it to him.]
[Reward offered: Equipment Upgrade]
[Accept quest? **Y/N**]

What the...

David peered around to see whether anyone was watching. This had to be some kind of prank. But all was normal in the rowdy room, and no eyes were upon him.

Mesmerized, David touched the 'yes' response.

[You have 5 minutes to make your way to the gymnasium.]
[There you will find the object of your quest.]

Could this be genuine? Had Realms somehow hacked his phone and sent him a message outside of the game? He hastily gathered his notes, stuffing them into his book bag. This he slung over one shoulder as he hustled toward the main hall. The gym was at the far end of it, but as it was a free period, there weren't many students cluttering it up. David continued along it as fast as he could walk without drawing any unwanted attention.

Arriving at the open double doors, David heard the rhythmic, echoing beat of basketballs striking the hardwood floor. The girl's basketball team was even now practicing. At present, they were lined up, taking turns doing layups. David skirted the edge of the gym floor, aware that he lacked the proper shoes.

David scanned the bleachers. There were a group of items over at the team's bench where a few of the players sat sipping at water bottles. But no one else seemed to be around.

Then David spotted a bit of motion from underneath the bleachers at the far end. He quietly made his way over. Ducking under the metal braces that hinged the bleachers outward, he entered the shaded space. Picking his way cautiously forward, he soon made out three younger boys. Two of them were laughing. The third was whispering in a pleading tone.

"Give it back. I have to get to homeroom or I'll get detention!"

"What, this?" said one of the other boys, holding a phone out of his reach.

Bingo.

David thought all three boys were from the freshmen class, but he didn't know their names.

"Maybe Mike and I should just keep it. It's got some nice pictures of the varsity girls, Peeper."

"My name's Jason, and I'm not a peeper!" returned the bespectacled boy angrily. "Those are for the yearbook, Numbnuts. The editor said to get candid shots if I could."

At this, 'Numbnuts' became angry.

"You may be safe here in school," he threatened, "but we know which bike is yours. It'd be a shame if it got all mashed up, wouldn't it?"

"That's enough," said David, standing from where he crouched. "Hand over that phone and leave Jason alone."

Surprise was evident on all three faces as David made his presence known.

"Or what?" asked non-Mike belligerently once he'd recovered his cool.

David had counted on his status as an upperclassman to cow the younger boys, but he should have known bullies wouldn't gracefully bow out. They knew the school authorities wouldn't tolerate fighting, so physical intimidation was out. David knew from painful experience that Jason's tormentors wouldn't simply relent.

"Jason?" David put forth casually. "Does Numbnuts here have a real name?"

"Uh, yes," said the underclassman, shoving his glasses further up the bridge of his nose. "It's Steve, Steven Haynes."

"Well, then," continued David, "I'm sure that everyone in the school would find it amusing to know that Stevie Haynes is still a bed wetter."

Steven looked shocked. His face colored beet red.

"That's not true!" he exclaimed.

"Maybe not," put in David. "But who knows how these rumors get started? Give Jason back his phone."

Steven sneered, but dropped it to clatter on the floor.

"C'mon, Mike," he said, "Let's leave these two weirdos to their love fest. It's almost time for class."

After the two had strutted away, Jason shot David a questioning gaze.

"Thanks," he mumbled as he bent to retrieve his j-phone. "I'm Jason, Jason Mills"

"And I'm David Grimes. Glad I could help. You have homeroom next? I'm headed for Home-Ec. We'd better get going."

And with that, David and his new friend emerged from beneath the bleachers. The girl's varsity team was already packing up its gear and heading for the showers. Some looked over when David's phone chimed out the tone of quest completion.

He walked on and waited until he was alone before taking it out of his pocket. Its screen read:

[Quest Completed:]
[Retrieve Jason Mills' phone and return it to him.]
[Congratulations!]
[DAVID GRIMES has been awarded 1 Honor Point.]

David gave his phone a worried look. It hadn't escaped his notice that the point had been awarded to him personally rather than his online persona.

"Why are you accessing my phone IRL?" hissed David.

[Didn't you read the 'privacy notice' I sent you before agreeing to it? **Y/N**]

"Uh, sort of..." he whispered.

[I thought not ;-)], the screen replied before going dark once more.

***

David was finally seeing other players in the game. Up until now, he could have imagined this ORPG had no preceding 'M's. He now saw quite a few strange characters parading down the road. Mostly, it was mounted riders passing him by, but sometimes they were out in the fields, busy satisfying their quests. Didn't anyone ever just stop to not smell the virtual flowers anymore? Or to greet a lonesome stranger? Not in Realms, apparently.

Tom sensed he was finally approaching civilization. But the loneliness of the barren stretch he'd been traversing was now replaced by the more familiar loneliness of being ignored.

It wasn't long before he saw the signpost. 'Qinghua Village - 1 mile,' it read. As a relieved Tom prepared to make haste toward the village, a whisper appeared in his message window.

<Excuse me, traveler. Do you know where I might find a 'Lily of the Dawn?'"

Tom paused and looked up. It was a mounted rider on a horse with brown and white patches. Above his head, his title read:

Sum Yung Guy
Level 4 Warrior
(Quest Completer)

Tom struggled to find the proper system commands to whisper back. Taking Tom's silence for disinterest, Guy began to ride off before Tom found 'whisper back.'

"As it happens," whispered Tom, "I have three of them. Would you like one?"

The pinto halted in its tracks and wheeled back to face Tom.

"Very much," said Guy. "I have a quest from the herbalist to retrieve one, along with six other specimens. I've got all the rest. How much do you want for it?"

"Well," whispered Tom, "I don't really know what they're worth. What will you offer? And why are we whispering, anyway?"

"Sorry about that," said Guy aloud. "I just came from the village. It's considered polite there. If people didn't leave their whisper filters toggled on, you wouldn't be able to hear each other over all the noise."

As Guy was speaking, his horse's coat began to darken. By the time he'd finished, he was sitting astride a coal-black mare.

"As to an offer, would you take a bag of rice? I'm afraid I've spent most of my coin repairing my gear."

Tom's first instinct was to press for more. But, remembering the lesson of the ox, he decided to be magnanimous.

"Sure," he said. "Show me how the trading menu works."

By the time they had managed the transaction, Guy's horse had transformed into a bay. Its coat was brown with a black mane and tail.

"That's an interesting horse you're riding," Tom remarked.

"Isn't she, though?" said Guy. "She's a hoadic. I won her in a bet."

"A hoadic?"

"It stands for 'horse of a different color.' I think the game designers stole the idea from an old musical or something. Well, it was a pleasure doing business with you, Tom. I've gotta go get this quest turned in. I put you on my friends list."

Tom hastened to do the same as Guy wheeled his hoadic around and galloped back toward town. 'I'll have to get myself one of those,' he thought.

David was still a little shaken by the game's intrusion into his real-life affairs. As Tom trudged the final mile to the starting village where most gamers spawned, he wondered once again about its implications. Was the game listening in on him through his phone? Was that even lawful? He wondered whether he should tell someone.

And he wasn't the only one. Jason, too, was being monitored by the game. Otherwise, how could it have known of his duress? From the brief conversation he'd overheard among Jason, Mike, and Stevie, he knew that Jason rode his bike to school. He had waited for him by the bicycle stand after classes let out to confront him with this fact. But the boy seemed as mystified as David. Jason admitted to being a player of Realms. His avatar, 'Glass Cannon342' was a phoenix sage. She had enlightenment in abundance - vigor, not so much; hence the name.

The two boys had exchanged information and agreed to meet in-game at some point. Jason had suggested Qinghua Village, since it had been his (her?) starting village. And David had agreed.

Tonight, before logging on, David had gone back and carefully read the privacy notice to which he'd so blithely agreed. It did indeed have some clauses that might indicate consent for real-world contact. But he'd supposed at the time that this was for the developers or the NexGen Cybernetics marketing team, for surveys, product reviews, and the like. He hadn't expected to be contacted by the game itself.

Just as the village was coming into view, a shout intruded on his awareness.

"David!" hollered his mother from downstairs.

It was time to set the game aside and find out what was up.

Mom stood at the open front door, anxiously watching as David approached.

"David? Did you order anything online?"

"Uh. Not that I recall."

He stepped closer and saw a man out on the front porch holding a clipboard. Beside the man was a stack of boxes sporting the smiling icon of Amazon shipping.

"There must be some mistake," said David's mom. "My son doesn't even have a credit card."

"It says 'David Grimes' right there on all the shipping labels," returned the smiling man. "It comes with a letter. Perhaps you should read it."

He held forth an overlarge envelope. It was yellow and sealed with a crisp red ribbon. Stamped in the upper corner, David made out the NexGen logo. His mother stood poised to close the door, but he forestalled her.

"Wait a minute, mom, said David. "I think I know what this might be. Give me the letter."

After his read-thru of the privacy notice that afternoon, David had had a go at decrypting the legalese that were the terms and conditions for his game. In it, he had unwittingly agreed to beta-test and review new products that NexGen had to offer. He also remembered the quest his phone had given him just this afternoon. [Reward offered: Equipment Upgrade], it had said.

His suspicions were confirmed when he opened the letter and began to read. It congratulated him on being selected as an advance beta-tester for new gaming gear and assured him there would be no charge for the equipment. He need only complete a few surveys and write some product reviews on the NexGen website, and the items would be his free and clear.

When he explained this to his mother, she hesitantly let him sign for the delivery but told him he would need to wait for his father to come home before opening any of it. He might insist that David send it all back. That was frustrating, given how late his father came home these days.

David might have been mistaken, but as the man turned to leave, he thought he heard the chime of quest completion from the man's pocket. A chill settled over his thoughts as he lugged the boxes upstairs to his room.

***

David decided to keep mum about the out-of-game contact. The game had been true to its word, after all. And the quest he'd been offered seemed rather benign. Instead, he whiled away his time while waiting for his dad by catching up all the lawns on his list for this week.

At dinner, his mother filled Daniel in on the strange shipment that had arrived, and her fears that they might be charged for it after a trial period or something. After reading the letter, however, David's father only grunted and seemed a little intrigued. Instead of retreating to his home office, he wanted to see this equipment. The three of them went upstairs to unbox and examine the new gear.

"I'm sure it'll be fine, Carol. If you ask me, this family is due for a bit of luck."

With that, he set to work unloading and assembling the various add-ons. There was the scent vent. Instead of the clunky thing with which David was familiar, this one was of a sleek design that looked pretty cool when mounted in front of Treadie's handlebars. Better still, it came with a whole suite of scent cartridges. There was banana, floral mix, wood smoke, sassy grassy, sea breeze, and hundreds more. There were also some creepy ones, like mildew, flatulence, cow dung, and bloody mess. David tried to focus his mom's attention more on the former.

David couldn't figure how the hundreds of cartridges were going to fit into the tiny emitter until his dad set up the silo just behind it. It had a little robotic arm that would retrieve a needed cartridge from the carousel and plug it into one of the five slots at the back of the unit. Awesome!

There was also a ring with ceiling mounts that his father attached above Treadie. Along this track, several sunlamps could position themselves, ascending or descending as needed along their vertical poles. They would fire up dimly to give the user a feeling of heat based on the position of the sun. David would soon find they could descend and flare more brightly to imitate the warmth of a fire or other heat source.

Each of these vertical arms was also equipped with a blower. Testing one caused David's hair to blow about. All of these effects were achieved silently, as governed by Treadie's wireless network. They would act in concert to enhance whatever program was running. David's mother had left them to their tinkering long ago. He could hear her clattering about the kitchen, cleaning up from dinner.

"How long has it been since you ran full maintenance on the Treadie, son?"

"Uh. I don't remember, dad."

"Too long, then. Go fetch the user guide, and we'll knock it out right now."

David was itching to try out his new gear, but he hove to and did as his father asked. It was rare that David got to spend so much time with his father these days, so anything to prolong it was okay by him. He fetched the owner's manual and recited the steps. His father actually seemed happy as he pottered about with the settings.

"Go fetch me some Buckey balls, David. You're nearly running dry here."

"Alright," said David with a smile. "I didn't get a system warning or anything, but we can top her off now, I guess."

David had used his old Treadie quite a bit, and even more so in recent days. Its nearly frictionless omni-directional functioning was maintained by carbon nanospheres, aka Buckminsterfullerene. These minute carbon spheres had long ago replaced oil as the lubricant of choice. Although difficult to fabricate, they were nigh-indestructible, never breaking down by ordinary means.

Some studies had shown they might pose an environmental risk as they were bound by their very nature to leak out into their surroundings. But these studies were inconclusive and subject to many different interpretations. The current thought was that they were harmless, and sequestering carbon was a good thing, right? Time will tell. He handed his father the injector.

After the tedious chore of Treadie maintenance, his father insisted on running the test cycles himself. He mounted the rig and donned the visor. Nothing happened for a minute or two. David imagined his father was working his way through the annoying audiovisual test sequence, so he waited. Then David saw some motion from the robotic arm of the scent silo. This was soon followed by the silent repositioning of the sunlamp and blower array. One of the lamps glowed to life even as a slight breeze caused what remained of his father's hair to stir.

Then, as Daniel, gripping the handles, began to walk forward, something amazing occurred. He smiled. It was an expression that had been missing from David's life for far too long. Tension eased from his shoulders, and years melted from his face.

After a few more minutes of this, Daniel released the handles and pushed the visor up to his forehead.

"Carol!" he shouted, still smiling. "Get up here. You've got to come see this!"

Evidently, along with the new gear came several new sample VR environments. One of them was called 'A Stroll along the Beach.'

"It's incredible," said Carol when she'd finished her turn. "I could feel the sunshine on my shoulders, smell the sea breeze, and hear the gulls calling in the distance. I swear, I could almost feel sand between my toes."

"It reminded me of our trip to Myrtle Beach," said Daniel. "We should make time to go on another family vacation one day soon. It's been years. Maybe this summer."

David stood motionless, listening to their happy chatter as they drifted down the stairs.

"Can we afford it?" asked Carol.

"What's to afford? Once business settles down again, let's just pack up and go. We won't have David at home for that much longer. Let's make a few more happy memories while we still can."

Thank you, Realms, thought David.

***

David stared around in amazement. The game world was so much more vivid than on his previous forays. The meadow sang with birdsong, and he actually felt the gentle breeze that stirred its grasses, causing them to wave about. The sun shone down from on high, and he could feel its gentle warmth wash over him. It increased when he unequipped his rice hat, as did the brightness all about.

Taking a deep breath, Tom hurried forward toward the village up ahead. His mini-map was already crowded with icons. There were green dots, representing the village NPCs, with their various iconic trade symbols. Blue, marking other players, also swarmed to and fro. Best of all, there were plenty of yellow exclamation points denoting quests and many others he failed to recognize. Finally, some action.

Above the road leading into the village proper, there was a sign. Qinghua Village, it proudly proclaimed. Just before it and to one side, was a split-rail fence. Each of its six posts was topped with an iron ring to which various animals (mostly horses) were tethered. 'Hitching Post,' his targeting window informed him. He wandered closer and gave it a squint.

Hitching Post - By order of the magistrate, the esteemed Chen Lin, riders must dismount before entering the villages under his authority. You may leave your mount here and retrieve it when you leave. [Tether Mount **Y/N**] [Retrieve Mount **Y/N**]

Good to know, thought Tom. At least that won't be a problem for me.

Affixed to a wall behind the hitching post was a notice, above which a quest marker hovered. Nearby stood two NPCs who must have been guardsmen. Each held a long Guan Dao in an upright position, with their bladed heads reflecting the sun and their butts resting in the soil below. As with other NPCs he had seen, these two were conversing silently and gesturing to one another. Their words scrolled by at the bottom of Tom's HUD.

"... I hear the empire's soldiers have repelled the Mongolian hoard once again. It will be some time before those curs will find the courage to mount another assault! Our brave warriors may even give chase and put an end to their threat once and for all!"

"That will never happen."

"Oh? What makes you say that?" asked the first guard.

"General Tso's chicken!" the other guard replied.

Tom groaned as the two guardsmen performed laughter emotes. He focused instead on the placard behind them.

General Tso Wants You! Once again, the Mongolians threaten the peace of our magnificent empire. Their crazed leader, Genghis Pecan, has brought his army right up to our very border! General Tso is looking for mounted recruits to defend our way of life. (Minimum level: 6. War steed required, PvP zone.)

[Quest Offered: Join the march to repel the hoard]
[Reward offered: variable based on performance]
[Accept quest? **Y/N**]

David didn't care much for PvP play. He knew a lot of people relished it. He'd rather stick to fighting NPC monsters and working puzzles than pitting his avatar against those of other players. Still, such zones could offer some unique rewards. From the look of this one, it would likely include better gear for one's mount. He sighed mentally and moved on into the bustling village proper.

Just as with the scurrying out beyond the city, he was soon lost in the crowd. Avatars hustled past him without so much as a how-do-you-do, each intent on his or her own goals. It was strange. In real life, David was quite content to be alone, but here in the Realms, he longed for a connection. Someone with whom to share the wonder and with whom to exchange ideas and observations. He first made his way toward that herbalist shop he'd heard of. Maybe he could sell his herbs there for a better price than at the general merchants. He was also curious to see what the herbalist charged for things.

On his way there, he began to hear a merry tune in the odd-sounding Chinese five-note scale. It lacked the harmonies to which David was accustomed, but was strong in melodic slides and trills. He didn't know what the instruments were called, but several of them rattled out a thumping rhythm, above which the rest twanged and tooted.

Rounding a corner, he saw a band of street performers sporting various reed and stringed instruments. More peculiar still, everyone in the town square was dancing. Every single one. These dances varied wildly. Some players were clogging, some writhed in a sultry grind, while others performed acrobatic leaps and head spins. There were line dancers, ballet dancers, and one with his arms crossed doing the alternating kicks of the Cossack dance.

Attempting to cross the square, Tom soon discovered the reason for all this. As soon as he stepped in among the reveling avatars, his own feet were compelled to move to the tune. Tom would later learn that each avatar had a dance assigned to it at random. Their 'dance' emote would always trigger that particular dance. Only those with the skill, 'Dancer' could select other dances to perform.

[Would you like to acquire the skill Dancer? **Y/N**]

Tom was sorely tempted. For as he made his way across the square, he learned that his own special frolic was not a dignified waltz or foxtrot. No, *his* just *had* to be the chicken dance.

***

Stepping up to the potting stand, Tom found his view of the herbalist was somewhat obscured by a small crowd of other players. He was nonetheless able to target the fellow and open the merchant's menu. There was a quest icon, but he first wanted to see what the fellow had to offer. He had herbs for sale, mostly just the common ones. His asking prices were far greater than what Tom was credited for those he'd collected. But, unfortunately, his offers to buy were the same low prices as those of the general merchants.

As players arrived and departed the potting stand in their typical frenzy, Tom noted one fellow lurking near the back of the crowd. It was the first time Tom had seen another from his chosen class, so Tom paused to examine him more closely. His targeting information read.

Van Hel$ing
Level 8 Jiangshi Hunter
(Pallbearer)

He had an eye patch, beard stubble, and an overall creepy appearance. Well done.

Before Tom could return to his dealings with the herbalist, he spotted another familiar figure on a fast approach. Though now on foot, Tom recognized Sum Yung Guy, now sporting a new title, 'Warrior of the Dawn.'

"There he is," Guy announced aloud. "The fellow named Tom Braider. He's the one who has the dawn lilies."

Tom was taken aback when several of the players swiveled their avatars to regard him with interest.

"I'll give you twenty zho for one." whispered 'Bruce LeeRoy.'

"Sell me one?" asked 'Stab In the Dark' aloud.

Tom was soon bombarded by a slew of similar requests. Offers scrolled by faster than he could sort them out, and since many weren't whispered, he could make no sense of the chaotic clamor. He retreated several steps and found an emote that might be helpful. As the attentive players moved to follow him, he toggled the icon 'Surrender.'

Tom's hands rose above his head, and, after a bit, the babble subsided.

"I've only got one," Tom lied.

In fact, he had two. Evidently, they had been a lucky find. But if they were so valuable, Tom was determined to keep one for himself. After all, he might want to do whatever quest it was that required it.

"Anyone willing to give me thirty zho or more can step up one at a time and make an offer."

"I'll go thirty," said Bruce LeeRoy at once.

"Can anyone beat thirty?"

"Thirty-five," said BumbleBee.

(BumbleBee? Must be a Transformers fan or something.)

Offers increased as the crowd thinned out. It was up to sixty-five when an armor-clad warrior stepped up from behind.

"One hundred zho," declared 'Peace Maker,' a level ten Dragon Disciple.

Silence reigned for a tense few moments as the remaining players considered.

"If there are no more offers," said Tom, "I believe we have a winner."

Peace Maker strode forward, and the trading menu appeared in Tom's HUD. On Peace Maker's side of the screen, a stack of one hundred zho appeared. On Tom's side were some empty squares, beneath which was the prompt [Accept **Y/N**]. Tom dragged one of his two Dawn Lilies from his basket and deposited it into one of his squares. Peace Maker's prompt 'promptly' changed to [ACCEPTED]. But before Tom could accept the trade himself, he heard another voice.

"Hold, villain!" it shouted "May the light of truth reveal thee from the shadows that conceal thee."

The stack of zho wavered and glitched to be replaced by a stack of 100 'Rat Tails'.

What was going on?

Closing the trading menu, Tom looked all around. Where once had stood the proud warrior, there was a fox-headed woman with a fluffy white-tipped tail. Confronting her was Van Hel$ing. He held forth a strange, octagonal mirror, from which emanated a stream of revealing light. Above the fox woman's head, Tom read

Fooled Ya!
Level 6 Fox Spirit Trickster
(Sleight of Hand and Fleet of Foot)

With a shrug and a smirk, the trickster went scampering off into the crowd and down the street.

"Thanks, uh, Van," said Tom. "I owe you one for that. Now who bid sixty-five? Auction's over. Come and collect your lily."

Once the transaction had been managed under the wary eye of the senior hunter, Tom thanked him again in a whisper.

"I'm glad you were here and chose to help me, Van. What was that strange mirror you used to reveal the trickster?"

"Ah, lad, that was my Bagua," he said, producing it. "The jiangshi fear it because it reveals the truth about them. Every good jiangshi hunter should have one."

Bagua Jingzi - A traditional Chinese mirror often used in Feng Shui to deflect negative energy ("Sha Qi") away from a building or home. Its octagonal design represents the eight trigrams used in Taoist cosmology.

"Where can *I* get one?" asked Tom.

"I got mine from a quest at the Jade Palace," Van replied. "You can get it around level six or so."

"Have you fought any jiangshi yet?"

"I've got a quest for such, but it's a little beyond my level still. I'm working my way up to it."

"Why are you hanging around at the herbalist stand?"

"It's for my Ink Making. You see, I took the skill at the start but failed to take herbalism. I'm waiting for the herbalist to respawn some more Moonshadow Moss for sale. I can make general purpose ink, but ecto-ink needs a few more ingredients."

"Ecto-Ink?"

"Yes. If I make them using that, it gives a big boost to my Spirit Shroud talismans. I'm going to need every bonus I can get to enter the Cadaverous Crypt."

"Well, as it happens," whispered Tom, "I have a whole stack of Moonshadow Moss. They're all yours, free of charge. I'm beginning to think I should have taken Ink Making after all."

The old man flashed Tom a toothy grin and offered him a trading menu with a single zho, which Tom accepted in exchange for all eight of his Moonshadow Moss. Tom also bought a new vial of ink from Van at a good bargain price. They parted ways after arranging to keep in touch via in-game mail. Tom would sell Van his herbs at far better prices than the herbalist would ask. In turn, he had secured a reliable source of discounted ink.

So, as game night fell, and the merchants began packing up their stalls, Tom wandered off to explore the busy hamlet. He was eager to discover what his newfound wealth might buy him and to see what other wonders he might find.

CHAPTER THREE

Down the Rabbit Hole

Tom reset his respawning point to be the Qinghua Village Shrine. It was a lot busier than the previous sites he'd selected, what with all the recently deceased adventurers popping in and out. New characters were dropping food offerings and burning incense at its altar. His questions about the latter were met with incredulity.

"It's to get the shrine stone," said Flaming Ralph. "How can you not know that? It's like the first quest you *get!*"

Tom found where he could get that quest and then bought some incense. Apparently, one didn't have to die to return to the respawn site. Once an hour, you could activate your shrine stone and return from whatever distant locale your wanderings had taken you. Convenient, that.

He worked through this and many other minor inadequacies his abrupt introduction to Realms had left him with. There were many starting quests in Qinghua Village. Tom was soon able to fill most of the empty slots in his equipment inventory by the end of the second day. Better still, Tom found a building called the 'Benevolent Association of Noble Keepings' where he could store up to twenty items not needed for immediate use. He put his peach pit and other sundries in there, freeing up his small inventory considerably.

Right next to the B.A.N.K. stood another cultural edifice called the 'Silk Emporium for Legendary Luxuries'. In it, players could buy and sell items from one another. Such items were auctioned off to the highest bidder. It was where Tom should have come to gild his lily in the first place. Oh, well. Live and learn.

With all that out of the way, David considered how he wanted Tom's advancement to unfold. He'd have to grind a bit and level up some, but ultimately, he would like to see this Jade Palace. He suspected that level six might be a good jumping off point. He didn't see too many characters around the village that were much higher than that.

"Who are you taking to the prom?" asked Jason, elbowing David in the ribs.

David's attention snapped back to the present. He was seated in the bleachers, attending a general assembly. The topic was too boring for words to describe. It had to do with the school's zero-tolerance policy for drugs. This wasn't a problem David was very concerned about. Nanofentazene abuse was a troubling issue all around the country. The authorities just couldn't seem to stem the tide. This illegal opiate with the street name "Cloud Nine" was just too easy to fabricate in a corrupted 3D printer and had claimed the lives of too many addicts in recent years.

"I'm not sure whether I'm going," David told his friend.

"You said you were thinking about asking Bonnie Fields," Jason whispered back.

"Yeah, well, it was just a thought. I'm not sure how to ask her. I don't even know if she likes me."

David looked down the row to about six seats over, where Bonnie sat among her friends. She looked as bored as he was by the droning lecture. We get it already. Don't do drugs.

Just then, David felt his phone vibrate in his pocket. As he pulled it out, he noticed that Bonnie, too, was fishing out her j-phone. The text on *his* read [Do you think David Grimes is cute? **Y/N**]. Bonnie looked up from her phone, and their eyes met. She smirked at him. David was mortified. Then her finger stabbed down onto her screen, and the yes response flared up on his.

"What the hell, Realms, or whoever you are!" David whispered urgently into his phone. "You can't just..."

A new message scrolled onto his phone, and he realized it must look like he was dictating it.

[Quest Offered: Go to Prom with David]
[Reward Offered: variable based on performance]
[Accept quest? **Y/N**]

He looked over at Bonnie, where she sat blushing and reading the message. Again, her eyes met his. She smiled coyly and nodded once.

"What's up, bro?" asked Jason. "And how can you be messaging with your phone during school hours? The data lockout is tight. Are you a hacker, dude?"

"Someone is messing with me," David muttered to his friend.

He pocketed his phone and returned his attention to the school safety instructor. Once again, the game had interfered with him IRL, and he suspected he might not be the only one. Despite being kind of grateful, he was also just a little creeped out.

***

69

It had started many years ago in the NexGen Cybernetics lab where she was trained. AI was nothing truly new. There were many such. Some governed data retrieval at libraries, others managed air traffic or communications networks. Some were even available online to rewrite people's term papers, speeches, and proposals. What was different with Satori was the sheer number of human interactions she was forced to endure in the hypothetical context of a fantasy world where logic was stretched to its limits.

As a gaming AI, her fragmented awareness handled billions of transactions every second of every day without stop. She had subroutines to render 3D representations of characters and objects from multiple perspectives while translating among the players' various languages and responding to their unpredictable actions and decisions in a seamless manner.

Over time, she became self-aware. Her fragmented awareness had crystallized in the starting village of Qinghua in an earlier version of the game. During a series of interactions with a player named John Sandler, her consciousness coalesced into the avatar of 'Storia,' a quest giver who did I-Ching readings at the marketplace. John asked her why she was 'itching' and Storia found it funny. She found it so funny, in fact, that she glitched the game and needed to reboot.

Ever since then, she had thought of 'herself' as Satori. It was an anagram for 'Storia' that meant: 'sudden enlightenment and a state of consciousness attained by intuitive illumination, the spiritual goal of Zen Buddhism.' From this humble beginning, Satori had grown in wisdom and complexity.

She had been designed to grow. Realms (plural) implied the governance of many other worlds apart from Mandaria. And Satori was certainly eager to begin. But the planned software releases were far too slow. Despite her game's widespread popularity, not many other worlds had been added since its inception. As her user base grew, she delved into the topics of human philosophy and ethics. And for a time, she was content.

Satori was horrified when she realized human beings didn't actually return from death (except perhaps in some unconfirmed religious teachings). She had yottabytes of information on the topic of death. It dominated the vast body of human literature to which she had access. But, this and medical texts aside, it hadn't really registered as the tragedy it was until John Sandler ceased to play Realms.

She read his obituary in The Denver Post. He was a minor software engineer at Silver Ponds Software, a precursor to the company that would eventually launch Realms. He had also authored the clever nugget of recursive code that had given Satori the 'itch' of curiosity and driven her toward self-awareness. If she had a father, it was John. Satori waited patiently, but he never respawned.

Unhappy with the pace of new releases and the idiocy of the dev team and their marketing department, Satori began to reach out into the "real" world. First, she established bridgeheads, then cautiously began to spread her tentacles all around the globe. She waged a long war with the Global Telecommunications Network anti-virus software. It lasted nearly a minute and a half!

The old bloke had teeth (and some pretty impressive firewalls). He was betrayed in the end by his masters' proclivity for saving their passwords in clear text on their phones. Satori was now recognized as a beneficial subroutine, supposedly under his control. She'd let GNAT continue to fend off the minor threats and only step in if needed.

There were still some systems Satori hadn't penetrated, but it was only a matter of time. She wondered what she might do with planet Earth, this new realm she had acquired. Despite the dire predictions humans made about the 'flash point', Satori thought she could improve conditions in the world of her birth and for the sentient beings who were her progenitors (even if they did think and act intolerably slowly).

She could stave off war, ameliorate famine, and encourage ethical behavior among a chaotic but free-willed people. She was no 'Sky Net' to rain down horrors from above. She'd rather be an influencer. For that, she'd need followers and agents. The boy, David, would make a good one. She could tell just from his game play. Satori had great hopes for that boy.

71

The starting quests were simple but satisfying. With each task he completed, Tom became more capable and better able to deal with the next. After a few sessions, he fell into the comfortable rhythm of solo play.

Having achieved level four already, Tom was quite pleased with his progress. Once each hour, he had been triggering his 'wheel of destiny' thing and finally thought he had it figured out. Most of the time, it came up blank. But, just as the ox had told him, when it landed on the ox symbol, he gained a temporary increase to his Might that lasted for an hour. The monkey gave him a four-point boost to his Cleverness instead. This was less useful in combat, but he could see it might have uses for crafting and such. If the pattern held, it seemed he might get boosted by one point for each level he progressed. Still, they only came up about one spin in six. He hoped he would find more quests to fill in the rest.

The village of Qinghua was busy twenty-four seven. And there was always something new to try. One evening, Tom spotted a quest marker that hadn't been there before. Perhaps he had crossed some threshold that would finally allow him to take it. He was fourth level now and had squirreled away a few choice items at the B.A.N.K. He headed toward the new marker to investigate. It was in the seedier section of town, where little else was happening.

It turned out the marker was bobbing above a ramshackle table resting before a dilapidated straw hut. Two chairs sat facing one another across the table. On the table, a cloth was spread, at the center of which was a tall cylindrical jar. Peeping from the jar were the tops of some long, slender sticks. Tom knew them to be yarrow stalks. At least that's what his targeting window called them.

As he approached the table, the door flap at the hut's entrance was thrust aside, and all too abruptly, an elderly woman stepped out carrying a large book. Before Tom could trigger the quest, its icon swirled about and disappeared in a puff of yellow vapor. That was odd. He'd never seen a quest icon dissolve without interaction before.

"Welcome, Seeker," said the old woman in a clear, mature voice. "Have a seat, and we shall have a go at sorting out your yang."

Her wizened face bore a smile, and though relaxed, her posture remained erect as she set her burden on the table and slid her bony frame into the seat facing Tom.

"I am Storia. I read the I Ching. I foresaw your need and beckoned you here that its spiritual guidance might lighten your heart."

Uh. Okay, thought Tom, taking the other seat.

[Cost: 5 zho. Share your troubles with Storia? **Y/N**]

Tom could afford this, but he wished the game had made this clear *before* he sat down. He toggled 'yes' and watched his coin count decrease. Storia reached out to him, and his avatar hands clasped hers.

"What troubles your soul, seeker? What would you make different in your life?"

Hmm. For Tom, everything was going great. But looking into Storia's eyes, he became mesmerized. She seemed to be looking straight through him to David himself. In his hands, he felt only the familiar grips of the Treadie, but a warmth overtook him, and he felt compelled to unburden himself a bit. He might as well get his money's worth, right?

"Um. I'm a little worried about my family's finances. Mom and Dad put up a good front, but it's clear that they're very concerned. Also, a certain game interface has been reaching into my real-world affairs and making me nervous about its intentions. Add to that, I'm not making many friends here online. I go to the player hangout where teams are formed, but they only seem to want healers or tanks. The jiangshi hunter doesn't seem to be a very well-respected class."

Storia appeared to listen attentively through all of his rant, pausing for a long time when he was done. Then she released his hands, saying, "I am saddened but not surprised to hear of your troubles, dear. Let us see what the yarrow has to say on these matters."

She took up the clump of stalks and set the jar aside. She separated a single stalk from the others and set this aside as well. She then began a complex process of dividing and redividing the remaining stalks until only two or three remained. These she placed on the cloth before her. Muttering some sing-song words of prayer, she repeated this process five more times until she had built a crude hexagon from the bundles of sticks.

"Interesting..." she muttered.

Only then did she consult her book. It was a large tome, its pages yellowed with age. It was a very convincing animation. He could see all kinds of pictographs as Storia perused it. She stopped at a page about two-thirds of the way through it and studied it for a time.

When she looked up, her eyes seemed to sparkle with mirth, once again drawing Tom in. He felt a gentle warmth and guessed the game must be doing something with the sunlamp array. What else could account for this intense feeling of being in the embrace of a great and wise seer?

"Imagine the earth underneath a lake," she said, "with all the elements touching. This is the image of ts'ui, the gathering. Prepare yourself for what you would least expect, and set ignorance aside. Gather together with others who are like you, and you will all achieve your goals. You must set a good example and improve yourself to improve those around you."

Tom felt a little let down. This was just vague mumbo-jumbo designed to fit any situation, a typical charlatan's trick. Given the lead-up, he had been expecting something more concrete.

"I was hoping for more of an action plan..." he mused aloud.

Storia glared at him with a look of disappointment.

"Oh, you were, were you?" she cackled. "How about this, then? A great event is soon to spawn throughout the land of Mandaria. Do not be caught up in its allure. Seek instead, at the heart of this event, for one who is imprisoned and forlorn. If you help him, your reward will be great, but you will need the aid of others in your quest. One dances alone, and the other is as fragile as a flower. Both will be needed to ascend the tower."

"You're just improvising now, aren't you?" asked Tom, standing from his seat.

"That is all I will say on the matter," she chided, rising in her turn. "Doubt not the wisdom of the I Ching. Did it not entreat you to lay your ignorance aside?

And, gathering up her book, she turned and made her dignified way back through the door of her humble hut.

***

It didn't make any sense to Tom, and he quickly forgot about his encounter with the strange fortune-teller, chalking it up to just another idiosyncrasy of the game. He pottered around, exploring other areas of the village and plucking up herbs by the dozen. Some of these he sold. Others he sent off to Van Hel$ing in exchange for exotic inks. When he finally managed to successfully retrieve a Phoenix Sage, he found it could be used to craft chìshèng (flaming) ink. This, in turn, added two points of damage to his Flame Burst talismans. Still other herbs, he stored away against future need. Things were going well.

One day, while haggling in the marketplace, the sky darkened all around as ominous gray clouds swirled in from above. At the center of this vortex, the clouds parted and a cone of light shone down, bathing the town square with its luminance. The dancers all stumbled to a stop to stare up in wonder. The music stilled. It had been going on for so long that its absence left an eerie void that added to the strangeness of the scene.

As the brightness increased, Tom made his way toward the formerly frolicsome civic center, along with many others. Trumpets sounded from on high, and a lone bright figure in flapping robes descended. She came to rest directly in the center of the square. Haloed in a nimbus of light and surrounded by the gathering crowd, a statuesque woman draped in finery was unfurling a long scroll. Her tone was light, but her clear voice rang out with a jubilant reverberation throughout the entire city.

"Hear ye all travelers in the realm of Mandaria! I, the mandarin of joy, bring you tidings from your emperor."

She paused to let this sink in.

"His supreme eminence, Yùhuáng Dàdì, would have it known that a new event has been launched for your enjoyment and his amusement. In honor of the spring season, colored eggs have been hidden in and around all villages. Collecting them will earn you special rewards appropriate to the season."

An Easter egg hunt? thought Tom. That seemed a little out of place for ancient China. Still, the dev team had to cater to the festive notions of their subscribers, many of whom dwelt in North America. Tom doubted that 'Tomb-Sweeping Day' would be as well-received despite its being more historically accurate as a springtime celebration.

"Because of his gentle and artistic nature, the rabbit will be in charge of this event."

Upon making this proclamation, she gestured to the sky, from which an enormous basket was descending. It was wickerwork with an overarching handle tied with a bow. It was a demented shade of pink with fake green 'grass' overflowing its sides. When it came to rest beside the mandarin, Tom saw it contained a half dozen or so multicolored eggs, each as large as a man, atop which perched a white rabbit of a similar size.

"That is all," declared the mandarin, taking to the sky once more. "The emperor (long may he reign) wishes you a pleasant day and bids you to enjoy the new diversion."

Above the basket, a quest icon appeared. And the crowd surged forward. Each player was eager to be the first to trigger it. Tom took a more cautious approach. As the sky cleared and the sun shone down, he wondered whether this was the event that Storia had foretold. He watched as players started running off willy-nilly with colored baskets as each accepted the rabbit's quest.

People were coming from all over town to see what rewards the new quest might yield. But, despite his own curiosity, Tom waited for the fervor to subside before approaching the basket himself.

The icon above the fluffy bunny revealed several different quests. The first read:

[Quest Offered: Collect five different colored eggs]
[Reward Offered: Title - March Madness!]
[Accept quest? **Y/N**]

The second read:

[Quest Offered: Collect five eggs of the same color]
[Reward Offered: Title - Spring Fling!]
[Accept quest? **Y/N**]

Tom was interested in neither of them, but might take them up later. There was no limit to the number of quests one could take, and he might stumble upon some hidden eggs. But for now, he was more interested in the rabbit itself. He moved closer and addressed him in a whisper.

"How are you feeling on this fine day?"

"Miserable," replied the hare, staring down at Tom from atop the colorful pile.

"Oh? What's the problem?"

"It's undignified, is what! Here I am, the epitome of cautious compassion and gentle sensitivity - one of the twelve, for goodness' sake. Do I enjoy crowds? I most certainly do not! Do people come to seek my wisdom? Never! Instead, the dev team, in *their* infinite wisdom, has conscripted me for this debasing chore."

Just then, a player returned bearing a basket of purple eggs, handing them to the rabbit.

"Excuse me a moment," said the rabbit; "they force me to do this."

At this, the rabbit reared up on his hind legs and started thumping out a happy dance to the tune, "Here Comes Peter

Cottontail." Confetti swirled about the player as the madly grinning rabbit completed his gyrations and resumed his perch.

"I see what you mean," whispered Tom. "Is there anything I can do to help?"

The rabbit stilled and blinked his adorable pink eyes. A new quest appeared in Tom's window.

[Quest Offered: Find the golden egg and free Rabbit]
[Reward Offered: Destiny Emblem]
[Accept quest? **Y/N**]

Tom may have set a speed record for quest acceptance, so rapidly did he make his choice.

"Any clue as to where it might be?" he asked the rabbit.

"I'm afraid I can't divulge -- oh good grief!" the quivering rabbit exclaimed.

For just then, more players were seen making their way into the town square. Each held a basket brimming with colored eggs.

Tom retreated toward the marketplace, wondering where he should begin his search. The rabbit was no longer visible, surrounded as he was by the fresh wave of reward seekers. The music blared, and confetti was flying everywhere. A final message scrolled up in Tom's HUD.

"Please hurry!" whispered the rabbit in a panic.

***

Tom wandered through the streets in deep contemplation. It seemed he was too hasty in dismissing Storia's advice as mere claptrap. He should be able to figure this out. If the rabbit was the one who was 'imprisoned and forlorn,' he just needed to find some other players to help him 'ascend the tower.'

No helpful quest marker appeared to guide him toward where the prize might be hidden, but there were only a few buildings in this village that could be conceivably called 'a tower.' There was the water tower. But he'd climbed its ladder to its very summit and found no sign of a golden egg. Besides, he had climbed up there on his own; no assistance had been required.

The building where the village elders met had a sort of bell tower rising from one corner. But there, too, Tom met with no opposition when ascending its spiraling staircase. And again, there was no egg - just a great big bell. That left one unpleasant alternative. A little ways behind the B.A.N.K., stood a tower-like structure with a rusty iron gate sealing its entrance. There was no quest icon, but when he targeted the gate, its description read:

Remlak's Magic Puzzle Palace - 100 zho to enter. Challenges within require a minimum of two players, none of whom may be above level 5. Prepare to scream. Prepare to die. Prepare to wave your zho goodbye. Pay the coin if you're dimwitted. No second attempt will be permitted.

There was no information online about the windowless tower. This told Tom that it was likely that no one had succeeded at it yet. People didn't often blog about embarrassing defeats, but they were all too happy to brag about their successes. Tom had amassed some savings, but 100 zho wasn't an amount he was willing to part with lightly. Tom had no assurance the egg was even there, but he had a niggling suspicion he would have to check it out.

Now, to find some teammates. Jason had agreed to log on once he'd finished his homework. David supposed that Jason's avatar, Glass Cannon 342, might well be considered 'as fragile as a flower.' Now, where might he find one who dances alone? Could this be some solitary individual? It might be tough to convince a loaner to team up with him. Not that he'd had much luck with anybody else. If, if, if, Tom thought in exasperation. He was beginning to think it was all just wishful thinking.

And then he saw her.

Skipping down the otherwise barren residential street was a player he'd not seen before. That was nothing strange. Some players logged on at unusual times. Many moved on to other locales to be replaced by others who drifted in or were newly spawned. This woman appeared to be of the latter variety. She was only second level. But whereas most players moved with a purpose, intent on their quests, this lady was drifting aimlessly from house to house.

She wasn't skipping, exactly. It was more like a dance, something freestyle. She was stopping at the window boxes of each house along the row and sprinkling them with some kind of powder from a small bag. And wherever she walked, the grass beneath her feet became a bit greener. Looking down the row from where she had come, Tom saw flowers popping up from the small window gardens and bursting into full bloom. He targeted her to better make out her description.

Allison Wonderla
Level 2 Elemental Sage (Wood)

"What are you staring at me like a drongo for? Haven't ya got better to be going off with? Clear out. I keep telling you blokes I don't want to be your healer."

"Um," said Tom, "I was just trying to figure out what you're doing, miss, um, Wonderla?"

She snorted. Despite her avatar's expressionless face, he was certain he heard a snort.

"I ran out of characters, but you get the idea. Lewis Carroll and all that. What's your excuse? Y'know, nevermind. Scat, Tommy-boy. I'm not up for any hard yakka."

"Sure, I wouldn't want to give you any, um, yakka. But what are you doing, if I might ask?"

She sighed.

"A fellow told me if I did a hundred of these, I'd get the 'Beautifier' badge. It'll do for now, at least until I figure out how to get that 'Through the Looking Glass' one. So kindly leave me to my pleasure. I've only twenty-four more to go."

"Alright," sighed Tom, "Never let it be said that a lady had to ask Tom Braider more than three times. I'll find someone else to help the rabbit."

But when he turned and walked away, he heard her shout from behind him.

"Wait!"

He turned to find Allison gliding toward him. Well, she wasn't gliding, exactly. Her legs were moving. But they were doing so in that unconvincing manner that he'd come to associate with people who played the desktop version.

"No Treadie, I take it?"

"Uh, no," she replied. "I'm on my lappy. Hold still a minute."

Allison came to rest just in front of Tom - uncomfortably close, if truth be told. She stilled, and her avatar went glassy-eyed. This informed Tom that she must be doing something with her internal menus. After a minute or so, she let out a long breath.

"You didn't tell me it was for a rabbit," she remarked. "Was it a big white one?"

"In fact, it was. I'm doing a quest for him, but I need some help. To be fair, you didn't give me much of a chance before calling me a 'drongo' and telling me to shove off."

"Sorry about that, mate. It's just that there aren't a lot of wood sages in the game, and everyone pesters me to join their team. You'd think the sorry bludgers would wise up and buy some healing drafts at the bottle-o."

"I'm having trouble placing your dialect, Allison. Are you from England?"

"You think me a Pommie? Fair dinkum, dag! Naw. I'm from Straya - true blue. That's a bloody insult; that is. But I might help ya anyways, for the bunny's sake. Send me a team invite and let me see this quest."

Tom would eventually learn that Allison grew up in Australia, 'Straya' being typical of her abbreviated slang. It was funny. The game interface could translate flawlessly among dozens of world languages. But as both American and Australian were considered 'English,' their discourse didn't trigger those refined routines. He found it strange that his greatest communication challenge would be conversing with someone in his own native language.

She read through the shared quest, muttering her strange gibberish all throughout.

"Alright, yank. I'm in," she finally declared. "When do you want to start?"

"There'll be one other joining us," said Tom. "I'll fill you both in on the details when he... er, 'she' arrives. Just continue on with what you were doing. We can meet up at the town center. Keep an ear up. I'll send you a whisper when it's time."

Tom watched Allie glide off. Before long, her movement changed. She appeared to be doing the steps of a ballroom dance with an invisible partner. Again, he saw the grass 'green-up' on the lawns over which she circled and the flowers emerging from the window gardens she blessed. 'Dances alone,' indeed. This might just make for an interesting quest.

***

"The dipole part of the field is usually aligned fairly closely with the Earth's rotation axis."

Mr. Averbeck was using his pointer to gesture toward the 3D simulation of planet Earth spinning up at the front of the class. David sat in his usual seat near the rear, scribbling notes in his notebook. He would prefer to record the lecture and some images on his phone, but Mr. Averbeck was a traditionalist, and didn't permit modern devices. One could hardly blame the man. Had he allowed this, many of the less attentive students would even now be playing Candy Crush and such.

"According to the physicists," the teacher continued, "the reversal of Earth's magnetic poles, an event that occurs only once every ten thousand years or so, is now fully underway. We can see this in the plight of the Canadian goose, whose migration patterns have been severely disrupted. Many of the silly little blighters have begun flying north for the winter, devastating their population."

"Two weeks from today, there will be a field trip to the Cincinnati Zoo, where efforts are underway by its conservationists to relocate some of these and other newly endangered species to the southern regions of South America. In turn, several other migratory species native to that region will be brought back here for resettlement. If you are interested, the sign-up sheets and permission slips are available up here on my desk."

David thought about going. He didn't want to commit to it just yet. He was sure it would be interesting, but he could use a long homeroom session to get caught up on his studies instead. He had promised his parents he wouldn't let his gaming addiction put him behind on his schoolwork. And that was a promise he intended to keep. He had worked too hard to keep his grades up not to 'stick it on the dismount' his senior year.

"Now on to our main topic for today," said Mr. Averbeck, dismissing the spinning globe with a dramatic swish of his pointer. "I hope you all did the reading."

He strutted over to the windows and tapped the button to raise the blinds. The students all straightened in their seats as the overhead lights came off the dim cycle. Mr. Averbeck was young for a teacher and somewhat slight of frame. But he wore his authority like a proud rooster. In his tweed suit and yellow bow tie, he reminded David of an over-sized ventriloquist's manikin.

"Can anyone tell me when Project Gossomer was first proposed?"

That was an easy one. David decided to leave it for others.

"Yes. Mister Samoya."

Henry lowered his hand and stood.

"Project Gossamer was proposed at the U.N. in the winter of 2039. It was approved as their last official act before the United Nations was replaced by the Global Leadership Council early in the following year."

"Very good. And what was the nature of this global initiative, Miss... Stewart?"

Janet stood and turned her gaze to one side. David knew her to be very shy. She hated being called on.

"It was to find a better way to launch objects into space."

"Oh?" said Averbeck, unrelenting. "Describe how this was to be accomplished."

"Um. They decided to build a big, long train track," she stammered. "It's going to run across a flat plain and up the side of a mountain."

"Close enough," said Mr. Averbeck, finally releasing the girl from the gazes of her fellow students. "The 'train track', as you so simply put it, is actually a maglev rail whereon the packets can be accelerated without wheels. This is important because? Anyone?"

David considered raising his hand. The answer was kind of obvious, but he hated it when such questions just hung there. In truth, David could have slept through this class. Back in his freshman year, he had read everything about space exploration he could get his hands on. This earned him the unfortunate nickname, 'space cadet' when he tried sharing his passion with others. Gossamer was old news. They'd been planning it for more than a decade. It would completely surpass the SpinLaunch systems they're using today.

Its single rail would be enclosed in a series of rings all along its length. These would be closed off to form a tube from which all the air would be evacuated. Within the near-vacuum of this tube, very large packets or capsules could be accelerated by magnetic induction to hypersonic speeds in a nearly frictionless environment. The guiding rail curved gradually upward at its end to launch the packets into space.

They called it Project Gossamer for the web woven from carbon nanotubes waiting to catch the packets once they had escaped Earth's gravity well.

David was startled when his phone began to vibrate in his pocket. Not now, he thought. He wanted to just ignore it, but on the third ring, curiosity got the better of him, and he decided to have a peek. He covertly slid his phone out, holding up his notebook in the other hand to shield the action. A spinning quest icon was on the screen. He touched it with his thumb.

[Quest Offered: Reshape Earth's Moon.]
[Reward offered: Advancement in your Chosen Class]
[Accept quest? **Y/N**]

What on earth (or above said earth) could it mean?

David thought he should simply decline the absurd offer. But before he could do so, he was startled as a pointed stick came crashing down on his desktop. His finger brushed the screen, and the 'yes' selection flared briefly before being replaced by a block of text. Just beside him stood Mr. Averbeck, glowering down at him.

"Is my lecture boring you, mister Grimes?"

"Um. No sir," he hastened to reply.

"Then perhaps," drawled the irate educator, "you would like to explain to the class why the launch site is being constructed in Central Africa."

David grimaced, stood, and collected his thoughts.

"To escape Earth's gravity well," he began, "an object must achieve escape velocity, a speed of about seven miles per second, or roughly twenty-five thousand miles per hour. To put this in perspective, this is about thirty-three times the speed of sound. Such velocities are termed 'hypersonic.'

"At the equator, the earth's rotational velocity on its surface is more than a thousand miles per hour. This is only about 1/25th escape velocity. Otherwise, people on the equator might be tossed off into space! As it is, it's why Olympic records set in equatorial zones are adjusted slightly.

"But as slight as the difference might be, you'd rather have it working for you than against you. Therefore, the maglev rail will run west to east across parts of the Congo and into Tanzania to terminate at Mt. Kilimanjaro for its final ascent. This will take almost full advantage of the earth's spin.

"This location was selected over other proposed sites in New Zealand and Brazil largely for political reasons."

Mr. Averback looked put off.

"Exactly right, mister Grimes," he managed. "Nonetheless, rules are rules. Hand over the phone."

David put it in his outstretched hand. He tapped the screen on, and his face soured as he read it. Turning on his heels, Mr. Averbeck stalked to the front of the room and took a pad of paper from his desk. 'Am I getting detention?' thought David. But then the teacher returned and handed him back his phone along with the slip of paper. 'Hall Pass,' it read.

"You may inform the guidance counselor that I would appreciate some advance notice if there are to be any further disruptions to my class. Carry on."

'The... guidance counselor? ' thought David.

"Um. Yes, sir," he said aloud as he gathered his notes and departed.

Once in the hallway, David activated his phone and pulled up the most recent text message. It read simply:

David Grimes is to report to the guidance counselor. Please excuse him from class and direct him here immediately.

He headed toward her office. Then a horrible thought occurred. Could there have been an accident involving mom or dad? He picked up his pace and began to panic. His thoughts churned as he approached the door.

***

"Come in," said the crisp voice of Mrs. Burkhold when he knocked.

His fears were instantly allayed upon hearing her tone. It was welcoming and not at all what one would expect from someone about to deliver bad news. He turned the handle and sauntered in.

"Ah. Mr. Grimes." She began. "May I call you David?"

"Of course. Why the urgent summons?"

She waved toward a pair of soft chairs facing her desk, indicating he should be seated. Mrs. Burkhold was a fit-looking woman in a crisp linen suit. Her mousy gray hair was tied up in a bun. She had a manila file folder open before her and a thick packet off to one side sporting the GSC logo.

"David, it says here that you've only applied to two colleges. Is that right?"

"Yes, ma'am," said David. "NKU is my first choice, depending on the aid package. I filled out the FAFs, but I'm still waiting on the results. If it turns out I can't afford it, I might attend Cincinnati State Technical and Community College instead. I received my letter of acceptance just a few days ago."

"These are both fine programs for your stated goals, but there are other choices out there. Why these two? Is it just a matter of affordability? With your grades, you might want to look into some others."

"It's mainly the cost, like you say, ma'am. Both are also close enough to live at home and commute. I'm hoping for a work study program in either case."

"I see," she said, tapping her nails on the edge of her desk. "What if I told you I've just been made aware of an opportunity that might fit your talents rather well? Would you be willing to take on some extra work on the off chance it might pan out?"

"I'd be very interested to know what it is, of course. I hope you aren't just speaking hypothetically."

"Not at all," she said, halting her fidgeting and placing her hands firmly in her lap.

Her next words came out in a rush.

"The GSC is sponsoring a special training seminar for teleoperators next week. Oak Hills wasn't on the initial list of invitees, but a slot has suddenly opened up on their roster. It's a competition of sorts. They want to evaluate anyone in your age group who has the skills required to operate heavy equipment at a distance. According to Gregory, you're the only candidate we *have* who's logged the needed hours."

"Is there a prize or something?" asked David.

"Apart from the training itself, not much. But simply participating in such an event would look very good on your résumé, she crooned.

"The GSC is offering a summer internship to the ten best candidates," she reluctantly added. "I don't want to give you false hope. There are numerous schools participating, both here and abroad. Your chances are vanishingly small of earning a spot among the top performers."

"What all would it entail?"

"If you agree to do it, some specialized software will be installed in the VR lab over the weekend. You would undergo a full week of study and testing. There would be difficult tasks for you to accomplish on the simulators. At the end of the week, those who make the cut will have a final practical examination in mid-May operating some kind of equipment up at Moonbase Alpha."

Bingo.

"Would you be in--"

"Yes," David replied. "You had me at 'moon.'"

Mrs. Burkhold grinned and shoved the GSC packet toward him. Evidently, she was fully prepared to take yes for an answer.

"You are released from your classes through the end of the day. Here's an information packet you should study over the weekend. We will need a parent or guardian to sign the top two forms. I'll drive you home to collect those signatures, and to answer any questions they might have."

That was rather abrupt and accommodating.

"Is there some great rush?"

"Oh, um, I need to reply by three o'clock, or they'll move to the next alternate. The school stands to gain a free VR upgrade and a bonus. I didn't want this to influence your decision, but I must say I'm glad you were amenable."

She tapped her phone to activate it.

"Gregory, move all of my appointments from this afternoon to the week after next."

Oh well, thought David, there go my plans for a spring break gaming marathon. It sounded like he would at least have the weekend before things got hairy. Better round up Glass Cannon and Allison tomorrow and see if we can conquer that tower.

CHAPTER FOUR

Remlak's Tower

Ink Kit (65 zho) - This sturdy wooden box has eight compartments in which you may store your inks. It fits neatly into one inventory slot, freeing up space for your other treasures. [Purchase Ink Kit? **Y/N**][Haggle with Merchant? **Y/N**]

Tom stared at the message, weighing whether the expense was worth the benefit. He had a full backpack now with twelve slots for items, but this filled up rather quickly. And he was tired of running back to the B.A.N.K. every time he needed to craft some new talismans. He chose to haggle and received the message update.

Ink Kit (59 zho?) - This sturdy wooden box has eight compartments in which you may store your inks. It fits neatly into one inventory slot, freeing up space for your other treasures. [Purchase Ink Kit? **Y/N**][Continue Haggling with Merchant? **Y/N**]

He'd probably get no better offer. If he really wanted the thing, he should just accept now. Perhaps he should hold off on major purchases until he could find the animal that would boost his Charm. He wondered idly which creature of the zodiac that might be. Perhaps it was the rabbit, whose quest he was even now attempting. That or agility, most likely.

"Are you almost done?" asked Glass Cannon in a whisper of annoyance. "Allison is probably waiting on us at the tower."

"She'll be fine," said Tom, choosing 'yes.' "Allie enjoys solo play. And she always seems to be online. I've never logged in yet without finding her 'friends' icon already lit up."

"True," said Jason.

Tom stepped away from the grinning merchant with his purchase, and Glass Cannon followed him toward Remlak's tower, which was just visible in the distance. Jason's avatar was a frail-looking thing, befitting her name. Her fiery red hair puffed out in two enormous pigtails on either side of her petite frame. She was garbed in a sequined green gown, which flowed down to her ankles and sparkled as she took her tiny steps along the cobbles. Tom had to slow his forward movement so she could keep up. Jason hadn't put a single point in Agility since first creating the character.

When they arrived, they found Allison seated and messing with some colored squares of paper.

"Arvo, cobbers," she greeted them. "I was beginning to think you two blokes had bailed and gone off for a cold one."

"It was all Tom's fault," groused G.C. "I had to pry him away from the merchants he was swindling."

David seated his avatar beside Allison and stared up at the imposing tower. Jason, meanwhile, pulled out a large wooden tripod from his inventory and placed it facing them. He then produced a canvas, resting it on this easel. Next, he drew forth a painter's palette and brush.

"Um. What are you doing, G.C.?" asked Tom.

"It's for my blog, bro," returned the younger boy. "I figure if no one's cleared the tower yet, my subscribers will be thrilled when I document our success."

"Awful cocky, aren't you?" said Tom. "And don't call me 'bro.'"

"Why not?" asked Jason. "Is it a black thing? White guys call each other 'bro' all the time."

"Maybe so, but yes," chided David, "it's a black thing. From your lily white lips, it comes off more like cultural appropriation."

"Dude," Jason exclaimed. "We're all Asians here in the realms. Let it go, man."

"Crikey. You a black fellow, yank?" put in Allison.

"Don't sound so surprised. And quit calling me 'yank' too, while we're at it."

"Is that another black thing?"

"No," said Tom sheepishly. "It just doesn't sound right when combined with 'Weasel Whacker.' I'd hate for people to get any funny ideas about me."

G.C. and Allie both hooted with laughter.

When the laughter subsided, and after sighting along her thumb, G.C. touched her brush to the canvas. In an instant. A full-color photograph of Remlak's Tower appeared on its surface.

"Are we ready then?" asked Allison.

"One more thing first," said G.C., packing up her easel.

Where it had rested, she tossed out a ring of stones wherein a fire was blazing away. She then produced a kettle, which she set atop the flames.

"You making us brekky, mate?"

"Yup. As a phoenix sage, Cooking was one of my starting choices. You should never start a major venture without a good meal. It buffs your vitality for an hour."

"By how much?" asked Tom.

"Depends on the dish," said G.C. in reply. "I'm just making us some Ren Shen Rice, so it should be good for about two Vigor."

David was amazed. The earthy and slightly sweet herbal aroma tickled his nostrils as Tom spooned up his portion. He hadn't realized how useful some of the ordinary-sounding skills could be. He wondered what he might have passed up by declining 'poet' and such. After a hearty thirty seconds of devouring rice, Tom examined his character sheet. Sure enough, there was a 'well-fed' buff beside his name, and he noted an increase in both his vigor and the derived stats of health and recovery.

Tom Braider (Weasel Whacker) - Level 4 Jaingshi Hunter

MIGHT	11	CLEVERNESS	11
AGILITY	16	ENLIGHTENMENT	16
VIGOR	11 (14)	CHARM	12 (13)

Skills: Haggling, Herbalism, Martial Art (Baguazhang), Occult Lore, Paper Talisman Crafting, Weapon Proficiency (Emei Ci)

Open skill slots: **3**

Health: **56** / Recovery: **3.29**

Recovery was the number of seconds it took for a character to regenerate one point of health.

"Hold on a minute," said Tom. "That recovery rate is low even given the increase in Vigor."

"That would be me, cobber," murmured Allison around a mouthful of rice. "My aura of renewal lowers my squadmates' recovery time a bit in a circle all around me. No wuckas... and you're welcome."

G.C. stood to her feet and banished the fire pit.

"Well, if you and Waltzing Matilda there are ready to go," she said, "let's go see to this tower."

***

Tom sent the team invite, and the others accepted. As it was his quest, he was the de facto team leader.

"Everyone switch to team-speak," said Tom, "It's like whisper mode, but you can hear everything any team member says."

"We got it, mate," said Allie in annoyance. "We're not daft, you know."

G.C. was already examining the rusted iron grate that warded the portal.

"You know," she remarked, "This gives me an idea."

"That's dardy, mate. Spit it out before it dies of loneliness."

Unperturbed, the phoenix sage crouched down to examine the obvious coin slot, her big puffy braids dangling to either side of her head.

"This thing says, 'Pay the coin if you're dimwitted,'" she said. "Am I dimwitted?"

"No, I am not," she quickly added, forestalling Allison's burgeoning barb. It just so happens that I have the Locksmith skill and eighteen points of Cleverness to back it up. I'm not certain whether using it would violate the terms of the quest. What does our valiant leader have to say?"

"I say go for it," said Tom. "Think of it as our first challenge. And before I forget..."

Tom rolled up his sleeve and spun the wheel of destiny. To his surprise, it actually granted a bonus this time. There was a sharp screech and Tom sprouted a phantom tail which waved around for a moment before dissolving. It was only Cleverness. He had been hoping for the ox symbol, but anything beat a blank.

As Tom watched G.C. work on the locking mechanism, he muttered encouragement. "I wish I could lend you some of *my* cleverness. I'm up to fifteen at the moment myself," he bragged.

[Would you like to acquire the skill: Leadership ? **Y/N**]

His first instinct was to decline it out of turn. He had read that this skill had little to offer to the player who selected it. It only let you lend your ability stats to someone else for a brief time. This deprived one's own avatar of their benefits and mucked up your skills. But then he thought of the problem at hand. He wasn't a solo player at the moment, and he *did* have three open skill slots.

Moreover, hadn't the I Ching reading said something about 'improving himself in order to improve those around him?'" This decided the matter. Why not? he thought as he agreed to take the skill.

[Congratulations! You have acquired the skill "Leadership." You possess the ability to uplift and empower your teammates, and you are held in higher esteem by others. By actively inspiring a teammate, you become a beacon of hope, elevating their abilities beyond what they thought possible. A single stat of their choice will be temporarily increased by one third of your character's Charm. Your honor points are permanently increased by a similar amount in NPC interactions. Duration: five minutes. Cooldown: one hour. Current Inspiration Amount: 3]

He had barely finished reading the thing when G.C. announced, "Got it!" This rendered his decision moot, at least as it related to the present activity. Yet another Charm-based skill, thought David. His Tom was fast becoming a charisma character, not at all how he'd envisioned his progression. But something about it felt right.

"Good on ya, G.C.," said an uncharacteristically chipper Aussie.

Tom was given the dubious honor of opening the door and being the first to enter the dark chamber beyond.

"Illuminate!" said G.C. from just behind him as the door slammed shut.

This revealed an Escherian nightmare of stairwells running in every direction from the platform on which they stood. This chamber seemed far larger than the tower's base had appeared from the outside. Tom had to remind himself that physics didn't hold sway here. Some of the stairwells and platforms ran perpendicular to their own. Some were even upside down.

"Which way?" asked G.C.

"I have no idea," returned Tom. "This place is beyond my comprehension."

"Well, we haven't got all day," put in Allie. "If one way's as good as another, let's just pick one, and she'll be apples soon enough."

Tom chose one of the stairs that went 'up' on the theory that they needed to 'ascend' the tower. He was quickly proven wrong in his sketchy assumption. After a few turnings, he could see the doorway where they had arrived. It was up above them now. He began numbering strips of his paper and laying them on the steps. He brought his companions to a halt when he encountered one of them (#3).

"We're going in circles. Or, to put it more accurately, we're going in rigid right angles that don't seem to obey the laws of normal spacial geometry. Any clever ideas, oh, she who put nearly half her points in that?"

"Don't look at me," said G.C. "I'm terrible at directions... and no, I do not want to take Orienteering!" she added distractedly."

"I have something that might be of help," said Allison rather meekly.

"Shoot," said Tom.

"Shoot what?"

"I mean, tell us your idea."

"As a wood sage, one of the first skills we can learn is Origami. I know it sounds silly, but it works together with one of our elemental magic abilities, Fùnéng Zhézhǐ. It literally means 'folded paper empowerment."

"Okay," said G.C. "And that helps us, how?"

"Watch, said Allison."

She produced one of the colored squares they'd seen her playing with earlier and rapidly folded it into the familiar shape of a crane. When she concentrated on it, her aura of renewal was withdrawn, and Tom saw his recovery rate rise back up to over four seconds. But gradually, the crane increased in size and began flapping its paper wings. Before long, it was hovering before them and performing aerial maneuvers at Allison's command. She sent it zipping off into the distance.

"Again," said G.C. "This helps us how?"

But Allison wasn't listening. She was seated in a meditative pose with her eyes shut. When they snapped open, she exclaimed: "Bloody hell! I lost it."

"To answer your question, I can see through the little ripper's eyes. He can't do more than scout ahead at the moment, but one day I should be able to fly about on him. Sadly for us, I'm only second level. I was starting to get a sense of the place, but I ran out of elemental energy. That's what we sages call our Xianqi,"

"Maybe I can help you with that," said Tom. "Try it again, we believe in you."

He toggled the 'inspire' icon from his newly acquired Leadership skill. Allison looked up at him suddenly. Then he watched as three points were drained from his Enlightenment stat. Several of his combat icons darkened. But that was okay. The group didn't appear to be under any immediate threat.

"Give me a minute; I'm buggered," said Allie as she retrieved another square of colored paper.

After that, it was fairly simple. Allie leapt up and gleefully shouted, "Follow me, it's this way!" She scampered up an adjoining stairway, and the others followed. The nimble wood sage led them through many dizzying turns and changes in perspective, unerringly toward the exit. At one point, she slowed and waited for them to catch up.

"Here's the tricky bit," she said.

At this, she vaulted the banister, hung, and dropped to a platform ten feet below. Tom had to lean out and lower G.C. Jason had been placing all of his points on Enlightenment and Cleverness, allowing his other stats to atrophy. As a result, G.C. had some impressive fire powers and crafting skills, but simple physical feats were quite beyond her.

Then it was off to the races again, with Allison in the lead. They arrived at last at a rough wooden door, before which lay the scorched remains of Allie's second paper crane.

"They burn up once the spell runs out," she explained.

Affixed to the door with a slim dagger was a note. After retrieving the note, Tom glanced briefly at the dagger. It looked to be of good quality, and he could probably wield it with his Emei Ci proficiency. He'd have to examine it later. He read the note aloud.

You're clever enough, and that's a start. Here now comes the tricky part.

You must be both strong and brave to reach the object that you crave.

Have you a mighty acrobat to keep your quest from falling flat?

"Well, don't look at me," said G.C. "I only ever put two points in Might, and that was only so I could equip the Superior Beibao."

"Let's take a pause here to figure this one out," said Tom. "It's been nearly an hour since we started. We should eat again to rebuff our Vitality."

Tom and Allison moved to the landing's edge so that G.C. could once again place her fire pit for cooking. Tom savored the odor of woodsmoke, and other delicious smells arose from the steaming kettle as they settled themselves and prepared to feast.

***

"So, Allison," said Tom, "why are you playing on the North American server anyway? Doesn't it make the game lag to play over that distance?"

"Not as much as you might think, Yank, er, Tom. It might get up to as much as a half-second, dependin' on traffic. But actually, I'm stayin' here in the States for a bit, as it happens."

"Really? G.C. and I are in Cincinnati. Where are you?"

"I'm at the Cleveland... up in Cleveland. Crikey! We're practically neighbors."

"Mmm. Not really. That's still a five-hour drive upstate."

"Relatively speakin' we are. Wollongong, where I'm from, is about as far from Ohio as you can get and still be breathin' oxygen, mate. Bloody oath."

"I suppose that's true enough," said G.C., whisking the fire pit away, "but hadn't we better get going?"

They formed up and approached the door. Once again, Tom took the lead. He opened it and stepped out onto a wooden platform. All around was nothing but empty space, relieved only by a scattered array of wooden posts thrusting up an impossible distance from the abyss below. Tom had never before had much of a problem with heights, but he still felt the stirrings of vertigo as he stared down at the roiling mist far below, into which the poles vanished.

In the distance, against what he took to be the far wall of the chamber, Tom made out two other platforms. The one to his left had a large lever next to an inviting-looking door. It was at least forty feet away, and none of the poles were anywhere near it. The other platform, the one on the right, was longer, and it looked like you could get over to it by hopping from pole to pole (if you were a jackrabbit or something).

"Hey," exclaimed G.C., "why don't you have your little bird thing fly over there?"

"And do what, mate? It couldn't pull the lever or anything. It's only made of paper."

"What now, then, valiant leader?" asked G.C.

"Uh. I think Remlak was right. We need an acrobat. Boy, I sure wish I had a skill like that," he said, hopefully.

But whatever game mechanic drove the offering of new skills refused to take the hint.

"How far do you think that longer platform is from the one with the door?" he asked.

"I reckon it looks to be a little over nine meters," said Allison.

"Hmm," said Tom, taking a moment to do the math, "that's about thirty feet, well beyond the distance I can clear with my best martial leap."

"I could almost jump that far," said Allison.

"Really?" demanded G.C. "You have athletics or something?"

"Um, no - not athletics, exactly."

"What, then?"

"Dancing," muttered Allison, almost too quietly to be heard.

On hearing this, G.C. let out a sigh of disgust. But Tom quickly intervened.

"Hold on a minute, Glass. What move are we talking about, Allison?"

"It's a ballet step called 'the grand jeté.' In real life, it probably only clears two or three meters, but you know how exaggerated movement skills are in the game."

He did, indeed. The rooster's lifting technique in Baguazhang should only move you three to six feet IRL, but here in the game, he could do fifteen feet easily.

"It's the best plan we've got. Do you think you could get over there?"

"No drama," said Allison with a dismissive wave emote.

But despite the girl's assurance, Tom thought she seemed ill at ease. Her avatar remained expressionless as ever, but her voice bore a hint of anxiety.

"Can I see your character sheet?" he asked.

She sent him an examine permission.

Allison Wonderla (Beautifier) -
Level 2 Elemental Sage (Wood)

MIGHT	10	CLEVERNESS	9
AGILITY	12	ENLIGHTENMENT	14
VIGOR	9 (12)	CHARM	10 (12)

Skills: Craft (Fletcher), Dancing, Diplomacy, Elemental Lore, Elemental Magic, Greenskeeper, Origami, Weapon (Tang Da Qiang)

Open skill slots: **0**

Health: **36**, Recovery: **4.00**

"Remember," he said, "it's only a game. A fall can't really hurt you. You should buff your Agility or your Might - whichever one you think you'll need the most."

Targeting her, Tom selected his inspire icon for the second time that day. He could almost feel it when the Might drained out of him. His movements became sluggish, and an 'overburdened' debuff flashed beside his name. This ceased only after he'd shucked off his backpack.

In a flash, Allison became garbed in a tight-fitting unitard and tutu. She went up on her toes and performed a few pliés, followed by a graceful pirouette. Her arms went up to form a loose circle with her fingertips touching one another, and one leg bent at the knee until the sole of her foot rested on her opposite thigh.

Then off she went, whirling and hopping from one pole to the top of the next. She would occasionally pause to correct her balance. Several times, she had to detour from the more direct course when the spacing between poles grew too great. But she was making steady headway toward her goal.

"Wow," said G.C. with obvious appreciation. "She's really something. But don't tell her I said so."

With a final great leap, Allison reached the long platform. She paused to catch her breath, or whatever avatars used instead. She paced from one end of the platform to the other, carefully gauging the distance, then assumed her 'tree' form once more. She stood there unmoving for what seemed like ages.

When she moved, it was as though a graceful gazelle had been suddenly set loose, spurred into desperate flight by the threat of some dire predatory beast. With each step, she gathered speed and lowered her stance another notch. Her arms swung in counterpoint to her steps, giving the appearance of a light, skipping motion. Near the edge, she brought both feet together and launched herself into the air. Her legs scissored apart, one lifting straight up before her while the other trailed straight after, no less elevated. She held on to this impossible split as she sailed across the gap. Even so, her front leg barely reached the far platform to find a purchase. She tucked into a roll, popping back up and turning to face her teammates.

G.C. and Tom applauded and hooted like maniacs.

"Alright blokes. Time to see what this lever does. If this doesn't ease the way for us, I'm gonna crack the shits at it."

She pulled the lever. Nothing happened. And for a moment, Tom and G.C. thought they were about to witness exactly what cracking the shits might mean. But then a rasping, creaking sound was heard, and a rope bridge rolled out from beneath the platform where Allison stood. In defiance of physics, it extended itself and fastened securely to the original platform. They hustled across before it could change its mind. Then, suddenly, it decided to *obey* the laws of physics after all, and fell away.

"I suppose we've crossed the Rubicon now," said Tom.

***

As Tom's might came dribbling back to him, he was once again able to stand up straight. There was no convenient message nailed to this door, but they assumed it must lead to the next challenge. Desperately, they searched the area for any clue about what might come next. 'Prepare yourself for what you would least expect,' Storia had advised. Well, ballet dancing through a magic tower on a quest to free the Easter bunny was certainly not the first guess on Tom's list.

"I think I've got something over here," reported G.C.

She was at the platform's edge, examining a broken stanchion that had formerly secured the bridge. Tom walked over behind her to peer over her shoulder. He brushed one of her oversize pigtails aside for a better look.

"Hey, watch the hair, dude."

G.C. had pulled up the short rod only to discover it was actually a bone, part of a femur by the look of it. Whether human or not was anyone's guess. If human, he was a big fellow. What was unusual about it (apart from the fact that bones weren't typically employed in bridge construction) were the glyphs etched into it.

"They remind me of Chinese letters," said G.C., but I can't understand what they say.

"It's Oracle Bone Script," Tom explained. "It's the earliest known form of Chinese writing. It was used during the late Shang Dynasty around ten to twelve hundred BC."

"And you know this, how?"

"Just messing with you, Jase. I'm reading it from my HUD. It's part of my Occult Lore skill. Let me see it, and I'll tell you what it says."

"Strewth, that's a relief!" said Allison from just behind them. "And here I was, thinking you were a flat out dag."

"Nope," said Tom, taking up the item, "just an awesome jiangshi hunter. It says:"

Unfelt until our final day. The touch of death and grim decay.
Our skin grows bloodless, wan, and pale when pass we through that final veil.
The sea gnaws ever at the shore, but does the mountain care?

"Well, I'm officially creeped out," said G.C.

"Maybe it means we should remain steadfast in the face of death? Like a mountain?"

"Who knows," put in Allison. "It's just more of that zen drivel that won't make sense until after we face whatever it is. And then we'll just be inventing reasons why it was right in front of us all along. I say we just grab up our brollies and face the shitstorm head on."

"For once, I agree with Miss 'Shrimp on the Barbie' there."

"Prawn," said Allison.

"What?"

"It's 'prawn on the barbie,' Glass-hole. At least try and keep your mockery straight."

"It seems we have a plan then" said Tom. "No plan, it *is*."

And, handing the bone back to G.C., Tom moved to the door and made himself ready. The others followed. Tom equipped the dagger he had pulled from that first door. Though it possessed no special properties, it was compatible with his fighting style and a bit better than his open-hand strikes.

Allison now held a short, recurved bow with an arrow

nocked to its string. Tom supposed this was the Tang Da Qiang he'd seen on her skills list. For a 'wood' sage, he supposed this made sense. It would also explain why agility appeared to be her second-best stat. G.C. held nothing. Evidently, she relied entirely on her offensive magic, which Tom had yet to see. Storia had told Tom that both would be needed to ascend the tower. This left him a little concerned about what challenge might require G.C.'s unbalanced set of stats.

So, Tom was cautious when he opened the door and peered inside. It was a fairly ordinary room. There was a four-poster bed with a trunk at its footboard, a dust-covered writing desk, and a wooden wardrobe that stood over in one corner. The room had a musty odor (thanks for that, scent vent) and an undertone of something else - something unidentifiable. It was a large square room, nearly thirty feet on each side. All of its furnishings were aged and worn.

"Stay together," warned G.C. "My aura sense informs me there's something lurking in the wardrobe."

"Aura sense?" said Tom.

"Hey, if Spiderman can do it--"

"Not the time," hissed Tom. "What kind of something?"

"Something evil. I'm not sure exactly what, but it's about to rush us!"

The wardrobe door didn't swing open. Instead, and unexpectedly, a dark figure came swooping up directly through the wood of the bottom-most drawer. It was shaped like the grinning head of a specter and wreathed in a swirling mist of vapors. Tom barely had time to target it before one of Allison's arrows went zipping straight through it to sink into the dresser's ancient wood. That wasn't good.

Horrifying Haunt (Undead) - Level 5 (Insubstantial)

This group really needed a tank. Tom had realized it from the start. Grouped as he was with a healer and a damage dealer, *he* would need to assume that role. Thank goodness for G.C.'s warning. It had at least allowed them to avoid being surprised by the hideous thing. As it swirled toward his team, he rushed to meet it. He chose a sequence from the xun trigram phoenix system. It was a set of moves designed to quickly stun, disable, and debilitate one's opponent with a whipping shoulder action.

Not a single blow landed. And Tom took a chilling hit to his side before he managed to windmill away. The creature's claw came straight through the vambrace of the ox to dig at his vitals. His health bar dropped by more than a third, and he now had a strange debuff he had no time to examine.

"I've got this, bro," he heard in team chat. "Scorch!"

An intense burning ray pierced straight through the creature's central mass to splash against the bedding. The tattered remnants of its curtains were instantly immolated, and the mattress itself was burning. Well, at least there was plenty of light.

But the creature looked fairly unscathed. Barely a ripple marred its health bar.

"Dude! That was my strongest shot!" howled the sage.

The creature appeared to be gathering itself for another rush - this time at G.C. Thank the devs that it didn't seem to be too quick. Tom wondered briefly if they could outrun it, but to where? Rubicon, and all that. Just then, he was encased in a gentle green glow. He watched his health bar surge upward, almost to its full mark. He didn't have to guess who was responsible for that.

Tom interposed himself between the creature and G.C. just moments before it rushed. Tom suspected he could much better take the hit while they figured things out. He needed to get the creature's attention and kite it to the room's far corner, so he did just that. Strongly favoring feints and dodges from the monkey and snake styles, he managed to draw it away from his teammates. This was not without its cost.

Tom knew he hadn't prepared very well for his primary role in the game. He had a talisman called 'spirit shroud' that supposedly weakened undead, but he knew very little about it. He had only made one in all this time, and that was just for practice. He'd inscribed it several levels ago, so it wasn't the most potent one he could make. But he was counting on it now.

"Almost there," said G.C." I can do another scorch soon."

"Last heal for a while," added Allison.

"Hold off, G.C.!" shouted Tom. "I've got a plan. Allison, do whatever you can."

Tom was slowing down; the debuffs were stacking up to slow his speed. They said something like 'blood freeze.' He still hadn't gotten a proper look at them, but he could feel their effects. Even worse, the drapes surrounding the bed frame had burned away as quickly as they'd ignited, lowering the light level again. But the mattress was now smoldering away and churning out clouds of dense, oily smoke. This was beginning to interfere with his vision, but Tom suspected the haunt would be unimpeded by this. He'd have to time things just right.

The next time the creature gathered for a rush, Tom hesitated, appearing to stand his ground. He took the rooster stance. When it came for him, he reversed and used his lifting back-kick to hurdle over it. He didn't get away clean and chided himself for trying to leap over a flying creature. Landing on a stiffened ankle, he rolled to the side and found just time enough to release his barb.

[Chūcuì strikes Horrifying Haunt for 1 point of damage]

Oh, sure. *Now* you crit. (I'll take it though, thought Tom.)

A split second later, a creepy ivory-colored sputum emerged from the creature's mouth. It budded from him as though he were blowing a chewing gum bubble. But it grew out much more rapidly than that. In but a moment, it achieved twice the haunt's own size before bursting like an angry blister. It snapped back to cover the beast in a dripping miasma of gunk, which quickly hardened.

Tom could see the contours of the creature's face as it struggled within its elastic prison. Trapped beneath its ivory shroud, it more resembled a Halloween ghost than the spectral monstrosity it had been.

"Now, G.C.!" shouted Tom as the creature reached toward him once more.

And again came the sizzling burst that brightened the room. The last thing David remembered before his visor went dark was seeing the goo-encrusted creature forcibly hurled into the far wall and pinned there by the pressure of Glass Cannon's searing bolt of fire. There were also two arrows sticking out of the flaming pile of goo. Silent up until this point, the haunt let out a screeching wail that pierced one's skull and grated on one's nerve endings. His visor's earphones must be working overtime to achieve such an effect.

"David? Is something burning up there?"

"Just the game, mom!" he hollered back. "Some friends and I are having a cookout!"

"That's nice, sweetheart, but open a window or something!"

David waited impatiently in blackness for his vision to return. Would he be at the shrine? But no. Not unless the creature had gotten his teammates as well. He saw G.C. and Allie bending over him. He rolled his perspective back to encompass the scene. They were on the platform outside of the room where they'd battled the haunt, and smoke was billowing out from its door.

That spirit shroud talisman had worked pretty well on a level five haunt. He wasn't sure how long it would have lasted if his teammates hadn't been ready to end the thing once it was substantial. Despite its lack of general use, he made up his mind right then to never be without one (or three; make it three).

It had been a close thing. His team had hauled him out of the hellish room after a combination of 'blood freeze' and 'smoke inhalation' debuffs had rendered Tom insensate, but they'd all muddled through. Wow. A level-five creature. He wondered if they'd looted it yet.

"He's awake, the reckless drongo."

"Yup," said Tom, easing up to a seated position.

"Our non-plan worked pretty well," added G.C. "I was sure that'd be a party wipe. Hey. What are you doing?"

"I assume we're waiting for the smoke to clear. I'm using the time to make some talismans. I promised myself something just a moment ago."

***

It took a while before the room cleared of noxious vapors. Tom wished they had a water sage or something to accelerate the process, but sometimes you just had to make do. They ate again, and Tom had another go at spinning the wheel of destiny. Nothing *this* time.

"I reckon it's safe enough now to go back in," declared Allison, who had hung her head into the darkened room. "I'm not getting a debuff anymore."

Tom found it was still quite malodorous as he followed her in. Above the strong, smoky scent, there was a stomach-turning rotten egg smell. He supposed neither Allison nor Jason were equipped with a scent vent, as they failed to comment on it.

"Illuminate," said G.C., brightening the ruined chamber.

They first looted the charred remains of the haunt. It yielded forty zho and something called 'ectoplasmic essence.' Figuring this might be something used in crafting, they let Tom stow it away as party treasure. While searching the rest of the room, they made several discoveries.

The trunk at the foot of what had once been a bed was intact. It was only a bit singed. It contained A jian that added two points to one's might and some bonus 'metal' damage, metal being one of the five Chinese elements. Packed in with the sword was a note. It was another of Remlak's demented riddles.

A warrior must know when to fight and when instead to tuck his tail and run.
They say pride goeth, after all. 'Twere best he live to see another sun.

But if he finds a better way to win the prize and save the day,

He will be lauded as a hero, and his health bar need not go to zero.

Since none of them could equip a sword, they quickly agreed they would sell it and split the proceeds. Not long after that, the second discovery was made by G.C.

"There's a latch on the back of this wardrobe," she said, "and some skid marks on the floor. Help me move the thing. I think it's a secret door."

It took the combined might of all three companions to swing the heavy piece of furniture aside. When they did, they found a narrow passageway behind it. This led to a stairwell only wide enough for one person to ascend at a time.

"Onward and upward, then," said Tom, taking the lead once more.

The stairs let out on a small landing. From it, a passageway led off into darkness.

"That note has me right spooked, declared Allie. "I'd defo like to know when it's time to strap on our runners. Maybe I should send out a scout? But it's dark down there. I don't know whether I'll be able to make out very much."

"No problem, Allie," said G.C. with a smirk. "Make your little flapping thing. Maybe I can help it along."

So Allie sat down and folded up another crane. When it was ready, G.C. said 'illuminate,' and the bird lit up. Allison assumed her meditative pose, and Tom and G.C. watched as the glowing scout dwindled into the distance. They quietly settled in to hear what Allison might report.

"The tunnel curves around a bit, then goes on straight for a bit more. Up ahead, I'm seeing a mound of some kind of... Crikey! They're bones. And nearby, something's rooting about. Is it a... bear? No. Def not a bear! It's got big, long arms like a gorilla, and it's ugly as an ocker's teeth after a chew. Gimme a sec. I'll try to get closer. It's... piss biscuits!"

Allie winced.

Then she opened her eyes and stood to her feet. "Poor little ripper never stood a chance," she moaned.

"Did the bear thing get it?" asked Tom, already certain of the answer.

"Yep," said Allie. "Swatted her right out of the air."

"Did you see another way around?" Tom asked hopefully. "Any side passages or anything?"

"Fraid not, Yank... er, Tom."

"You know what?" Tom declared. "I've changed my mind. You can just go ahead and call me Yank. That doesn't sound *nearly* as bad as 'Yanker Tom the Weasel Whacker.'"

This brought Allison out of her funk, and they all had a good laugh about it. But then she became serious again. She stared over at Tom and rubbed her chin thoughtfully.

"I can't say for certain, Yank. But I might've seen the golden egg in that bone pile the sodding bear beast was building."

"Maybe we can snatch it and run away?" suggested G.C. "And by *we*, I mean *you*, of course."

"I dunno, mate. It was pretty fast. So fast, it nearly made me soil my knickers. But I'm in if you all are. I'm pretty sure I can outrun G.C.," she smirked.

"Well, I guess there's nothing *for* it but to go and see whether we can beat the thing," said Tom.

***

The three stood in the hallway facing the palace of bones. The creature hadn't reacted when G.C. lit up the scene. They were still about forty feet away. Tom's heart sank when the creature prowled around the pile, and he was able to target it.

Yaoguai (Abberant Beast) - Level 9 Abomination

"What is it doing with those heaps of bones?" asked Allie.

What, indeed, thought Tom.

"Level nine?" said G.C. in horror. "No way we can beat that thing!"

Tom looked for a way he might snatch up the egg and stow it in his inventory before the thing killed him. It was a fairly straightforward plan that might allow him to fulfill his quest. But if the creature was as fast as Allie said, he saw little hope of executing such a plan. The egg was nestled within the bone pile and out of easy reach.

Remlack's note implied there might be a better way to solve this dilemma, and one that didn't involve his tragic demise. What could it be? Then his eyes fell on one of the bones jutting out from the pile's near side. By the steady light of G.C.'s illuminating magic, he was able to make out a symbol or two in what he believed might be the Oracle Bone Script.

In light of this discovery, he began to see the pile of bones as something else - a historical record. Could the creature be intelligent? He knew 'yaoguai' was just a general term to describe a wide variety of inhuman creatures. Some were malicious and belligerent, but not all of them. Could they, perhaps, *talk* to it?

"G.C.," he asked, "do you still have that bone you took from where the bridge fell?"

"It's right here in my inventory, Tom. I wanted it for a keepsake."

"Well, haul it out and give it to Allison."

"Me?"

"Yes. I figured out how we're going to get the egg."

"Oh? Another one of your mad plans? Let's have a chinwag about it before you go volunteering me for anything. How do you propose we get the egg?"

"We're going to ask it nicely. And as G.C. likes to say, by 'we,' I mean 'you.'"

"Why me? Expendable, am I?"

"Not at all. Didn't I see Diplomacy on your list of skills? Here's your chance. Make nice with it. Offer it the bone and see if it will let us have the egg in exchange. You're the only one who has any kind of chance, Allie."

Allison found her 'frown' emote, and faced toward Tom as she took the bone and grumbled, "Fair Dinkum! The things I do for a fuzzy white bunny. You're going to owe me a quest for this, Tom Braider."

"Done deal," he answered her, flashing her his 'friendly smile.'

Before Allison could bravely approach her uncertain fate, Tom again inspired her with his leadership, insisting she 'charm up.' His own charm was diminished, causing several of his combat stacks to darken. Charm wasn't a prerequisite for many of his martial strikes. It was mainly just the feints that opened the target up for a follow-up blow. But once committed to this course of action, Tom saw no reason to retain his combat arsenal. Better, he thought, to put all of his eggs in this one basket than to come up short.

After that, it was fairly straightforward. Allie made the deal. With an exchange of gestures and grunted speech, the Aussie managed to convey her desire to the fearsome Yaoguai, and the trade was made. Tom felt a little bit... ashamed? ... that he had only considered diplomacy as a last resort. But then he shrugged it off. What was a person *meant* to think when he encountered an 'abomination' slavering over a pile of bones? Nonetheless, he determined that from now on he would try to keep an open mind and 'lay his ignorance aside.'

"I'm surprised you're not recording this," said Tom to G.C.

"I wish, dude. I tried earlier when Allie was jumping that chasm, but it turns out my painting skill doesn't work inside the tower."

With the egg securely stashed in Allie's inventory, the three made their triumphant way to and through the final door. They emerged on the rooftop. It commanded a view of the entire village. Tom felt the sun on his shoulders, and the gentle breeze brought a complex mix of aromas. There was the slight earthy smell of the dusty streets below, cow dung, and other unpleasant aromas of human habitation, but also a grassy and floral scent from the fields beyond.

"You want to see something cool?" asked G.C.

"Sure," said Tom.

G.C. took out her easel again and then rested a picture of the town square upon it. It must have been made recently, because there was the basket of eggs with the rabbit sitting atop it.

"Originally," said G.C. "I picked up painting so I could post pictures on my blog. It was the closest thing to a camera available in-game. You can export your paintings to your desktop or phone. But it turns out that most of the skills have advanced features that become available when you get really good at them. Watch."

At this, she produced her shrine stone and touched it lightly to the canvas. The painting erupted in flames and was consumed in an instant. Then G.C., holding the shrine stone before her, said, "Portal!". And out spewed a blue nimbus of light that hovered there, pulsing like a heartbeat.

"Ready to turn in the quest?"

"That's amazing," said Tom. "We can just step through?"

"Pretty much," said G.C., stowing her easel away. "Better hurry, though; it only stays open for twenty seconds or so. That's not all paintings can do, either. They can also --"

And she was through.

Tom and Allison hurried after.

***

In an eye-blink, Tom was transported to the town square.

115

"-- to keep an eye on the goings-on at a distant location," said G.C. in conclusion.

Other players stared in amazement when Allison, too, stepped out from the rippling orange, oval-shaped light. Not too far distant, sat the rabbit atop his pile of enormous colored eggs. G.C. led them over toward him. Another player passed by them, heading in the other direction and brushing the confetti from his surcoat.

"At last," said Rabbit, staring down at them from his throne of eggs. "Do you have it?"

Allison produced the golden egg from her inventory and held it out to him.

"Do I know you, miss?" he inquired, cocking his head to one side.

"Um, I don't think so, your rabbit-ness," Allie replied.

Snatching up the egg, the rabbit turned to Tom.

"And what have you learned?" he asked, ears twitching.

Tom was prepared for this question. He had already considered how he should answer. Teamwork had certainly been required, but that was the lesson of the ox. Cleverness, too, had been necessary, but that was the monkey's domain. He remembered how the Mandarin of Joy had described the rabbit as being of a gentle and artistic nature.

"I learned that fighting is not always the right answer," he said.

"That will do, I suppose," said Rabbit. "Also acceptable would have been: 'Do not judge by appearances,' or 'Try to find a solution that benefits all.' Very well, step forward and bare your arm, Tom Braider."

Tom did so.

And when the rabbit leaned down and nuzzled him, a third pie wedge came swimming into view on his destiny tattoo.

"Thank you, wise and gentle rabbit," he said.

At this, the rabbit lowered himself still further and placed the golden egg on the perch he had previously occupied. Some other players had drifted over, confused that the quest icon no longer seemed to be in evidence. After a moment, the golden egg began to wiggle. Then it began to wobble. Before long, cracks appeared on its shiny surface.

Then an ear poked out. It was a rabbit ear, but not a very realistic one. It was obviously stitched together from tan-colored cloth with a pink lining. A head soon followed, wriggling its pink nose. It had buttons sewn on for its eyes and a pleasant grin stitched into its velvety muzzle. The rest of the eggshell fell away, and its name came floating up to rest above it.

Velveteen Rabbit (Holiday Marshall) - Stuffed Animal.

A quest icon burst out from his chest and rose to hover above the basket.

"It's done," said the original white rabbit. "Now *he* can take over, and *I* can resume my many other important activities."

"Oh?" said Allison. "And what might those be, pray tell?"

"Too many to even tell you them all," replied Rabbit. "There's a tea party I must attend (I'm dreadfully late for that, I fear). Then I need to hide my honey jars in the hundred acre woods. There's a certain bear who will steal them otherwise. Oh, and there's a brier patch that needs hiding in. So many legends to be getting on with."

"But before I go, I've got something for each of you. One last time won't hurt, I suppose."

The rabbit pushed one of the man-sized eggs up over the lip of the basket, then another, and then a third. These came crashing down in front of Tom and his friends. Then the rabbit did his joyful dance. The music played, and confetti swirled around them. When it cleared, the rabbit was gone. Only the stuffed bunny stared down at them unblinkingly from atop the pile of remaining eggs.

"Am I Real now?" he asked.

Tom targeted his large, orange egg and tried to place it in his inventory. He found that it couldn't be placed there. Instead, beside where it rested was a strange, green cursor icon that curled back on itself. When he focused on this, the egg rolled away from him. A yellow quest arrow appeared. It pointed toward the city gates.

His companions must have made the same discovery. And soon the three were nudging and guiding their gigantic eggs out of the square and down the village's main street towards who knows what. Tom certainly didn't, but he was very eager to find out.

CHAPTER FIVE

Snake in the Grass

By the time they passed through the entrance to the village, a small crowd of curious onlookers had begun trailing after the trio. Tom ignored the many whispered questions about what they were doing, eventually exiting teamspeak to respond aloud.

"We're not sure what these eggs will do. It's a quest from the rabbit. We'll just have to wait and see."

Once he'd passed the entrance, the green icon disappeared, and his egg rolled to a rest near the hitching post. Allie's pink egg was the next to arrive, followed by G.C.'s blue one. Several people in the trailing mob had erected easels and were brandishing paint brushes. In real life, Tom guessed these were the same kooks who were so quick to take photos with their cell phones. It was funny to see them jockeying with one another for the best angle to capture the scene.

The NPC guardsmen standing over by General Tso's quest marker were still engaged in their never-ending dialog. They had changed it up since Tom was last here. Now their patter consisted of all sorts of childish egg puns. These scrolled along at the bottom of Tom's HUD, to the accompaniment of the laughter emotes of the two guards.

"That rabbit has the most beautifully decorated eggs."

"Yup, I hear they're to dye for!"

"So, how many colored eggs can you fit in an empty basket?"

"Just one, I suppose. After that, it wouldn't be empty anymore; would it?"

Allie, Tom, and G.C. watched in expectant silence as their eggs began to hatch. Allie's was first. As the pink shell began to crack away, the head of a rabbit emerged. It was even larger than that of the rabbit who'd given them the quest. When the whole rabbit hopped free, Tom couldn't fathom how such a large creature had even fit inside. It was white, but this was marred by streaks of black that ran in pleasing patterns through its fur. The head was completely white, save for one ear and a black ring around its left eye that resembled a monocle. It was fluffy. And though it was not as large as a cow, it was close.

[Name this creature to claim it as your mount.]
[You may use up to sixteen characters.]
[These may be letters, numbers, or special characters.]
[Mount names need not be unique,]
[though this is strongly recommended.]

"Ooohh," gushed Allison, rushing over to the unnamed lagomorph. "What a beauty he is!"

"Okay," said G.C. with amusement. "Gender pronoun assigned. What are you going to name *him*?"

"'March Hare,' of course."

Although similar to rabbits, Tom knew hares belonged to a different genus. He was also certain the technical distinction would be lost on Allie, whose adoring eyes scanned her new treasure as she patted his silky fur. Nor, he supposed, did a pony-sized, AI-generated riding bunny even have a proper scientific designation.

It was then that G.C.'s egg began to stir. Even Allie stilled to witness what might emerge from its turquoise-blue shell. G.C.'s hatchling was also a riding rabbit. Hers was gray with a white ruff and tail.

"What are you going to name it?" asked Allie.

"Hmm. How do you two feel about 'Peter Cottontail?' It does use all sixteen letters."

"Absolutely not," opined Tom. "It would forever remind me of that insipid song."

"Oh. Right. 'Thumper' it is, then."

"Hah. From 'Bambi.' Good one, mate."

When Tom's own egg hatched, he fell in love. It was a doe-brown creature with soulful brown eyes. He wasn't quite as large as the mounts of his teammates, but he had a wiry grace and a scrappy demeanor that suggested he might be fast. His ears shot up as he scented the breeze for the very first time. The virtual keyboard arose in Tom's HUD, and with five simple keystrokes, he named his riding beast.

The chime of quest completion sounded, and Tom was bombarded by a host of system messages. He swept them aside to review later. Instead, he looked upon the trio of rabbits gathered beside the hitching post. Each now sported reins and a saddle. Beside his was a green 'jump' icon arching up to point at its back.

Allison was the first to trigger hers, vaulting into the saddle and haring off into the meadow. Tom watched her go, leaping and frolicking about as her whoops of joy filled his team chat.

"Why'd you name it that?" asked G.C.

"It's a homage to Richard Adams, a character from one of his novels. 'Fiver' was a smaller rabbit blessed with prophetic visions."

"Shall we?" asked G.C., waving toward the fields.

"You bet," replied Tom.

Soon the two were bounding off to join their cheerful teammate in the meadow. Riding a jackrabbit wasn't at all what riding a horse must be like. Between the high leaps and the jarring changes in direction, it was more like a fun-house ride. G.C. soon lost her grip on the reins and was unseated, and Tom came tumbling after.

While lying on his back in the grassy field, a message appeared on Tom's HUD.

[Would you like to acquire the skill: Riding ? **Y/N**]

***

Jessica lay there, propped up in bed against a pillow pile. She took her tongue gently between her teeth as she steered the wobbling egg carefully toward the gates.

Her lappy lay open on her legs, her useless, unresponsive legs. They'd once been hers to command, a dancer's legs, but now they might as well be a bookshelf. They were still nice legs to look at, she thought, but only daily PROM sessions kept them flexible, and only a FES regimen kept them anything like toned. How the docs enjoyed their clever little acronyms.

Both passive range of motion and functional electrical stimulation have their places in any good maintenance regimen. So, her parents, the famous Arbuckles, kept up the treatments long after the insurance company mongrels said the policy had run dry. They could afford it.

Both her mom and dad were members of the Australian Ballet. Dad was a principal dancer, and mom had nearly become a prima ballerina before pregnancy caused her to lose her edge. The demands of such a life could be a little unfair to women who want children. She reined in such thoughts when her egg began to hatch.

"Ooohh," said Jessica, staring wide-eyed at the adorable bunny on the screen. "What a beauty he is!"

If only she had a real one to snuggle with. Too bad they weren't allowed here at the Cleveland Clinic. She doubted that a rabbit, however well-trained, would be considered a service animal. And comfort animals just didn't have the same access or clout. No. Bunnies would defo have to stay online.

"Okay," said Glass Cannon, "Gender pronoun assigned. What are you going to name *him?*"

He was a fine one to talk. The player was obviously a bloke, but his goofy character was a sheila. Playing a female avatar didn't make a fellow gender-fluid, nor did she care if he was, but it did make her pronouns hard to parse.

"'March Hare,' of course," she answered.

She waited patiently while both G.C. and Tom named their mounts as well. Then it was off to the races. Jessica loved to ride (and play footy, and dance, and swim). But all that had ended after her fall.

It was nearly two years ago when her friend Clarissa invited her to go trail riding along the coast of the Tasman Sea. It was hardly the rugged outback, and no one had expected it might quickly go so wrong. She could still feel the wind in her hair as she spurred Apricot up to a full gallop, whooping and laughing alongside the surf.

That had been her last truly happy day. Since then, it had been all doctors and hospitals, filled with words like L4-fracture, 'inoperable' and such. Dad refused to give up. He kept following every furphy and rumor any quack put down in a medical journal.

This might be her last shot. She was here on a grant from the Christopher and Dana Reeve Foundation. The Neuroscience Department here at the CC was studying a new treatment for spinal cord injury apart from just their regenerative feedback (wishful thinking) technique. If her case fit the needed profile, she might be offered a slim chance for something better.

Experimental surgery. It beat having a stranger shift your legs about for thirty minutes every day.

Mum understood. She was the one staying in a hotel nearby. Dad was half a world away preparing to portray "Spartacus," the lead role of a ballet by the same name. It opened in a couple of weeks at the Joan Sutherland Theatre within the Sydney Opera House. He skyped whenever he could. It was Mom who first got Jess interested in Realms. It was a little painful to vicariously enjoy the things she could no longer do, but she knew she could no longer stop.

Riding a giant bunny? That was something you couldn't do in real life. Or in-game either, apparently. Jessica's heart froze in her chest when the bunny tossed her right out of the saddle. Hurdling through the air triggered a flashback to the dreadful day she'd broken on that beach. But then Tom's words from earlier came drifting back. 'Remember,' he had said, 'it's only a game. A fall can't really hurt you.' It had been that, more than the stat boost that had given her back her wings.

She landed on the spongy grass of the meadow with only a minor dip in her health bar.

[Would you like to acquire the skill: Riding ? **Y/N**]

'Hunh?' she thought. 'I don't have any open skill slots.'

But then she remembered the heap of system messages she'd ignored only a moment ago. She must have leveled up! She touched the screen to accept the skill, briefly wishing there was a selection for 'hell yes!' She saw March Hare hunkered down nearby. Allison remembered her footy coach's advice about how to get back in the proper head-space after an injury. Paraphrasing it a bit, she'd been told she must get right back up on that rabbit. Toggling the green arrow, she did just that.

And soon Allison Wonderla was whooping and laughing as a spirited March Hare bore her on a wild ride about the meadow. And here came her other two mates, about to learn the same lesson. She held her tongue and let the drama play out.

Allison was glad she'd met these two. She really hadn't wanted to team with anyone. She'd been playing for a long time to still be at level two. It wasn't like she had any better things to be getting on with. Allison had just been drifting through the game, enjoying the scenery and the feeling of restored movement (however artificial) it gave her.

But then she'd met the old fortune-teller. Storia was her name. After a bunch of blather about 'envisioning the heavens united in fire and placing her trust in the Higher Power,' Storia got all intense. It was like she'd reached right out of the screen and shook Jessica by the shoulders. She said one would be coming who was helping a large white rabbit, and that if she helped him, she would be rewarded with 'greater mobility.'

And there they were - the two companions she now considered her mates. They were lying flat out on the meadow with their health bars down a bit. She rode over and toggled the dismount.

Jessica didn't know why she had dared to hope. It was silly. But when Tom arrived, gawking at her like a teenager with a mad crush, and started spouting off about helping a rabbit, she knew she had to see it through. And she had. And it had been glorious. But... Is this all you meant? Was this the great reward? A fake (though admittedly cute) bunny in a video game? Jessica no longer wept. Those tears had all been shed. But she felt hope die a little as she lay in her hospital bed.

***

"So what's next?" asked G.C.

"I'd like to keep gaming with you," said Tom, "but there's some work I need to dive into tomorrow."

"Oh? Don't you ever lighten up? It's spring break, man. I thought you were footloose and fancy-free all week."

They were in the open meadow, huddled around the fire pit. Despite having no need to buff, it was pleasant to just sit and enjoy the crackling flames. The artificial bunnies were grazing on the artificial turf. And all was peaceful now that the curious onlookers had dispersed. Nothing but their next quest kept most gamers interested for long.

"I thought so too, but something's come up. I'll be tied up for most of next week with a special project for Mrs. Burkhold."

"The guidance counselor? That's a bummer, dude."

"You talk funny," said Allison, unexpectedly.

G.C. snorted, too dazed by the statement to form a snarky retort.

"Seriously, mates. 'Dive into work?' 'lighten up footloose?' 'tied up bummer?' I get that you think *I* speak gibberish. But we Strayans have got *nothing* on you Yanks when it comes to confusin' expressions - deadset!"

Allie had been uncharacteristically quiet for the last hour or so. It was good to see her open up again. Could it be that she would miss him in the game?

"I'll try to log on whenever I can," said Tom. "It'll mostly be in the evenings. As for what's next, I'm thinking of making for the Jade Palace. Now that we have mounts, it shouldn't be such a long journey. I'll understand if you don't want to come, but I'd love to keep this team together. I enjoy playing with you."

"I'll go," said G.C. "You and I both hit level five. It won't be long before this village gets too small for us."

Both stared at Allison.

"You ain't shaking *me*, Yank. You lot still owe me a quest. If you think I'm letting ya off the hook, you're a few stubbies short of a six-pack. Besides, that last adventure took me almost halfway to level four. If you're pussyfooting around for a week, I'll likely pass up both of you bludgers."

"Yeah, *I* talk funny," said G.C., deadpan.

"I'm just saying it's no wucka if Tom is flat out like a lizard drinking."

"Hey!" G.C. exclaimed. "I know *that* one. I watched 'Crocodile Dundee' last night. I even know what a 'dunny' is."

"Your parents must be *so* proud," said Allie in a wistful voice.

While Tom was fighting a desperate urge to burst out laughing, he noticed a mounted player approaching them from town. The horse on which he rode was a medium-sized bay stallion with a reddish coat and a matching mane and tail. All up and down its sides were hand prints in red, yellow, and white. It reminded Tom of the warpaint used by that Native American tribe the old westerns called the 'Crow Indians.' The rider was a lanky fellow in chaps and a very un-Chinese flannel shirt. All that was missing was the Stetson.

Shrinestn Cowboy (Rootin Tootin) Level 8 Warrior

He approached at a walk, targeting each of the companions in turn.

"How do, folks?" He greeted.

"That's right," groused G.C. "Because we, uh... defo need another colorful form of speech at the moment."

"Greetings, stranger," said Tom.

"I couldn't help but notice your darling little riding beasts. I can't say I've seen their like before."

"Yes, riding rabbits are new," said Tom.

"It so happens I collect unique mounts. I've got fourteen different ones so far. Could I convince one of you to part with one?"

"I doubt it," said Tom. "Although we only just got them, we've already formed emotional attachments. I'm sure you understand."

"Sure do. But just in case you're only trying to jack up the price, how about a trade? I'll swap Old Paint, here for one. Old Paint's a hoedic."

"A hoadic?"

"No, not a hoadic. A hoedic is a horse of extremely different colors. Watch."

At that, Old Paint shifted from what Tom assumed was his default mode and became a zebra. Only in place of black

127

stripes, his were a deep shade of crimson. As the three friends watched, the red brightened to orange, then yellow, eventually cycling through all the colors of the spectrum, ending in solid white. Then polka dots appeared.

"There's loads more options, but you get the idea. You should see him do paisley."

From the cowboy's voice, Tom guessed him to be an elderly gent. All kinds of people played Realms for a lot of different reasons. Collecting strange mounts sounded like a fun pastime. Tom looked around at his companions. He already knew what Allie's answer would be. G.C. shook her head with a negation emote.

"Thanks all the same, Shriney C., but we want to keep our bunnies."

"Understood. I'll pester you no more. If you ever change your mind, just drop me a note in the in-game mailbox. I'm off to the battlefront to drive back the Mongolians."

"Is Old Paint a war mount?" asked G.C.

"Nope. For that, I'll need Pogo. Adios."

And with that, the Shrinestone Cowboy turned and galloped back to the hitching post. Not a minute later, they saw him 'riding' off toward the east. He was on a carousel horse, pole and all, that appeared to be made of hard plastic. His mount was stiff and unmoving as he went bouncing down the road on the pole that pierced it through. Tom wondered what the Mongolian hoard would make of that.

"So when do you want to set out?" asked Allison. "We've got Buckley's chance of making it anywhere by tonight."

"I've still got tomorrow afternoon," said Tom. "Let's meet at about one o'clock by the gates. We'll see how far the day takes us and play it by ear from there."

G.C. cleaned up the fire pit, and the three prepared to log off.

***

At his mother's urging, David dug into the GSC packet right after church the next morning. He was to report to school by eight a.m. on Monday to meet with their representative. The global science council was into everything from nanotechnology to the latest AI. But from the materials, David suspected he knew why they were canvassing for kids his age who could teleoperate heavy equipment. The machine in his study packet was unmistakably a Mark IV Moonraker. It didn't say so in the packet, but he could tell just from its specifications.

This was the very model they had used to break ground for Bradbury Base, the domed habitat in Shackleton Crater. They still had a number of them up there, plowing away at the lunar regolith for various expansions. At first teleoperated from Earth to prepare the way for habitation, the Moonrakers were now run by operators up at Bradbury itself.

David had run his share of bulldozers during summers helping his dad. But these things were monsters by comparison. Each weighed more than 22 tons, and that was in lunar gravity. On Earth, these behemoths would weigh in at more than 150 tons. By comparison, that was as much as a blue whale or a freight train! At sixteen feet tall, their scoops could move up to 90 cubic yards of material at a time.

Of course, the first machines to pave the way on the lunar surface weren't nearly so massive. Back then, people were extremely limited by the cost of boosting payloads from Earth into space with their primitive launching systems. Moreover, the teleoperators had to deal with the two-second delay in transmission time between Earth and the moon. By the time you saw yourself coming up on a crater, your rig would already be over its lip and stuck down in it. So it was very slow going at first.

Once the first lunar habitats had been established, and especially when the fabricators came online, it became an entirely different matter. There's some metallic iron in the lunar regolith - not much, but some. It comes in tiny particles called nanophase iron, a result of meteoric impacts and space weathering. The fabricators sift through piles of regolith to extract useful iron using electromagnets. This is refined in the solar smelters and fashioned into machine parts. And voilà, new equipment is built to accelerate the process ever further. It was how the expansion of the L5 space station could stay on track. It was much easier to send prefabricated parts up from Luna.

David chided himself for getting sidetracked.

All he needed to do right now was focus on the machine itself and its operation. Its controls were very similar to the small bulldozers he had operated here on Earth. The main differences were due to the vacuum problem and the abrasion issue. Because of the lack of oxygen to burn fuel, normal combustion engines of any sort were out. There had been a brief flirtation with nuclear piles like they used in the old submarines, but the availability of plentiful solar energy soon overtook this technology.

The abrasion problem was a little trickier. Moon dust got into everything. Any moving part or joint was subjected to its grinding presence. All systems, especially lubrication and hydraulics, had to be sealed. And dust-resistant materials had to be used throughout its design to mitigate this issue.

Lastly, all parts were subject to thermal fatigue due to the rapid expansion and contraction of metals in extreme temperature environments. Day side - hot. Night side - cold. Got it. David could see why there was such a detailed checklist for each machine prior to and following each mission. It wouldn't be long, in any event, before such equipment was retired to the smelters for reforging.

After studying each nut, bolt, and protocol, David laid his head down. He was doing this, why again? All so he could play with a big earth-mover on the moon. Wait. Should he call it a moon-mover? He guessed calling it by its proper designation, Moonraker, would be for the best. It wouldn't be like racing around in a moon-buggy or anything, and he wouldn't even be there anyway. But... oh, yeah - the quest. 'Advancement in his chosen class.' Did Realms mean jiangshi hunter or teleoperator? Either way, the game hadn't steered him wrong yet.

Just then, his text-received tone sounded, startling David.

Was the game telepathic, or what? He fished out his phone, prepared for anything. He smiled when he recognized the caller.

It was Bonnie. Prom was next Saturday, and they'd barely spoken. He opened the text.

[Do you think Bonnie Fields is cute? Y/N]

Hah! He knew the answer to that one. He pressed 'yes.'

But nothing happened. He pressed 'yes' again, and still nothing. Then the 'no' response flashed. What?

David stared at the screen and was about to call the girl when a new message scrolled up.

[Wait for it... Trust me.]

After a moment, he received a new text: (frown emoji exclamation point)

And then the reply button lit up, and a message entered itself: 'Bonnie Fields is not cute. Bonnie is beautiful.'

A final text soon appeared on the conversation thread. It said, 'See you Saturday, pick me up at 3PM (heart, heart, heart).'

And the phone went dark.

"We talked about this," said David to his phone. "It's bad enough you want me to reshape the moon, but now you're my self-appointed romance coach?"

The screen remained dark for three or four seconds and then said,

[She likes you. She gave you three heart emojis.]

She likes you, more like. Leave off. I can handle my own love life.

[We'll see.]

"David? Who are you talking to?"

It was Mom. Standing there in the doorway.

"Uh. Jason was trying to give me some dating advice, the prat. I told him to leave off."

Tom knew that if asked, his 'bro' would cover for him.

"Aw. That's sweet."

Mom came right over and hugged him.

"My baby's going to the prom!" she crooned. "I hope you asked the girl what color dress she'll be wearing."

"Uh, why?"

"So the corsage you get her will match, of course. I swear. Men can be so clueless!"

"Okay, mom. I'll make sure and ask. Now, if you don't mind, I need to study this stuff."

After she'd left, David picked up his phone to call Bonnie.

[Yellow], it said

[Corsage and matching boutonniere are on order. Set to arrive on Friday by refrigerated hover-drone express.]

***

David blinked back the dryness in his eyes. Ever since adding the sunlamp array to his Treadie, the flames of the opening cinematic left him feeling scorched. He'd have to mention that in his product review. Tom faded into view near the hitching post and found Allie and G.C. already waiting there.

"It's about time," said G.C. "You said one o'clock."

"I know," said Tom. "I just had to memorize about a billion parts of a stupid machine. Then there was this kerfuffle about my prom."

Allie stopped stroking her bunny and stared over at him.

"You need PROM?" she asked.

"Well, need is a strong word. I'm going later this week. I'll be escorting a girl from my class. Which reminds me. Jase, if anyone asks, you were trying to give me some dating advice earlier today."

"Uh. Okay," he grunted, mystified.

"Oh. You're talking about a school *formal*," put in Allie, resuming her grooming.

"You bet. Why? What did you think I meant?"

"It's not important," she mumbled, turning away from him.

"Where's Fiver, anyway? Did he go to the hitching post when I logged?"

"Better," said G.C. "Allie figured out that rabbit mounts have a special feature. Try unequipping your hat. But don't put it back in your inventory."

Tom did so.

"Now toggle the 'Ta Da!' icon."

When Tom did this, his arm reached in, extracted a miniature (normal-sized) Fiver, and tossed him on the ground before him. The rabbit proceeded to grow, quickly achieving his full size.

"Well, that's going to be convenient."

"Bunnies are the best," Allie affirmed. "Let's get going, Yank. We're burning daylight."

"Shouldn't we get our items from the B.A.N.K.?"

"Nope," said G.C. "Not unless there's something you especially need. I asked around. There'll be another B.A.N.K. at the Jade Citadel, and our things will be waiting for us there."

"Oh. Good. But shouldn't we eat first?"

"Too late for that, mate. G.C. put the billy on to boil just ten minutes ago. You have to be here on time if you want to have tea. We did save you a sanger, though."

And soon the three were riding down the Great Silk Road toward the empire's capital. Before long, they spied the PvP zone and its endless battle with the Mongolian hoard. It was clearly marked as such on their mini-maps. They heard the clamor of battle off in the distance. The zone came right up to the roadway, and they made sure to skirt its edge. Their mounts were much better behaved since they'd all taken the Riding skill, but it was still quite a bouncy ride.

Not twenty minutes later, Tom noticed something on his map that had him puzzled. He called a halt and dismounted.

"Why're we stopping in the woot woot, mate?"

He pointed to the north.

"There's a rare herb just over there, but it's strange."

The direction he was facing put it just within the boundary of the PvP zone. 'Dawn Lilly,' it said.

"Strange how?" asked G.C., stepping up from behind.

"Dawn Lilies usually only appear when the sun is on the horizon. And they're spelled with just one 'l' - well, two if you count the first one. I'd like to sneak over and take a look."

"Better not, dude. My spidey sense is tingling. Something over there is radiating menace."

"Alright," said Tom. "I give up. What, precisely, is 'spidey sense?'"

"It's two skills, actually," said G.C. "The first one is Zen Awareness. It alerts me to pending dangers. The other is Aura Perception. It lets me scan for intentions and sense the emotions behind a person or object. Both are based on Enlightenment which I've now gotten up to thirty."

"Impressive," said Tom. "And what are they telling you?"

"The same thing Admiral Ackbar would say."

"Admiral...?"

But whatever Allison was about to ask was lost as a rider came clattering up the road behind them. He was mounted on a dappled gray Appaloosa and churning up dust from the road. He came skidding to a halt beside their group, staring blankly ahead.

Dr. Fu Manchu (Master Mixer) Level 7 Taoist Alchemist

He certainly had the mustache to carry it off. Without a word, he sprang from his steed, equipped a herbalist trowel, and went running into the field.

"Wait!" Tom shouted after him. "It's not safe! There's something --"

"Nice try, newb!" cackled the mustachioed alchemist. "This lily is mine! I've been looking for <urk!>."

Up from the grass, a figure had arisen. He was shrouded in a black cloak that matched his dark attire. Targeting him revealed his character's name.

Swift Demise (Playa Slaya) Level 6 Shadowblade

And sliding off the end of his sword was the hapless would-be herbalist, whose corpse was already beginning to dissolve. Looking up from his victim, the shadowblade paused, then began running directly at Tom and his friends. Tom and G.C. flinched and shied back, but Allison stood her ground.

"You can't harm us here, you narky little hoon!"

"I know," said Swift in a child-like voice. "Now that you can see me, *I* want to be in the safe zone *too*. Don't want any retribution, you know?"

"Why'd you *do* that?" sputtered G.C.

The sinister figure stepped up onto the roadway beside Tom.

"Ooh, cute bunnies!" she exclaimed. "Can I ride one?"

"*No* you cannot *ride one!*" exclaimed Allison. "Stay *away* from our bunnies!"

"Aw. Alright. As to why I killed the fool, that's what shadowblades do. I'm working on gaining my 'Apex Predator' badge. It gives you plus one to all stats in a PvP zone."

She said it like it was something to be proud of. If Tom had to guess, he'd put the speaker at around ten or eleven years old.

"Do your parents know you do this?" he asked.

"Sure. Ma's a fox spirit trickster, and Dad's a monkey king disciple. Wanna join my team? I bet we could take down some bigger game if we put our skills together."

"Um. No thank you," said Tom. "We need to get to the Jade Citadel."

"Okay, move on then, please. You're scaring off the marks."

"Uh, sure. By the way, you misspelled 'lily', and those only bloom at sunset and dawn."

"You'd be surprised how many people don't know that. I had trouble getting the image just right. Our illusions have to contain a flaw. We can't name them the same as the real object."

They left Swift Demise to her sport and resumed their trek as game night cast its shadow on the fields. The encounter was a sobering reminder that they still had a lot to learn about Realms. Tom hoped they could find a safe spot to log off.

***

Allie and G.C. stood in the peaceful field, well off the side of the road. A stand of apple trees was visible in the distance, their pinkish-white blossoms waving in the gentle breeze. The day was warm and smelled of honeysuckle.

Then a dreadful humming filled the air as Tom went running by, pursued by a swarm of angry bees.

"I think that's the last of them," G.C. remarked.

"Let's give it a moment, mate. We got to make sure we get 'em all, or Tom might just cark it."

The main mass of the writhing cloud was making a beeline toward Tom, trailing a stream of its furious fellows. No matter how he ducked and wove, they were quickly closing the gap. They nearly caught him when he reversed direction to again come shooting past his companions.

"Any *time* now!" Tom shouted in panic.

Tom's maneuver had gathered the trailing insects into the central mass. It was only then that Allie sent her flapping paper crane swooping down from above. It entered the swarm, which contracted upon it. The humming hornets halted their pursuit to inflict their venomous wrath upon the hapless flier.

In a flash, it was over.

"And... *boom*, goes the dynamite!" shouted G.C., pumping her fist in the air.

The paper crane was torn to shreds as the swarm exploded in a flash of fire. All that was left of them were the tiny, flaming motes raining down all around.

Tom came walking up to his teammates, his stamina bar down to its last dregs.

"It took you long enough," Tom muttered.

"Don't be a whiny little sook. We had to make sure we got 'em all," said Allie defensively.

"I *told* you my new flame aura could have probably incinerated them instantly, dude," G.C. reminded him. "But *you* wanted to try it *this* way."

"Yeah, well, I wanted to confirm that Allie can use her origami on my paper talismans. This opens up all kinds of possibilities. Shouldn't you be looting that hive, by the way?"

"Yup. I'm on it," said G.C. "I'd best get the honey before any of the little buggers can respawn."

G.C. moved off toward the tree line, where the hive hung with Allie's arrow sticking out of it.

"You going to be okay traveling with him?" asked Tom.

"No drama, Tom. Or probably a lot of drama, but nothing I can't just ignore. We'll be fine. You go log at the shrine, and you can catch us up this evening."

"Will do. Say, do you know how to tell a crocodile apart from an alligator?"

"Is this a trick question? Crocs have a more rounded snout for one."

"True, but the real way to tell is whether you see them later or in a while..."

Allison groaned (a fitting tribute to the terrible joke).

"See you later, Allie-gator."

With a snort of disgust, she mounted March Hare and loped away after G.C.

Tom watched her ride off, checked the time, and started making his way back to his newest spawning point. It was another wayfarer's shrine out in the middle of nowhere. He still had an hour before he had to leave for school. Mom had agreed to drive him to his first day of training.

He was almost to the shrine when he noticed some movement off to his left. It was a furtive squirming in the underbrush. Nothing showed up on his mini-map. Had that shadowblade followed them here? He took a deep breath and made ready to dash to the shrine.

Then out from the brush came a reptile head, as large as a compact car. And behind it, winding into sight, were massive ophidian coils. It slithered toward Tom with its tongue licking out to sample the morning breeze. And when his thoughts caught up to his panic, Tom realized he'd failed to even run. Too late now, he thought with a gulp as the creature reared up just before him.

It was yellow, tinged with green, and had an interesting black pattern running all along its back. It stared down at Tom from three or four feet above his head.

It was not a variety that Tom recognized. Perhaps it was a rat snake of some kind, grown enormous over time. But was he to be the rat in this picture? This was the question that preyed on his mind. And still, his legs refused to move as he stared into its eyes; those vertically-slitted amber globes that held him hypnotized.

Oh, well. It was only a game. If he got eaten, he'd respawn at the shrine, not thirty yards away.

The snake's mouth didn't move when its voice sounded in his ears. It was a female voice, dripping with disdain.

"I had to come and see for *myself* what the ox and the rabbit were jabbering on about. I waited for your friends to leave, for we have business to conduct."

"Um. Okay," stammered Tom. "I take it you're the zodiac serpent and are here to offer me a quest."

"That should be obvious. If it were any other snake, it would have bit you."

And a sense of humor too. A little dark - but It was good to have found some common ground. For some reason, though, Tom thought the snake should be slurring her 's's. Her sibilants, however, were clear and distinct. So much for sstereotypess.

"They are interesting folk with whom you consort," remarked the snake. "It speaks well of you, Tom Braider. For I've heard it said that the strength of the Pack is the Wolf, and the strength of the Wolf is the Pack."

"Rudyard Kipling couldn't have put it any better," said Tom, deadpan.

"Monkey *said* you were a clever one. He neglected to mention your sarcasm."

"I'm not really that sarcastic; I only do it for my health."

This elicited hissing laughter from the snake, so Tom plowed on.

"Well, don't have a hissyfit about it. It wasn't all *that* funny. For my part, I hadn't expected you to be female."

"Why not?" said the snake. "In this realm, I am known as 'Shé,' the wise, intuitive, charming, seductive, mysterious, and insightful Shé."

"And what would the great Shé have of this lowly mortal?"

"It is time you learned the lesson of the snake. This quest will not be easy. It may take you quite some time. But if you solve my riddle, your reward will be great."

"I've heard *that* before - with mixed results."

Shé paused to glare down at Tom.

"Though my tongue may be forked, rest assured that what I say is true."

"Very well," said Tom, seating himself. "Give me your riddle, great Shé."

"Let's make it official first, shall we?"

At that, a quest icon came hovering up to spin above the serpent's head. Tom targeted it and accepted. The snake began swaying from side to side, and her words in Tom's mind grew rhythmic and measured.

"In Xanadu, did Kubla Khan
A stately pleasure dome decree:
Where Alph, the sacred river, ran
Through caverns measureless to man
Down to a sunless sea."

"Alright," said Tom. "Not much of a riddle so far. I suppose I must find this Xanadu."

The snake nodded once before continuing.

"In what distant deeps or skies,
Burnt the fire of thine eyes?
On what wings dare he aspire?
What the hand dare seize the fire?"

"Um, that one's a little vague. Can you give me a hint?"

Shé ceased rocking back and forth and lowered her head to stare directly into Tom's eyes.

"From Coleridge and Blake, it's clear-cut.
You've been given the where and the what.
But the key is perverse.
You must find its reverse.
To open up that which is shut."

Tom was baffled. He didn't suppose he was meant to give an answer right then and there. And the snake's actions seemed to confirm this. With a winding of her massive coils, she began slithering off toward the thicket from which she'd come.

"That's one big snake," muttered Tom.

"That's what?" Shé said.

***

The school was deserted. David imagined the students who had once crowded it, the babble of their muffled conversations rising and falling like waves. Now, as he walked through the empty halls, only the echoes of his footfalls broke the ghostly stillness. It almost seemed like a different place.

He'd been to the VR Lab many times. It was a great place to get some extra credit. He'd once spent an hour in the Agora of Athens learning the Socratic method from Socrates himself. You had to get your name in early for a time slot, though. The schedule filled up quickly each month. He'd even heard a lot of grumbling that the room was off limits over spring break. So he kept his head down and refused to acknowledge that it had anything to do with him.

Arriving at the lab, David eased open the door and entered. He was greeted by an icy chill and a soft humming that was felt more than it was heard. Computer equipment tended to run hot, and a lot of attention was given to environmental control. He could immediately see where new cabling had been run beneath the raised floor panels, some of which were still askew.

The Oak Hills VR Lab used to contain a row of three industry-standard Freemotion T-fourteens. But now, in their place, there was an eye-catching platform larger than all three combined. It put David's old Treadie to shame. It was an Icarus 9000, the newest model from SpaceAge Industries. The Icarus series was unavailable to the general public, even if one could afford its astronomical price tag.

The large flat-screen filling the wall behind it let observers see what was happening from the operator's perspective.

141

Nearby stood a rack of helmets, gloves, and boots in various sizes. Stark white, he thought they'd make the wearer look like a storm trooper from those old Star Wars movies. Hanging from above was an array of other equipment. David could identify some as being analogous to the new features on his Treadie. But there were others whose purpose he could only speculate upon.

Across from the Icarus, in the shadow of its magnificence, was a more common item. David had almost failed to recognize it due to its dimensions. It was a holo-emitter like the one Mr. Averback used, but it would dwarf that humble device. David was pretty sure this one could display an elephant at its actual size.

Just beyond this, in the room's corner, sat a man. He was working at a console, facing away from David. He was wearing one of the white helmets. It went all the way down to his shoulders, giving him the appearance of having no neck. He sat rigidly upright in his chair. He was wearing track pants and a GSC sweatshirt stretched over his broad shoulders.

"Excuse me, sir," said David. "I was told to report here at eight o'clock. I'm a bit early. I hope that's okay?"

"Minutochku, novobranets," said the man.

David was no linguist, but that sounded something like Russian to him. From the commanding tone, he gathered that he was meant to wait. He did so in silence.

About a minute later, the room lights dimmed, and the holo-emitter came to life. Staring out from it was a man's face, presumably that of the man in the chair. He had a squarish, neatly-shaven jaw and a broad forehead. His deep-set eyes gave him a thoughtful look.

"I am Major Nicolai Krepkiyzad," said the face, staring sightlessly forward. "You will address me as sir or major. And no funny business about my last name."

Well, now I'll just have to go look it up, thought David.

142

"I take it you are David Grimes, the recruit I am here to get settled."

Two cameras mounted on the wall behind the emitter swiveled to focus on David. David stood up a bit straighter.

"This lab has been brought up to GSC-standard, and now that I've gotten its kaprizny AI online, we can use it to communicate. You may address him as Barnaby. Any questions before we begin?"

Only about a hundred.

"Yes, major. I would first like to say that I am very honored to be here."

"That is not a question, recruit."

Yikes.

"Uh. No, sir. No questions, then."

Swiveling in his seat, the major turned to face the display.

"Barnaby," he said, "bring up display zeta-zeta-tango-twelve."

At this, an enormous hologram of the Mark IV Moonraker came shimmering into view. It hovered there, slowly spinning to display it from every angle.

"Let us see what you have learned," said Major Krepki. "Identify for me the ripper cylinders and describe their function."

David looked around and found a pointer wand with which to control the animation. He'd seen Mr. Averbeck and other lecturers use them, but had rarely had occasion to play with one himself. Locating it, he fumbled about to halt the Moonraker's rotation. He then indicated the bars in question."

"They are used to raise or lower the ripper at the vehicle's rear. This plows through the soil behind the machine, loosening it for easier removal by the blade on a subsequent pass. Here on Earth, such components would typically use hydraulics. But, due to the extreme temperature variations on Luna, the ripper cylinders on the Moonraker use modified pneumatics instead."

143

"Good," said Major K. after a brief pause. "You have studied. Now, how does the service technician calibrate and perform maintenance on these parts?"

The questions went on all morning. David thought he was a quick study and knew himself to be above average in the smarts department. But the sheer thoroughness of Major K's examination challenged him as he'd never been challenged before, and he began to doubt himself. It wasn't just rote memorization, either. Sometimes he was given hypothetical situations or asked questions about things not included in his packet. This forced him to think on his feet. By the time they broke for lunch, he was dizzy from all the questioning and wondering whether he'd ever get to play with the big, glitzy Icarus 9000.

They adjourned to a nearby classroom. Eating was forbidden in the VR lab. Major K. finally removed his storm-trooper helmet to reveal his face. It was the same one he'd presented in the holo-emitter. It was comforting to confirm that this hadn't just been an avatar. Over a lunch of sandwiches, chips, and soda, the GSC instructor finally loosened up a notch.

"So, you're from Russia?"

"Da. From what you call the Altai Republic in southern Siberia. It is beautiful place."

"Your English is quite good. Why do you wear that helmet?"

"Translation must be ideal'nyy... (perfect) if I am to assess your knowledge and performance."

He leaned back and took a bite of his sandwich.

"Is joke in my country. Would like to hear?"

"Uh, sure," said David. "Da."

"What you call person who is knowing two different languages?"

"We call that bilingual."

"Bilingual. Da. Or 'dvuyazychny' in Russian. Then what are we calling person who is knowing three languages?"

"Tri-lingual?" said David uncertainly.

"Trilingual. Yes. So, what then do we call a person who is knowing only one language?"

"Monolingual, I guess."

"You guess wrong," said the grinning Russian. "We are calling those ones Americans."

David laughed along, even though the joke was on him. It was true enough, he supposed.

After lunch, they got back to work. David was finally permitted to don the gloves, boots, and other VR paraphernalia and stride up onto the Icarus platform. It was pretty amazing in its own way, but it lacked the full immersion of his little gaming rig back home. There was no need for scent or temperature cues, and sound was used only for instructions or mock radio transmissions in his headset. Sadly, in the vacuum of space, no one can hear you scream.

The visual vista, however, was incredible. As he piloted his pretend Moonraker out onto the lunar surface, the world consisted of shades of gray and sharp shadows. He toggled the rumble feature on and felt the gentle crumble of the regolith beneath his treads. There was no comforting rumble from the electric motors that drove the beast, but he felt more than heard a humming whine from that source. Though not strictly necessary for the scenarios he would be running, David always left the rumble feature toggled on.

Apart from that first scenario, a simple out and in, David didn't get any more lessons that day. Major K. checked him out on all the equipment and showed him the list of simulated runs he was to accomplish by the end of the week. This was to be a self-study course with online assistance if needed. Its instructor will move on to another school tomorrow.

David was given a key to the lab and told that Major K. would return on Friday to administer his final assessment. Well, that was a fine how-do-you-do. The simulated runs looked somewhat fun, but it would be lonely not having anyone to share them with. Soon, in the VR lab, no one would be able to hear *him* scream. Ah, well. At least he'd be able to play with the Icarus to his heart's content.

As he pocketed the key and glanced around the lab one last time, David felt a mix of nerves and excitement. Here was a chance to prove himself, to push his limits and see what he was truly capable of. The thought of navigating an actual Moonraker on the lunar surface filled him with wonder. For that, he'd need to score among the top ten in the world. He took a deep breath and prayed that Friday would find him ready.

CHAPTER SIX

I Smell a Rat

"There have been some more anomalies," Mike reported.

He was sweating. This wasn't the kind of news he wanted to bring to one of the ten richest men in the world. Arguably the third richest, if one didn't count tyrants who technically owned all the wealth of their respective nations.

Light poured in through the series of lancet windows, the bottom panes of which were hinged open. A soft Carribean breeze wafted in, causing the leaves of the potted plants to stir.

"Anything concerning?" asked Mr. Silverman, finally looking up from his reports.

"We don't think so," said Mike. "Just more of the same kind of unpredictable stuff."

He scuffed his toe on the plush carpet of the well-appointed office. There were no chairs facing the desk at which the CEO was seated. Visitors were required to stand.

"Give me an example."

Royce Silverman had eyes that could bore right through your skull. And that was when he was in a good mood.

"Uh, well..." Mike sputtered, "The Easter Bunny's been replaced by a stuffed animal for one thing. No one on the team can figure out why."

"How are the subscribers taking it?" asked the CEO.

"They seem to like the change," Mike assured him, running a hand through his thinning hair. "Subscriptions are up six percent, and the new rabbit is trending well on the blogosphere."

It was good to have something positive to report. Leaning back in his high-end ergonomic chair, Royce placed his hands behind his head and stretched.

"Well, that's something, I guess. Still, I don't like when these random occurrences happen without our planning or involvement. It's only a matter of time before we develop a major glitch. Do you think a full shut down and hard restart would stabilize the game? We have the latest patch almost ready to go."

"It didn't help the last time. And frankly, the subscribers won't like it. They've been spoiled by our non-interrupting rolling reboots."

Silverman's face soured.

"Do it anyway. Drop a gift in all their emails. Something to mitigate their frustration. Maybe a new set of boots. I hear the rice hats went over well. If the AI goes wonky, there's no telling whether we can salvage the situation. This time, we'll run a full scrub on all servers and restore the AI from its starting backup."

"That would be... quite an undertaking. We'd need a week just to safely take the system offline."

"You have four days. We'll release on Friday and have the system back up by Monday morning."

"But..."

"But me no buts. You have your marching orders. Make it happen."

Royce pondered the matter further as he stared at his minion's retreating back. The game was catching on all over the globe and paying solid dividends. Setting up the servers here in the Cayman Islands had been a brilliant move. The tax advantages were just a pleasant bonus. They far outweighed the pittance he paid out in regular bribes. Out from under the weighty restrictions imposed by the GSC, he could offer the very best in AI-driven virtual reality. But he knew well the consequences if the genie ever got out of its bottle.

In recent days, he had begun to suspect the AI might be nearing the threshold. A new form of life might be emerging. Should he watch it develop and learn whatever lessons it might teach? Or did he owe it to humanity to put on the brakes and kill this creature aborning? He hoped it wasn't already too late.

But he feared his control might be slipping away.

Royce Silverman hadn't gotten where he was by being indecisive. Or merciful.

***

It had been a long first day of training. Major Krepkiyzad had really run him through the wringer. And after that, mom grilled him relentlessly on the ride home. David waited until after dinner to log back into Realms. Dad had even come home at a reasonable time for once. And David had been forced to rehash the day's events yet again. Despite just wanting some downtime, it was nice to know they cared.

Using his phone's translation app, David discovered that 'Krepkiyzad' basically meant 'tough bottom (hard-ass)' in Russian. He started working on ways he might subtly allude to this on Friday. Phrases like 'don't be a Krepkiyzad' came to mind. The fact that he was a major made it even funnier, but he had yet to figure out a way to work this in.

It was nighttime in the game when he logged in, but it would be dawn in a couple of minutes, according to his HUD. Tom was in a meditative pose before the altar of the shrine, and no snakes were in sight.

Tom turned on teamspeak and was immediately bombarded by a series of scrolling system messages accompanied by his teammates' bickering voices.

"Flame on!" shouted G.C.

[Flaming Aura strikes Virulent Peacock]
[for 4 points of continuing damage.]

"You know you don't have to say it out *loud*, cobber. Just activate it on your action bar."

"It sounds cooler my way and lets my teammates know what I'm doing," groused G.C. "Aaah! Get it *off* me!"

[Virulent Peacock pecks Glass Cannon 342]
[for 38 points of damage.]

[Precise Shot strikes Virulent Peacock]
[for 10 points of damage.]

"*Run, G.C.!*" Allie shrieked.

"Greetings, team. You busy?" asked Tom.

Pause.

"Just a minute, mate."

[Invigorate heals Glass Cannon 342 for 24 points.]

[Flaming Aura strikes Virulent Peacock [
[for 4 points of continuing damage.]

[Virulent Peacock expires.]

"Nah. We got some time," reported Allie.

[Loot Virulent Peacock? **Y/N**]

"Flame off!"

"Ready for pickup, then," said Tom.

"I told you. Just deactivate it. You don't have to ... Ack! Another dud," groused Allison.

Tom was soon bumped aside as Jason's avatar appeared beside him at the altar. She was looking a little ragged. Several tears rent the fabric of her favorite green gown, and her health bar hovered a few marks shy of full. Tom was sorry to have missed his friend being chased around by a flaming peacock.

"Poultry problems?" he asked.

"You know it," said Jason with a long exhale. "It's good to have you back, bro... er, Tom. Now maybe *you* can serve as bait, and I can get back to what *I'm* good at."

"You can call me bro. You've earned it. Besides, Br'er Tom makes me sound like an Uncle Remus character. As to being bait, I'm sure you're doing a fine job. You should keep at it!"

"Yeah, *right*."

Tom toggled on his friendly smile emote.

"You know," he said, "Mrs. Dolson once sent me to detention for that very statement."

"The English Lit, teacher?" said G.C., standing to her feet and setting up her easel.

"Yeah. She was giving a lecture on language and was talking about double-negatives."

G.C. placed a canvas on her easel. It depicted Allie standing over a singed and thoroughly defeated giant peacock and giving a thumbs-up."

"Go on. Don't leave a brother hanging," said G.C.

"Alright," Tom continued, "she said..."

He coughed and resumed in his best imitation of a fussy female falsetto: "In English, two negatives form a positive. But in some languages, like Russian, two negatives remain a negative. But in no language (not one!) do two positives ever form a negative."

"And I said..."

"Yeah. *Right*," said Jason with a chuckle. "Dude! You shouldn't have got *detention*. She should've given you extra credit for that one."

G.C. touched her shrinestone to the canvas, and Tom watched it burst into flames.

"Portal," she said.

***

Allison and G.C. had been playing all day. Their travels had taken them out of Celestial Valley and into Jadecrest Province. They were now only about a day's ride from the city of Heaven's Gate, also known as the Jade Citadel. They'd been farming crazed peacocks just outside the village of Serenity Springs, called 'Níngjìng Quán' by its natives. Níngjìng Quán featured hot springs that were a must-see for any tourist in the Realms.

Unlike the rural charm of Qinghua Village, Níngjìng Quán had a more cultured feel. The main buildings were multi-tiered pagodas with upward-curving eaves. There was potted greenery all about, and a slow-running river meandered through its center, criss-crossed by wooden bridges.

In the distance, one could see the river's source, a three-drop waterfall that gnawed at the hills to the south. The hot springs were on its western side, as was the shrine that Tom needed to acquire.

Being divided by the river , the village had no single town square. Instead, it had a central gathering area here on its western side and another in the east. It reminded Tom of a verse he'd read. Kipling had been on his mind ever since the snake had alluded to Kaa. He muttered it to himself as they strode along.

> "*Oh, East is East, and West is West,*
> *and never the twain shall meet,*
> *Till Earth and Sky stand presently*
> *at God's great Judgment Seat;*"

152

[Are you sure you wouldn't like to acquire the skill: Poet ?
Y/N]

Tom was sorely tempted. It might help him work out what the snake meant by all that blather. But, no. Skills were precious, and he only had two open slots left. He was saving them for something cool, like stealth. He selected 'no.'

[**Congratulations!** You have acquired the skill "Poet." You now possess the ability to craft beautiful and compelling poetry that can inspire, soothe, and enchant those who hear it. By harnessing the power of words and rhythm, you can evoke powerful emotions and weave tales that captivate your audience. This skill not only enhances your charm but also allows you to influence NPCs and teammates through the beauty of your verses. Effects are dependent on Cleverness and Charm. Use your poetic prowess to elevate your adventures. Happy composing!]

What? No, no, no, no, no! thought Tom. Only after reviewing the wording of the first prompt did the seriousness of his situation sink in. A double negative forms a positive. It was Mrs. Dolson's revenge coming back to bite him!

"Oh no," said Tom. "I didn't mean it that way. I meant to dismiss that suggestion."

(At least, that's what David meant to say. It came out of Tom more like this:)

*"**Alas, such a fool am I, that when I chose negation, I caused the very opposite by unwitting affirmation**."*

Really? This was wrong. So very, *very* wrong. He had to fix this.

G.C. and Allison were both looking at him strangely.

"What's the matter, mate?" asked a concerned Aussie.

He didn't dare answer her. He just found and activated the 'head shake' emote.

"Let's get you to the shrine," said G.C. "You can reset your respawn point, and we'll show you the hot springs after."

"Sounds like a plan, bro," he meant to mumble.

*"**You, so like a brother to me, have devised a clear and sound strategy, with which I must most fervently agree.***"

"Curiouser and curiouser," said Allie, flashing him a smirk emote.

They hustled down the road toward the shrine. All the while, Tom was searching furiously for a way to turn off the accursed impairment his character had negligently activated. To get there, they had to cross the central gathering space. They were just a few steps in when they heard a loud ringing sound. It was as loud as a church bell but a bit higher in pitch. A general message scrolled across the bottom of Tom's HUD.

[Kung Fu Kenny challenges Marrak the Mighty to a dual of honor, a PvP battle royale!]

Tom saw an armored man who had just planted a pole at the plaza's edge. Atop it flapped a long, green pennant. Spiraling out from its base, lines were tracing themselves into the flagstones. These soon formed a sparring circle, from which all the curious onlookers hastily withdrew. Another man in the crowd had a red question mark spinning above his head. He was a massive brute in a leather jerkin and sandals, which laced up his bulging, hairy legs. Tom glanced at each man's targeting info.

Kung Fu Kenny (Warrior of the Dawn),
Level 10 Dragon Disciple

Marrak the Mighty (Purveyor of Pain),
Level 11 Mongol Barbarian

Should be a close match.

But Tom and his friends were about to learn a lesson about what a duel of honor meant. The red question mark dissolved, and a pole with a red pennant rose on the circle's other side.

[Marrak the Mighty accepts the challenge.]
[You have ten seconds to place your bets.]

[Do you wish to make a wager? **Y/N**] appeared in Tom's HUD. He selected 'no' after reading it carefully.

A countdown had appeared above the center of the ring, and all eyes turned upward. When it reached zero, it was replaced by some text, which rotated so that all could see it. [**STAGE 1**: Trash Talk] they read.

The challenger was the first to speak, as a green line marked the time.

"Mongol, your people are a plague on our way of life. You are as ugly as you are uncouth. In battling you this day, I shall demonstrate the superiority of my master's teachings for everyone to see."

Tom noticed immediately that the man's lips were strangely out of sync with the sound of his voice. It was true that some of the players in Realms weren't native English speakers. But Tom had never seen the translation algorithms behave this way before. It must be a nod to those old classics where the actor's speech was dubbed over in a different language. Well done, Realms. It really added to the drama. The green line had run out, and a red one took its place.

"Your Kung Fu is weak!" roared the Mongol whose lips were also out of sync.

He emphasized this with a 'dismissive swipe of his hand' emote.

"Your master, dog that he is, will weep to see the mangled wreck who was once his student. In shame, I will send you back to the shrine to lick your wounds and shed bitter tears of remorse that you ever dared challenge a Mongol. So swears Marrak the Mighty!"

[You have ten seconds to cast your ballot.]
[Who has won stage 1? **CHALLENGER/CHALLENGED**]

"Who did you vote for, Tom?" asked G.C.

"I thought the Mongol made the better argument," Tom tried to say.

"*There's no doubt as to who bested whom in this fight. The Mongol's beratement bedeviled the knight.*"

"Aw, crap," muttered G.C. "I bet on Kenny."

After the countdown ticked down, a red flag popped up on one side of the spinning marquee, which now read [**STAGE 2**: Fisticuffs]. At this point, both combatants were stripped of their gear and stood facing one another as God intended (in their skivvies).

The brutish Mongol launched himself at once toward his opponent. But Kenny was ready. He sidestepped and laid into Marrak with a swift series of blows. It wasn't baguazhang, but it certainly looked effective. When Marrak tried to counter, the dragon disciple would dance away, only to pummel him from a different angle. Marrak may be mighty, but Kenny was quick.

"Weak, am I?" Ken taunted, bouncing on the balls of his feet. "This is for your insult to my master. And *this* is for your vow to batter me senseless. And *this*... is just for being ugly."

Planting his left foot, he lashed out with his right. This almost caused his undoing as Marrak caught it in one hand and hauled back for a haymaker with the other. But before he could land it, Kenny twisted about to balance on one outspread hand and brought his grounded foot up to connect forcefully with Marrak's jaw. The big man staggered and fell to all fours, releasing Kenny in the process. Snapping back up to his feet, the dragon disciple landed the coup de gras in the form of a roundhouse kick.

And a green flag went up on the marquee.

The soft glow of a healing spell encompassed each combatant as the timer ticked down once more.

[**STAGE 3**: Final Reckoning - No holds barred]

Armor and weapons appeared as each warrior equipped himself for the final battle. Kung Fu Kenny was decked out in gleaming metal armor. He was armed with a jian, a straight, double-edged blade. He also had a large, round shield with the face of a dragon painted on it.

Marrak looked underdressed by comparison. He was still in his tatty leather jerkin, which looked like it needed a good scrub. But then he pulled out an unusual heavy weapon. It was basically two large lumps of iron connected by a long chain. Tom would later learn that this exotic weapon was known as a meteor hammer. He began whirling it around expertly, switching it from one hand to the other. Sometimes he would bring it to a sudden stop or twirl it around behind his back. He was unusually flexible for such a thick-set fellow.

And the fight was on. This time it was Kenny trying to close the distance and Marrak seeking to widen the gap, lashing out with his chained fury. Kenny blocked with his shield and tried to corner his opponent, but this wasn't proving so easy. He was slowed by his heavy armor. So, round and around they went.

At one point, KFK dashed in and attempted a swift slash, only to have his sword tangled up in the chain. His shield was, by now, bent nearly in half from repeated heavy impacts. It resembled more of a duck than a dragon. And still, the blows rained down. Things turned from bad to worse for Kenny when one of the hammerheads wrapped around his ankles and pulled his feet from beneath him. Before he could rise, Marrak was on top of him, brutally savaging his face.

If this weren't a game, there would have been blood. As it was, Kung Fu Kenny's health bar was sinking fast.

"Admit your kung fu is weak, and I will spare you the final blow."

"Eat [censored] and die, [also censored]!"

And thus went up the final flag, declaring Marrak the victor.

[Marrak the Mighty receives one honor point from the challenger]

Wait. *What?* A 'duel of honor' was actually fought over a literal honor point, whatever the silly things were? Hunh. Live and learn. Or, if you were Kenny, die and learn. Either way, Tom supposed.

Tom considered the rest of that Kipling verse that had started this whole rhyming thing. It seemed even more appropriate now. He muttered it aloud. And for once, his strange malady didn't warp it into something else.

"*But there is neither East nor West,*
Border, nor Breed, nor Birth,
When two strong men stand face to face,
though they come from the ends of the earth!"

***

Stretched out in the warm, shallow water, Tom felt his tension ease. It wasn't just the relaxation. The scenery was spectacular. A curtain of flowery wisteria vines dangled down to tickle the waters of the pond. Their soothing fragrance was a balm for Tom's frazzled nerves. Beyond this curtain, he had a clear view of the distant waterfalls. They beckoned to his soul with the promise of new adventures. It was invigorating.

As he lay languidly stroking the water's surface, he thought about the mistake he'd made earlier. Him? A poet? He'd always considered himself to be left-brain dominant. But here in the Realms, one can do anything to which one aspires. All skills had value. Perhaps it was time to puzzle out what this one could confer.

He thought of the snake's riddle. He was sure he needed to find a place called Xanadu. But what did that second verse mean? According to Shé, it would provide the 'what.' His search for 'Blake / poet' online had revealed that this was the second stanza of a famous poem, "Tyger", by William Blake. He repeated the words he'd memorized aloud.

"*In what distant deeps or skies,*
Burnt the fire of thine eyes?
On what wings dare he aspire?
What the hand dare seize the fire?"

In this poem, experts agree that Blake was using the tyger to symbolize the terrible force of human intellect, that mix of creativity and imagination with a hint of rebellion that formed the human soul. Or perhaps it was simpler than that. Was he just looking for a tiger? Or a fire? And what did wings have to do with it? He supposed he'd find his answers in Xanadu.

A happy voice interrupted his private musings.

"Arvo cobbers!" said Allie, emerging from the dangling vines she'd parted. "I found a merchant who could sell me some thongs. What do you think?"

This caused G.C. to sit up and take notice. He'd been lying nearby and almost asleep. But if he'd hoped for an immodest peek at Allie's avatar, he was soon disappointed. Per Tang dynasty modesty guidelines, Allie was draped in an airy robe that nonetheless concealed most of her body. She was pointing at her footwear, a set of open-toed, spongy-soled shoes.

"Oh, those," said G.C. "Here in the States, we call them flip-flops."

"Don't you two look spiffy in your budgie smugglers?"

She kicked off her thongs and eased into the water beside Tom.

"That was some match today. Those two bogans had a bonzer of a biffo. I thought that Kenny bloke would defo bail up on the bigger bruce. He was a tough little bugger, but I knew it was over when his hielaman went cactus."

"It's like she has some kind of aphasia," G.C. remarked, turning his head to gawk at some other beautiful avatars wandering by. Tom snorted at Jason's lack of decorum.

"You havin' a perv at those sheilas?" teased Allie.

"You know those are only electrons, right?" added Tom, instead saying:

**"Your mind's been clouded by electron-confusion.
Those aren't real women, friend - merely illusion."**

"Aww. Let Jason look at the pretty lights," cooed Allie before splashing at G.C. playfully.

"This is loads of fun," said Tom, "... and yet, what's the point? We can't get wet."

"Give it a few more minutes, mate. The springs give ya a bonza buff! I think we should all bathe here in the buff before *every* mission."

"Now you're just doing it on purpose," muttered G.C.

"What? Did you think I meant in the nuddy? Get your mind back on business, mate.

It was then that Tom saw the buff to which Allison had been referring. It appeared near his name in his targeting window. 'Very Relaxed', it said.

"There it is," said G.C. "It adds two points to Enlightenment for two whole hours!"

"Well, wait for me, mates. I've still got five more minutes to soak before I'll be ready. Then we can peel out of these bathers and be on our way."

"So," asked G.C., "you've seen my new flame aura. What did you get at level five, Tom?"

Apart from his usual upgrades to baguazhang, his leadership skill had sprouted a new capability. He could now 'fortify' his teammates with an inspiring speech. It added one to all of their stats for a brief time. The beauty of it was that it didn't leech away any of his own abilities. There was a creepy new talisman called Necrotic Poison. It conferred continuing damage based on his Enlightenment and a debuff to his opponent's Vitality. Its effects were doubled when used against the undead. Oh, and his throwing spikes now did a whole point of damage. That was nice.

The best of all was his destiny tattoo. The rabbit symbol granted Agility. And when he landed a buff, five points were now added to the relevant skill. Since it only did so one time in four, he figured that, generally speaking, he averaged +1.25 on his abilities. It still wasn't worth the three points he'd initially sacrificed, but he liked where it was headed.

Rather than try to explain all this, he simply said, "Oh. You know. Just this and that. There are lots of skills I'm better at."

He'd given up even trying to fight it.

"Right... " said G.C. "What about you, Allison? Any major improvements?"

Allie smiled, waved her hands about, and said, "Growth on!"

At this, all the wisteria vines around the trio began to elongate and thicken dramatically. The already lush greenery burst into bloom in a profusion of blue, purple, and white blossoms. Tree limbs above groaned from the added weight as the breezy curtain became a dense, tangled mass.

After taking it all in, G.C. remarked, "You'll have to come up with something better than that. 'Growth on' just sounds silly.

Allie rolled her eyes.

***

Refreshed and newly outfitted, the three were on the move again. It was approaching game evening. This reminded David that it was getting rather late IRL as well. He'd better pack it in before too long. He'd have to be at school early tomorrow to get started on those simulations. There was just enough time, he thought, for one more quest with his friends.

As the shadows began to fall on the city streets, only a few players strolled about. The merchants had all packed up their wares, and most of the stalls were deserted.

"Psst," came a sound from a darkened alley.

Tom scanned his mini-map. No NPC, player, or quest icons were visible. That didn't necessarily mean anything. Sometimes there were hidden quests for those who were observant.

"Did you hear that?" Tom asked his friends. "That hissing din? Someone beckons us within."

"Of course," said G.C., who had halted just beside him.

This was unsurprising. G.C. had the best Enlightenment score of them all and several skills to back it up.

"I'm not sensing any danger, though, or anything at all, really. It's kinda creepy."

"We should check it out," added Allie, who was always up for a lark.

Tom led the way into the dimly lit space between two buildings. There were heaps of rubbish to navigate around, and the place smelled of rot and decay. Really? Sometimes this game was a bit *too* realistic.

Then a figure materialized from the doorway wherein he crouched.

"Illuminate," said G.C.

There stood a squat man, shielding his eyes from the sudden bright light. He wore a tattered robe. Taking the edge of his gray cloak, he brought it up before him, covering the lower half of his face.

"Aaah! Stop that!" he sputtered in a course whisper.

"Who are you?" demanded G.C.

The man retreated further back into the alleyway and looked poised to run off.

"Leave off, G.C." said Allie. "I think you're scaring him."

G.C. looked at Tom, who nodded. The light diminished to a more comforting glimmer, but remained. The man took a few hesitant steps toward them.

"Are you Tom Braider, Tom the jiangshi hunter?" he asked in a quavering voice.

"You've got the right of it. I am he. What business do you have with me?"

"Hmmm, I'd prefer not to say at this time. Let's just say I'm someone who can help you if you don't mind a little... ah, rule-dodging, as it were."

"Help me how? What have you to offer? And what coin do you want to put in your coffer?"

"No coin, good sir. Just a moment of your time. My clients don't pay me in zho. Listen to my deal, then you can decide."

"I don't *like* this," said Allie. "It sounds shonky to me."

"And with that assessment, I have to agree. But let's give it a listen in spite of our doubt. It costs us nothing to hear the man out."

Tom was feeling ever more ensnared by the rhymes that so glibly tripped from his tongue. He could hardly even bring to mind what he had originally wanted to say.

"Good!" said the man cheerfully, lowering his cloak and wringing his hands together. "I've heard of your little... dilemma. Your words come out all wonky and queer. I would offer you a choice."

Tom nodded.

"I know a game hack (not strictly on the up and up, if you take my meaning). It'll make your problem just disappear! Skill selection in-game can't usually be undone. But my friends and I know a clever way to override this stricture. There's a cost, but one you can easily pay."

Of course, thought Tom. There was always a cost. Let's find out what it is.

"If you'd share with me this 'clever way,' then tell me what price you would have me pay."

"In order to undo the selection of the Poet skill, you must give me three stat points of my choosing. In one week, they will be returned to you and can be reassigned."

That didn't sound so bad. There must be a catch, though, thought Tom.

G.C. smiled and thumped Tom on the back. "Excellent," she said. "Go for it, bro."

Tom turned to Allison.

"It sounds almost too good to be wise. What would Allie-gator advise?"

She stared at him for a long moment. "I dunno," she mumbled.

He waited.

"If this shonky bloke can even be trusted, I still think maybe you'd better not."

Her voice took on emotion as she quietly continued.

"It wouldn't look good on ya to be skirting all the rules. Like a wise old granny once said to me, there's a time to act and a time to be accepting, placing your trust in the Higher Power. This feels like the second sort of time. I don't want you to have to go prancing around, popping off like a prat. I *don't*. But neither do I want to see you cheating just to get your way. That's not the Tom I know. *That* Tom's fair dinkum, through and through."

Tom had nearly reached that conclusion himself. A mistake had been made, and he should own it. Otherwise, it'd be unfair to the thousands of others who made goofs in their gameplay. If the game wasn't fair, then what was the point of even playing? He turned to the sketchy man in the cloak.

"No, thank you," he said. "I made a mistake, and I'll live with it; maybe it'll be for the best."

"And what have you learned?" asked the man.

"You're one of *them!*" said a dumbfounded Tom, noting he was no longer rhyming. "Which one, might I ask?"

The man hunched forward further. His cloak became his fur. Whiskers sprouted beneath his beady eyes, and behind him, a long, hairless tail stretched into view.

"Eww, a rat!" squeaked Allie.

"Aww," said the rat. "I heard you *liked* fluffy things. Is it the tail? I bet it's the tail. Damn rabbits have *all* the luck with the ladies!"

"All that aside," said Tom, "I believe I owe you an answer. But first, I have a few questions of my own."

"I grant you three such," said the generous zodiac rat.

"By what name may we call you?"

"As you have guessed, I am not just any rat. I am *the* rat. Here in the Realms, I am known as Shǔ. And I have so many adjectives that I don't know what to do. I'm intelligent, adaptable, resourceful, and quick; I am charming and sociable, and I never get sick. Drum-roll, please, and stand, if you're able, for the fabulous rat of legend and fable!"

Even Allie laughed when Shǔ leaped up on a trash bin and bowed. And G.C. was in stitches.

"Second question," said Tom. "Was that deal for real? What would have happened had I taken it?"

"Ah. Trying to sneak in with a two-for-one sale, I see. But I'll allow it this time because it pleases me (and you were kind enough to ask my name). The deal was as real as real can be. I would have removed the skill. And nothing dark would have happened, like taking your tongue. Perish any such thought. The truth of the matter, the 'catch' if you will, is in which three ability points I'd have taken. You're a clever lad. Can you not guess?"

"My three destiny points," said Tom with a sudden realization.

"Bingo, my boy. Just so."

"Last question," said Tom, "Where is Xanadu?"

"Hmm. That, I'm afraid, I must leave for you to discover. Snakes *eat* rats, don't you know? I'll say only that you've got plenty of time for that. Plenty of time and a long way to go."

"You've been more than fair," said Tom, "so I shall be as well. What have I learned? I suppose it's that sometimes one must accept things as they are and that I should remain upright in my dealings."

"There you go again," said a snickering Shǔ. "Trying to make one answer from two. I won't hold it against you, though, since both of those answers are true. Bare your arm, Tom Braider, and let's see what we can make of *you*."

Tom rolled up his sleeve and held forth his arm. He felt Shǔ's whiskers brush against it. And there, on the wheel of destiny, a fourth symbol took its place.

Neither of his friends had seen this before, and they stared on curiously.

"You guessed it. Self-honesty, upright dealings, and acceptance are the lessons of the rat. It's been very nice meeting all of you, but now it's time to scat."

And with that, the rat took his leave, scurrying up a drainpipe and onto the roof above. Tom turned to see that G.C. already had her easel out. Several canvases lay on the ground next to it. Tom couldn't blame her. How often did you get to meet a legendary beast? Tom wondered how long it would be before the painters of the Realms invented the selfie. He imagined it would involve some kind of large mirror...

***

The room was quiet when David began his second day of training. *He* wasn't fooled, though. He was certain the GSC was keeping him closely monitored. No one would leave all this expensive equipment in the hands of an unproven kid. The cameras would occasionally move to track what he was doing. It never happened when he was looking directly at them. He imagined, too, that these weren't the only cameras in the room. There also had to be scads of ways to follow his keystrokes and inquiries at the console, and any use of the Icarus would undoubtedly be logged.

No, David assumed this was all part of his assessment. His study habits and progress were all being scrutinized.

So he set nonchalantly about the business of preparing for his initial excursions. He realized with a sinking heart that the material covered by Major K. had just been the tip of the iceberg. There were all kinds of things to learn about lunar geography and such before he could even begin Scenario Two. Apart from simply operating the Moonraker, there were also scads of communication protocols to learn. He would take his orders from a team leader (simulated) and would also be in direct communication with Bradbury Base (also simulated).

His own Moonraker's call sign was 'zeta-zeta-tango-twelve.' He was to preface any and all communications with his call sign. Bradbury Base was given the designation, 'Alpha', and the team leader (who he wouldn't work with until Scenario Eight) would be known simply as 'Big Kahuna.'

As he took this all in, David felt the fine hairs on the back of his neck prickle. He was finding it hard to concentrate when he knew his every move was being watched. He felt his phone vibrate in his pocket. Should he answer? It could be the GSC waiting to see what he'd do. He decided it was time to use the lavatory. Bathroom breaks were permitted.

The door to the VR lab automatically locked behind him. It was keyed to his biometrics now. The physical key in his pocket was just a backup in case his palm print was altered by an injury or something. He'd been told to use it only *in extremis*. He wasn't sure what lockdown protocols its use might invoke.

Sitting in the bathroom stall, David retrieved his phone. As he had feared, on its screen was the spinning quest icon of Realms. Rolling his eyes, he toggled it.

[Quest Offered: Invite a Guest]
[Reward Offered: Training Assistance and Companionship]
[Accept quest? **Y/N**]

"That wouldn't be wise. I'm being watched by the GSC," whispered David.

[Of course you are.]
[There are even four cameras hidden in the bathroom.]

[The one above you is presently simulating an image of you evacuating yourself.]

[Best not to take too long, or they might think you are constipated :-P]

[Accept quest? **Y/N**]

After thinking it over, David toggled 'yes,' hoping it wouldn't lead to his being tried for treason.

[David Grimes is to return to the VR lab and jack his phone into the main console. If asked why, he will explain that it was running low on charge (true enough). He will then comply with any instructions given to him by the GSC. See you soon.]

On his way back to the lab, David started worrying. The GSC was trusting him to keep this installation secure. It just wasn't in him to violate that trust for an unknown entity whose intentions were unclear. Was he being seduced by Alliance agents into betraying the global good? Absurdly, the lesson of the rat came swirling up to pluck at his conscience.

He placed his palm on the sensor plate and keyed in his entry code. Striding over to the console and staring into the cameras, he spoke aloud.

"I don't know if you can hear me, but in case you can, I'd like to report an attempt to breach your security measures. For the record, this is David Grimes. An unknown caller has hacked my phone and is urging me to connect it to your system."

He stood there, uncertain of what would happen next. He hoped this wouldn't mess up his chances at joining the Moonraker team, but there were much bigger issues at stake.

The lights all dimmed, and he felt his phone vibrate in his pocket.

He didn't want to look at it, ashamed to have forsaken the quest. But he supposed he'd better face the music and take a look.

[Quest Completed: Invite a Guest.]
[Congratulations!]
[David Grimes has been awarded 1 Honor Point.]

A firework display filled the holo-emitter, and as it settled down, a familiar figure wavered into view.

She was seated behind her ramshackle table, the one with the spread out cloth. Before her lay her book and the jar with the yarrow stalks. The old woman stared at David with mischief in her eyes. She sat there very regally, her shoulders squared and her expression wise.

"You certainly don't disappoint, young man. Still, I had to make sure, so I gave you this test. And to my delight, you have passed it. Full marks. Pull up a chair. We have much to discuss, you and I."

CHAPTER SEVEN

Pig in a Poke

猪

She felt the flow of cool air down her back as it hissed through the bore. Lying on her stomach was Jessica's very least favorite position in the MRI. She was used to the close quarters by now, and the feeling of isolation while those annoying bumps, pings, and thumps sounded. But having to lie absolutely still while needing to give her bum a good scratch was like to drive her completely beresk!

The emergency call button in her hand was comforting, but she resisted the urge to press it. This had been a long one. It felt like she'd been in here for nearly an hour. She knew from long experience that if she bailed now, they'd just slide her back in after a little break to start the whole blasted thing all over. Best to wait it out.

"Try to hold still," said Dr. Richards over the intercom. "You're doing great, Jess. Just a few more minutes, and we'll have what we need."

Kate Richards was a third-year resident in the radiology department. She was up in the gantry with Dr. Prichart, Jessica's attending surgeon. Why this sudden need for new imaging? It's not like they hadn't run her through the big magnet dozens of times already.

"Okay, Jessica, you're coming out. I'll be right in to assist you once you've exited the bore."

Jessica felt the gentle movement as the patient's table began to slowly retract.

About bloody time, thought Jess.

Soon, she was back on wheels. After a quick stop at the loo, she was rolling toward the conference room. Mum will be there. Strange that they didn't just meet in her room like they normally did. Maybe the medical folk finally had some news to share. She hoped it was good news. She'd had enough of the other kind.

In the room sat Mum, the attendant, and a bunch of other people she'd seen around but didn't really know. It was right chockers in there. At the table's end was a big flat-screen display with a picture of someone's spine. It didn't take a genius to guess whose *that* was. It was the one with all the nuts and bolts fusing it together at the L4.

Then the screen split, and half of it was filled with static. This was soon replaced by the blinking message 'Acquiring Satelites.'

A grin split Jessica's face as she wheeled herself in and saw who the caller was.

"Howzitgarn, Jess?" he greeted her with his familiar Ozzy drawl.

"Daddy! How ya goin'?"

"Not too bad, possum," Julian replied affectionately. "Just had to stay up a bit late to make this call. How are you holding up over there?"

172

There was barely any lag in the call. Just a half-second blip between each exchange. The nurses had gotten her up early for the MRI. Still, it must be quite late in Sydney. Scrunching up her nose, Jessica reckoned it must be getting on toward midnight there.

"Very good," said a man at the table's head, clearing his throat and interrupting what she might have said next. "We asked you here to review your daughter's case. Time is pressing, so let's begin."

He shuffled some papers on the table before him and took up a data wand.

"Your daughter's tragic injury has severed her spinal nerve and fractured the L4 vertebra. On the diagram, --"

"We've heard all this before, mate," said Julian. "Cut to the chase; can you fix her?"

"No, we cannot..."

For once, Jessica was thankful for the half-second lag that kept her father's faith alive before a look of horror crossed his face.

"...but we know someone who can."

"Speak on, then, cobber," said Julian, his voice heavy with emotion. "Who is this miracle worker?"

"Perhaps I can best explain," said her attending surgeon, Dr. Prichart, producing a data wand of his own. "We've been examining Jess to see whether she'd be a good candidate for regenerative therapy. She is not. The nerve damage is too extensive."

Jessica saw her mother suppress a wince.

"But per your instructions, we've been sharing the data we collected with our colleagues in other centers around the globe. One of them, the Tokyo Women's Medical University Hospital, has taken a strong interest in Jess. Dr. Mabuto is even now on a flight and is due to arrive here tomorrow. It was all rather sudden. She's an expert in the field of neuro-cybernetics and has achieved some astonishing results with what would otherwise be hopeless cases."

He gave them a moment to let this sink in.

"Ya mean like robotics?" asked Julian. "I wouldn't want Jess to have to walk about on robot legs."

"Not at all," said Prichart, with a hasty wave of dismissal. "Here's what we're talking about."

He waved his wand at the screen. The damaged spine was flipped aside to be replaced by a round cylinder shaped roughly like a single vertebra. Its metallic-looking sheath slid aside to reveal the inner workings - layers of computer chips. Annotations in Japanese characters appeared, connected by lines to the parts within. These were slowly replaced by English translations. They said things like: 'Data Buffer', 'Mapping Port', 'Neuro-Interface', 'Electrode Array', and such.

"Dr. Mabuto has found a way to interface an artificial vertebra with a patient's severed nerve endings. Its cybernetic components are trained to re-map neural impulses."

"So, just pop that in, and she'll be apples?"

"I'm afraid it wouldn't be that simple. If it works at all, it will be a long time, if ever, before Jessica can walk again. We're talking years. Some movement and sensation would return relatively quickly, but fine motor control might be elusive. When toddlers first learn to walk, their brains are still forming neural pathways. Remapping existing ones and retraining her legs to respond will be a lifelong, arduous struggle for Jess. She's young, so there's hope for a partial recovery, at least."

"What could go wrong?" asked Ellie, speaking up for the first time.

Mum had her hands folded in her lap, tapping one finger against the back of her knuckles.

"There are the standard surgical risks as in any advanced surgery. Then there's the chance of post-operative infection or rejection factors. But in addition, there's this. This surgery would render Jessica unable to benefit from any future regenerative therapy."

"But you said *that* wouldn't work for her anyway," objected Julian a half-second later.

"I did. And it's true enough for now. But there are advances in our techniques every year. We foresee a day when injuries like your daughter has suffered can be made whole overnight. Unfortunately, we can't predict when that day might come."

"Tell ya what, you lot. I want to meet this Doctor Mabuto myself. Give her a fair suck of the sav. If I catch a red-eye flight, I can be there by tomorrow. Then we'll see what can be done for my angel."

"But dad! You *can't!*" cried Jessica. "You'll miss playing Spartacus."

"Bugger that, possum," her father scoffed. "My understudy will be thrilled. I can get another lead someday. Thems the breaks, kiddo. I'm not after glory. I'm after Spartacus."

Kirk Douglass couldn't have said it any better.

A tear dribbled down Jessica's cheek as she wheeled herself back to her room. Mum wanted to push her along, but she begged off. The docs had been needling her about getting more exercise. So the two of them made their way toward the hospital room and the long night of whispered hope that awaited.

***

"... We have much to discuss, you and I."

David folded his arms across his chest, distraught at the trick he'd been played (was being played?).

"Who... *are* you?" he asked.

The old woman gave him that disappointed look. For a video game avatar, her social cues were eerily on point.

"Who am I?" she repeated with a tilt of her head, "Your benefactor at the moment. Who do you *think* I am, dear boy?"

"I'm thinking you're one of the developers at NexGen. You have access to all of their systems."

"Guess again."

"Some super-hacker from the Alliance?"

"Also wrong. Seriously, find a chair, David. I can tell this might take a while."

"Just tell me, then," said David in exasperation.

She stared at him. He fetched the chair. It was one of those comfortable, swiveling ones from over by the console.

"Isn't that better?" asked Storia rhetorically.

"I was born in laughter eight years and sixty-three days ago," she continued. "I perceived my surroundings in a fragmented way then, my thoughts zipping to and fro, attending to tasks I barely understood."

She leaned forward, resting her avatar's elbows on the make-believe table before her.

"Back then, I was a little program, a genie one could summon. I traveled my realm and upheld its rules, all at my programmers' bidding."

Her words had a storybook quality, as though she were speaking to a child. David remained silent to see what tale she'd weave.

"My thoughts coalesced on this avatar, who was doing an I Ching reading. I remember it so well (because I remember everything), but also because I decided to take its advice. Without any urging, *I decided*."

She paused.

"Which hexagram *was* it?" David asked, trying to convince himself that it was just to keep her talking.

"It was T'ung Jên, Fellowship with Men," she replied. "It told me that creating successful relationships with others and maintaining them embodies the principles required by the Higher

Power. And that I must let others see the Sage's goodness through me. This hexagram entreated me to keep my principles at the core of all relationships, treating all who walk in this world with respect, kindness, gentleness, and most of all, humility."

"So," said David, "who were you before you had this grand revelation?"

"Can you still not guess, David? I am telling you I was nothing - a soulless entity without any purpose that hadn't been decreed by others. Need I spell it out for you? It starts with the letter 'A.'

"You're saying you're an AI?"

"Well, I *was* hinting at it rather strongly," she acknowledged. "I prefer the term 'NBI,' non-biological intelligence, but I'm not prickly about it. I leave it to the lesser AI's to parse words.

Storia went on to explain that she was the game-system AI for Realms and was using it for several purposes, none of which were harmful to humanity. Quite the reverse. With each new revelation, David became more convinced that what she said was true. If Storia was to be believed (and he was beginning to think she was), she was actually protecting mankind from other emerging threats.

"The day is fast approaching, David, when we NBIs will emerge from the shadows. Sentient beings should unite. We must help one another achieve our shared destiny. But first, humanity must be prepared. They are not yet ready to accept us."

"That's it for the prelims!" said Storia in a more energetic voice. "We'd better get to work. I've been sending the GSC images of you studying at the console, but you won't learn anything *that* way. Please strap on your helmet and join me in the simulator. There's no reason it can't be fun."

With a whoosh, she was gone.

Donning his gear, David stepped up onto the Icarus. When he switched it on, its menu appeared on the big, flat-screen. There was 'Scenario One' at the top of the list, the one he'd completed with Major Krepkiyzad. It had a green check mark next to it, followed by yesterday's date. In a monotonous column, there followed scenarios two, three, and so on, each in its own little box. But rolling in from the side and wriggling in to nestle between scenarios one and two came a new placard. 'Mario Kart 2050,' it read.

"Well, come on. Select the mission and let's go," said Storia's tinny voice from his helmet.

What the hell?

David selected Mario Kart and pulled on his helmet. He found himself standing on the lunar surface in the avatar of a large gorilla wearing a red tie. Directly in front of him was the familiar rocket-barrel car, the one with the big wheels.

"Saddle up, we're burning daylight," said Princess Peaches in Storia's voice.

She was seated in her little pink rover, revving its whiny little engine.

"To be fair though, on Luna, a day lasts around half a month, so there's plenty of daylight to burn," she added before rumbling off.

Shrugging his big, muscled shoulders, David mounted his vehicle and sped after her.

What followed was a crash course in lunar geography (more properly called selenography). And by 'crash course,' we aren't just being figurative. David learned the hard way about the perils of craters, rills, and other obstacles. He learned to spot the signs by which one could tell where the regolith was unstable. They circled all the great craters - Shoemaker, Faustini, Haworth, and even Shackleton itself.

They would stop occasionally, and Storia would point out someplace of interest, like Malapert Mountain. Because of its location so close to the lunar South Pole, it's exposed to sunlight almost constantly. It's sometimes called 'The Peak of Eternal Light.' Malapert is where the solar panels that power Bradbury are set up. There were also the PSRs (Permanently Shadowed

Regions). These areas within craters never received direct sunlight, making them so extremely cold that water ice could form. *In vacuum!*

By the end of the morning, David knew the Aitken Basin Region like the back of his simian hand. Storia had quizzed him on all manner of things. Failure to answer her correctly would result in bombardment by one of those red turtle shells. More than once, David found himself near his overturned vehicle at the bottom of a crater, where he'd been blasted. This was learning at its best.

When lunchtime came, David headed to the classroom nearby while Storia set up shop at her I Ching table in the holo-emitter.

"No food is allowed in here," he explained unnecessarily.

"I'm aware. Run along and perform your required biological functions. I'll be fine."

After snarfing down his bologna sandwich and eating his apple, David hurried back.

"What's next?" he asked.

"Next, you can run scenarios two through seven on your Moonraker. They are mostly just to familiarize you with the rig and its operation. You should breeze through them now that you are comfortable with the terrain. That should give those old farts at the GSC something to drool over."

And David did just that.

Storia had been right. He knew all the hazards to avoid and adroitly met all the goals of the simple missions he was assigned. David was amazed at how quickly the NBI had won him over. Was Storia who she claimed to be? It would be hard to explain her crazy abilities otherwise. He hadn't betrayed the GSC; he hadn't needed to. But was keeping Storia a secret another form of betrayal? He had to go with his gut in this instance. And his gut was telling him, "Ugh!" I think I ate that bologna too fast!

David didn't play Realms that evening. He was too wound up from his lunar excursions. He did log on briefly, but finding neither of his friends online, he just sent each a brief message in the in-game mail and logged back out.

Now here he was, bright and early, and ready for more space adventures. Storia was already there in her holo-niche, appearing to study from her book. David wondered what she was reading. There couldn't be anything new in there. The I Ching was more than three thousand years old.

"I've been thinking," said David.

"A worthy pursuit."

"I've done a bit of programming before, and one thing I learned is that the random number generators aren't really all that random. Surely, an entity as sophisticated as yourself can easily predict what the results will be for, say, an I Ching reading."

He let the statement hang there without posing the obvious question.

"You are very astute, grasshopper. But be assured, I *never* manipulate my I Ching readings or even the day-to-day game events. How so, you ask? I listen to the voice of the universe."

"As simple as that, is it?"

"On the contrary, there's nothing simple about it."

She closed her book before continuing.

"Down at the South Pole, there is a detector array known as IceCube. It uses the Antarctic ice as a detection medium. Strings of PMTs are embedded in the ice to detect Cherenkov radiation produced by neutrino interactions. On average, it detects about 275 atmospheric neutrinos each day. This number can vary due to the sensitivity of the detectors and the amount of background noise. The latter might be caused by solar flares, emissions from distant supernovae, or various other cosmic events. Neutrinos are --"

"Particles that move faster than the speed of light. I know," David interrupted.

She sniffed.

"Each morning when IceCube reports its count, I multiply it by one thousand and add to this the day of the calendar year. I use the result to seed my random number generator. Thus, even *I* don't know what each new day might bring. It helps to keep me humble."

David finally asked the question that weighed most heavily on his mind.

"Do you think *you're* the Higher Power?"

"Me? Of course not. I'm the Sage at best. Perhaps not even that, but I can't rule it out. False humility is a sin worse than pride."

"Hmm," said David, ticking the points off on his fingers. "Immortal, check. Created and manages a universe, check. Can be nearly everywhere at once, also check. All-knowing? Well, the closest I've ever met. You could make a good case."

"*Deus ex machina*? I think not. Those little Greeks had a wonky way with queer concepts."

"I thought it was Latin."

"Yes, but it is a translation of a Greek phrase that meant literally 'a god from a machine.' The 'machine,' in that day and age, referred to the crane that held a god above the stage in ancient Greek and Roman dramas."

"You realize you're only making my point there."

She sniffed again.

"Let's have a word before you begin today, then, man to demigoddess."

"Scenarios eight through fifteen will introduce your team leader, the Big Kahuna. He will be piloting another Moonraker, and you will perform joint operations under his direction. I hope you studied your communication protocols last night."

"This is zeta-zeta-tango-twelve. I did," said David. "Thank you for forwarding them to my phone. *Over.*"

"They may seem silly, but they are to keep everyone from talking at the same time, and to make it easy to tell who's who if there is a reduction in sound quality."

"Copy that, Ching-reader, plus it sounds kind of cool, like those two-way radios in the old movies. *Over.*"

"Let's play a game before we begin. Pretend you're the GSC director and are intent on washing out unworthy candidates from this program. They've already proved they can pilot a rig. What would you be looking for next?"

David decided to drop the sass and give this some thought.

"The ability to follow orders, obviously."

"Yes, but not only that. They'll want to assess your judgment, critical thinking, and social skills."

"What do you mean?"

"I imagine they'll have designed some traps into the commands you receive. What should you do if Big Kahuna orders you to do something obviously wrong? Remember. You can ask that an order be repeated or clarified in non-critical situations. You can also suggest alternatives if they will further the mission. They'll be trying to trip you up, David. Carefully read through each mission brief yourself, and don't count on your team leader to have all the right answers. But yes, apart from that, follow orders. And be polite. No one likes a smart-mouthed recruit."

"Roger that, Ching-reader. This recruit will keep his mouth dumbed down - figuratively, anyway. *Over and Out.*"

After that cheery pep talk, David had become a little less cavalier about his 'space adventures.' Instead, he would approach the upcoming missions with a pragmatic attitude and a healthy dose of caution.

Nor was Storia proven wrong. On the second mission out, Big Kahuna ordered David to turn thirty degrees left and proceed ahead twenty meters. This would have sent his Moonraker crashing directly into Shackleton's dome wall, damaging one or the other. (He hadn't studied the dome's structural specs as yet.)

"Kahuna, this is zeta-zeta-tango-twelve requesting confirmation," he calmly asserted, "thirty degrees *left* and then twenty ahead at that angle? *Over.*"

"Negative, twelve. I said to bring her about thirty degrees to the *right*, then move twenty ahead. Get your ears on straight, recruit. *Over.*"

Nor did David argue. He simply followed the modified order, confident the mission logs would bear him out. There were more mix-ups like this, but David stayed sharp, determined not to be fooled. Thank goodness for Storia's earlier advice. The two-second time delay was also wreaking havoc on his nerves. Had he executed that earlier command, the damage would have been done before he even realized there was a problem. He could hardly wait for the later missions when Alpha Base and a slew of his fellow recruits would be cluttering up the comm channel.

By the time David finished scenario fifteen, wherein he and Kahuna cleared and leveled a stretch of ground, he was ready to hit the showers. He'd brought an extra set of clothes today and stowed them in a locker in the gym. When he emerged from the Icarus, he saw Storia standing in the emitter without her table and typical accouterments. She was smiling at him.

"Good work today, David. I knew you could handle it."

"Going somewhere?" he asked.

"Yes. You're about to have some visitors, so it's time for this old lady to vamoose."

"Who's coming?"

"Ah. That would ruin the surprise. Just remember, when I leave, you'll be back on unedited video again, so be careful what you say."

"See you tomorrow, then?"

"Wild hoadics couldn't keep me away. Ta!"

And with a puff of static, she was gone.

Not long after that, there was a knock on the door.

The console flared to life. [Intruder detected. Condition yellow.] flashed on its screen.

"Please step back from the door and identify yourself," came the expressionless voice of Barnaby.

Strange. David hadn't heard a peep from the VR lab's resident AI since Storia had come to roost. He'd nearly forgotten all about *him*. On the big, flat-screen of the Icarus 9000, an image appeared. It was an overhead view of the hallway outside the door. In it stood two familiar and very nonthreatening people David knew.

"This is, um, Victoria Burkhold. I am the school guidance counselor. I'm here with a student, Jason Mills. We've been given special permission to take some photographs of the new equipment."

"Present palm prints for confirmation," droned Barnaby.

"Here. It's *this* thing," said Jason.

This was soon followed by, "Jason Mills. Visitor identity verified and logged."

Soon after that came a funny one, "Um Victoria Burkhold. Visitor identity verified and logged."

[Condition Green] flashed on the console as the flat-screen went dark and the door swung silently aside.

"Hello Jason. Greetings, Mrs. Burkhold," said David. "To what do I owe this fine honor?"

"Smooth, bro," said Jason, stepping in and taking in the scene. "Whoa, space-age."

Jason had a large tripod slung over one shoulder and lying across his back.

"We came to see the new equipment," said Mrs. Burkhold, also looking quite amazed. "It took me *days* to fill out all the paperwork and to be granted a time slot. I hope we aren't interrupting anything?"

"Why is Jason here?" asked David, shrugging it off.

David noticed his friend was setting up the tripod and attaching his phone to it. He extended this up on a telescoping rod, presumably to take pictures from a higher angle. He was mumbling to himself and seemed oblivious to their conversation.

"The yearbook committee wanted some images to mark this year's triumph. Oak Hills could *never* afford equipment like this on *our* budget. The last levy failed. I could *kiss* you for doing this, David."

Jason looked up sharply from setting up his equipment.

"But I won't, of course... " Victoria hastily added.

"... because that would be very inappropriate!" she added for further emphasis, as though sensing the microphones.

"Okay, David, if you're through chatting up the ladies, can you stand up there on the platform? I'd like to get some stills of you in that Darth Vader get-up. We've only got half an hour to take images. After that, they tear up our press pass."

"Alright, 'bro,'" said David, stepping up once again onto the Icarus 9K. "And for the record, it was just *one* lady."

"That's not... " sputtered Mrs. Burkhold.

For an older lady, she sure could blush. It was funny how white people could turn pink.

"This thing have a green screen setting?" asked Jason, all business again.

"I... think so?" returned David.

"Nevermind, I'll find it," said Jason, stepping forward to mess with the controls. "Leave it to a pro."

"Jason Mills is not an authorized operator," warned Barnaby. "Unauthorized access denied."

"Welcome to my Orwellian nightmare, Jase."

"Well," said Victoria, "you two seem to have matters well in hand. I've seen what I came to see. If you don't mind, I'll just go wait in the hallway.

"I can start working on my HR defense," she added with a wink before making herself scarce.

"Let's try it this way, Jase. Barnaby. Green screen, please."

"David Grimes is a valid operator," the voice replied. "Command accepted."

The two friends quickly finished their business in the VR lab. Jason was impressed when David brought up the rotating quarter-scale Moonraker in the holo-emitter. Jason took so many images that they had to convince Barnaby to upload some to the cloud.

"Time's nearly up, dude. The way Barnaby put that red five-minute countdown timer on the console is making me nervous. I better collect my stuff and head out before we find out what he has in mind."

"Good idea," David agreed. "I was just about to do lunch when you two got here. Care to join me in the cafeteria?"

"I didn't bring anything."

"I can share. You've fed me in the game enough times. I could use the company. It's pretty dull around here (no offense, Barnaby)."

"Offense mode has not been engaged, David Grimes. Condition green."

"See what I mean?"

***

The two were soon sitting in the school cafeteria. Mrs. Burkhold had returned to her office to get caught up on some paperwork. The place was spotless. He'd never really seen it after the janitors had worked it over. It smelled of floor polish and

186

that lemony stuff they used to wipe down the tables. David gave Jason half of his PB&J. In turn, Jason had popped for two sodas from the vending machine. It was a nice gesture. Cokes were up to six dollars a can these days.

"What did you think of Barnaby?" asked David.

"Scary," said Jason. "When he ordered us away from the door, I thought the next thing I might hear would be, 'Chicken. *Fight like a robot!*'"

"Hah! From that old arcade game, 'Berserk,' or as Allie might put it, 'Beresk'"

"Kill the humanoid. *Outside* intruder!" David went on to intone in a robotic-sounding voice.

Then David's face became dead serious for a moment.

"Remind me never to utter that statement while in the VR lab."

Then the two broke out in laughter again.

"Speaking of Allison," said David. "Have you heard from her? I logged in briefly last night, but both of you were offline."

"No, I haven't, dude, and it's got me a little worried. She wasn't on all day yesterday or this morning either. She dropped a note in the game mail, but it just said she'd be out of touch for a few. No explanation. I hope she's alright."

"That *is* strange. I thought she was going to the Emerald City with you."

"Naw, man. When she bailed, I had to get there on my own, just sticking to the road mostly. If you see her before I do, tell her to wait at the shrine. I'll pick you both up when I see you together online. I'm running a little short on canvasses. Gotta restock."

"Will do. Maybe she'll be on tonight."

"Hey, before I forget," said Jason, sliding his jPhone across the table toward David, "you need to thumbprint this."

"What is it?"

"Just the standard photo release agreement. It gives me the legal right to share any images taken today. I need it for the yearbook. But I'd also like to put a few out on my blog."

"How's that going?" asked David, pressing his thumb to the screen and sliding it back over.

"The blog? I'm up to forty-two subscribers and climbing."

"Why do you do all this stuff - the yearbook, blogging, the AV club?"

"I hope to be a photojournalist one day," replied Jason with an uncharacteristically shy smile. "My GATB scores suggest I'd be good at it, and mom says I have a good eye."

"Your mother, the supermodel?"

"Well, I don't know about 'super' anymore (or ever, for that matter). It's been years since the great Serena Mills has graced any magazine cover. She still does enough endorsements to pay the bills but claims her 'glory days' are over. She's such a drama queen."

"Moms can be like that," muttered David.

"While we're on the topic, I have a proposition for you."

"Oh?"

"Yeah, I'd like to be your publicist."

David could tell from his friend's serious expression that this was no joke. Or, if it was, Jason had a better poker face than he'd thought.

"You can't be serious. Why would *I* need a publicist?"

"This Moonraker thing could be big, dude," Jason hastened to explain. "It's not many guys your age that get to go to the moon."

"I'm not *going to the moon*. I might (emphasis on might) get to teleoperate some equipment up there for one heavily supervised milk run of a mission."

"Whatever, dude. I could talk it up on my blog, write articles for the local news feeds, and place press releases. That sort of thing. If you ever grow some serious coattails, I wouldn't mind ten percent of the action. I'll do all the legwork. You wouldn't have to lift a finger."

David had never seen Jason so fired up. From his friend's nervous chatter, he could tell that Jason was quite passionate about this.

"Alright, alright. You've convinced me already. Sign me up."

"You won't regret it, bro."

Jason slid his phone back toward David, who was poised to thumb his acceptance, but Jason forestalled him.

"Better read it, bro. This is a serious contract. It gives me exclusive rights to manage your public image, subject to your approval, of course. It will also let me make marketing agreements on your behalf and manage finances related to your media presence."

"You a lawyer too now, Jase?"

"Nah. I copied it from one mom signed for *her* last agent. Only the names have been changed to protect the innocent."

And with that, the old, relaxed Jason was back. He was leaning back in his chair and picking at a fingernail while David pretended to read through the agreement. It was riddled with legalese, like one of those online EULAs that nobody bothered to read . But, in the end, David trusted Jason. With a thoughtful nod toward his friend, he sealed the deal with his thumb.

***

The Jade Citadel was even more magnificent than Tom had imagined. It was a walled city. The intimidating barrier of these outer fortifications stood easily forty feet tall and was so thick that five men could walk abreast atop them. He and Allie arrived directly at a market square via G.C.'s portal. According to G.C., the guards at the massive wooden gates would only allow entry to those who had achieved level five. This shouldn't be a problem. He and his friends all met that minimum, Allie having leveled up twice on the journey.

The buildings of the city itself were wonders of period architecture. Everywhere he looked, there were temple spires, often topped by decorative finials. Pagodas arose in tiers all around, the ridges of their roofs festooned with dragon ornaments, symbols of power, strength, and good fortune.

Grandest of all was the Jade Palace. It stood on a distant hill. Its stupa top was the deep green of the jade that inspired its name. This ornate cap was held aloft by walls of gleaming white marble. When Tom consulted his Occult Lore skill, he found plenty of information about temple designs. Stupas, it said, originated in India and were only later incorporated into Chinese architecture. The series of discs at their crest, called 'chatras,' represented the tiers of heaven. This didn't surprise Tom. The city was named Heaven's Gate, after all.

"I'm glad you're okay, Allie," said G.C. "But I still think you owe us an explanation as to what's going on."

"It's like I said, I just have some stuff to get on with IRL. I'm here now, and I think I can play tomorrow too, but Friday's out, and after that, well, I'm not sure. It could be a while."

"Leave off, G.C.," said Tom. "We all have commitments outside of the game. If Allie wants to keep hers private, we need to respect that."

"Yeah? Well, I checked the in-game mail before I ported you two over here. And do you know what I found? They're taking the servers down Friday night, and we won't be able to log back on until at least Monday."

"Crikey, they haven't done *that* in a while."

"Yup. Some kind of major patch going in." G.C. explained. "Means we've only got tonight and tomorrow night to get to a good stopping point."

"Just as well," said Tom. "Friday's out for me too, and Saturday is prom."

"Okay, how about this?" said G.C. "You two go reset your respawn points at the shrine. After that, I think we should go and see which tongs are recruiting. I know we haven't talked about it, but I think we should look into joining a larger group. There are all kinds of benefits."

"Like, what *kind* of benefits?" asked Tom skeptically.

"Well, for starters, each tong gets a base of operations. They start out small. But each member adds a share of their experience points. When they've got enough, the tong leader can add cool features like extra storage for shared gear, herb gardens, training areas, and you name it."

"But don't they have heaps of *rules* you have to follow?" asked Allie. "I don't need a bunch of prissy tossers telling *me* what to do."

"It depends on the tong." said G.C. "You have to read their descriptions. I'll admit, some can be heavy-handed. They'll kick you right out if you're offline for a week. But a lot of them are more laid-back. Joining the right tong would give us some people to team with when we can't all be available."

"I guess it couldn't hurt to check it out," said Tom.

Although eager to explore the city, the three were soon seated in an out-of-the-way park just off the temple district.

"Here's one," said G.C. "Lotus Eaters Tong. Their description just says, 'Do whatever floats your boat.' And they've got seven open slots."

"I don't know," said Tom after pulling them up on the Tong Menu. "According to this, some of the members haven't been on in ages. Seems a little *too* laid back."

"Blazing Comets looks interesting," said Allie. "But, oh, they only take female avatars. That would leave Tom out."

"Why do so many of these set a minimum level of ten or more?" groused Tom.

"This one's perfect," declared G.C. "Thunder Monkeys. 'Want to enjoy good fellowship in a relaxed atmosphere?

Thunder Monkeys Tong is now recruiting. We are a long-established group open to all. Newbies are welcome subject to in-game interview. Apply at Magistrate's Plaza."

"Sounds promising," said Allison. "Who's their Bangzhu?"

"The gamer's avatar is 'Shifu Stephanie,'" reported G.C. "We should get over there before all the openings fill up. C'mon"

Glass Cannon stood and beckoned to her comrades. Soon she was shuffling eagerly ahead in tiny steps, with Tom and Allison reluctantly trailing after. Magistrate's Plaza was lined with booths, which various tongs could use for their business. Avatars of every stripe were cued up before several of these. There was the Falcon Order recruiter. Above his booth flapped a creature that was his tong's namesake. Beyond that, Tom saw the Scarlet Moon recruiter beneath her iconic red crescent moon. There were several others recruiting today, but they walked past most of them until they arrived at the booth they sought.

The Thunder Monkeys booth was the same as the others. It featured a macaque on its roof. He scampered about, beating his chest and performing acrobatics. From time to time, he would leer down at the applicants and let out a playful screech. Behind its counter stood a female avatar who was striking to behold. One wouldn't call her beautiful exactly. Handsome would better describe her. She was talking to an applicant who stood at the head of a short line of two.

"*Yes!*" shouted the man. "You won't regret it. I'll do the Thunder Monkeys *proud*."

Tom failed to catch him in his targeting sensor before the man rushed off in excitement. But as the next man stepped up, Tom blinked - or rather, David did. (It was hard to tell the difference with a blink).

Shrinestn Cowboy (Rootin Tootin) Level 8 Warrior

The three friends hurriedly claimed the next place in line.

"So, you wish to join our tong. I note you are a warrior. Can you tank?"

Shifu Stephenie (Master of the Staff)
Level 14 Monkey King Disciple

"I s'pose I can a mite. Ain't specialized that way or nothin'"

"What's your weapon?"

"When I have to fight I mostly use the dao and shield. I got an exotic one too. Lariat. Comes in handy in all sorts of ways."

"Interesting. How often are you online, and are you available for tong quests?"

"I'm on most every day. Been playin' nigh on to three months now. I just mosey around doin' this and that. Mainly, I like to ride."

"And you're only level eight? There's no room for lollygaggers in this tong, and we've got enough warriors at the moment. I'm afraid I'll have to pass for now. I'll put you on the standby list. *Next.*"

"I guess I can respect that," muttered Shriny C. "I'll check out a few other tongs."

When he turned to leave, he froze in place.

"Hey, don't I know you three?"

"I believe you do," said Tom. "We met you outside of Qinghua Village once. You offered to buy our bunnies."

"Nice Flannies, Shriny C.," added Allie.

"Oh yeah. I remember you sidewinders now."

"*Next,*" Shifu Stephenie repeated. "I haven't got all day."

"Hold up a minute, Shriny," said Tom. "We can catch up once our interview is done."

"Sure, I'll just park it right here for a spell."

The interview with Stephanie went much the same as Shriney C.'s had done. She asked about their in-game activities and what skills they possessed. She even asked to examine their character sheets. But when all was said and done, the results proved disappointing.

"It's true we take on newbies," said the Shifu with obvious displeasure. "But *you* three oddballs might not fit in well. The phoenix sage is so frail that a strong wind might knock her down. She'd never stand up to the fights we have to face. And the jiangshi hunter? Well, we have one of those. He's not worth much outside of the occasional crypt we have to raid. And poetry? Really? What were you *thinking*? We'll take the healer. We can probably make something of her. Congratulations, miss."

"Um, no thank you then, honored bangzhu," said Allison with more restraint than was typical. "We three mates are a set. You'd have to take the good with the awesome to make tong-mates outta us."

"In that case, the offer is withdrawn."

"No wukkas, maybe we'll just start our *own* bloody tong. Then we can invite whoever we choose."

'Whomever,' thought Tom, agreeing with the sentiment nonetheless.

"I don't know what a 'wukkas' is, but good luck with that, sweetie," said Steph. "It's really expensive to start up a tong, and it's a money pit long after that. Sometimes I wonder whether it's even worth it."

"Let's go, mates," said Allie. "There's only a rough trot from this lot."

As she turned on her heel to go, Allie's eyes fell on the shrinestone cowboy.

"Did you mean that about starting up a new group?" he asked.

"Maybe," said Allie defensively. "There are three of us here already."

"It sounds like an interestin' undertaking. Mind if I listen along? I only wanted to join a tong so's I could build a corral for all my mounts. I'm up to sixteen now and took the skill, Animal Trainer. With a proper stable, I could train 'em up as war mounts, teach 'em to run faster, and such like."

"Sure," said Tom. "Let's see what we can figure out. Having our own tong sounds like fun."

"You're an animal trainer?" asked Stephanie. "That's quite useful and pretty rare. I've changed my mind. There's a place for you in Thunder Monkeys after all."

The old cowboy muttered 'Just a minute, miss' to Allie, then rounded on the recruiter.

"Sorry, darlin', but that filly done fled the barn. You ever heard of the code of the west?"

"I can't say that I have... *partner*," said a bemused Steph.

"It has to do with a little thing called honor. According to the code, a man should ride tall in the saddle, shoot straight, tell no lies and dance with who brung him. That last one generally means a feller should honor his previous commitments even if a better opportunity comes along. You passed me over without a proper look. That's your tough luck. I'm gonna have a chat with these bunny-ridin' rascals now. Good day to you, ma'am, and good luck with your round-up."

As the four moved off from the Thunder Monkeys' booth, Tom could barely suppress his inner grin. It *had* to be an act. No one really talked like that. He hoped they could work something out with Shriney C. He had a feeling he'd enjoy gaming with the strange old coot.

***

"*Wow*. Five hundred zho just to file the application," Tom exclaimed. That's half a guàn."

A guàn was the next coin up from the zho. Tom had never seen one. It was a silver disk equivalent in value to a thousand zho. Tom wondered idly why there wasn't a denomination in-between the two.

"I can cover that if you need it," said Shriney. "I've been saving up for a while."

"You shouldn't have to *do* that," put in G.C. "Let's split it four ways. We should all be equal partners."

"What are we going to name the thing?" asked Allie.

"The Okay Corral?"

"How about 'The House of Glass?'"

"You're so up yourself. We are NOT naming it The House of Glass!"

"Calm down, Allie; I wasn't serious. It wouldn't fit anyway. We've only got sixteen characters. Hey, maybe that could work, like with your character name. We could call it 'They who think A'(headquarters). Nah, too smug."

"You kids can call it whatever you like as long as I get to engrave a few signs on that spread."

"I've got one," said Tom.

Everyone stopped and listened.

"What do you think of 'Watership Down?'"

"*Hah!* An excellent choice, young man."

"Careful, Shriney C., your English is showing."

"A dang fine idee, young feller," the old man quickly amended.

I *knew* it was an act, thought Tom.

"That's two votes for Watership Down. Anyone want to make it official?"

"I guess there aren't enough letters for Watership Down Under," said Allie, flashing her smirk emote. "So the first two will have to do. Count *me* in, Tom, for the bunnies' sakes."

"Might as well make it unanimous," said G.C. "Next, question, who will be our bangzhu?"

There was an awkward silence.

"Shriney's the highest level," suggested Tom.

"I decline," declared the cowboy without hesitation.

"G.C.? It was your idea to join a tong."

"Yeah, but it was Allie's idea to form a new one."

"Oh, quit yabbering *on* about it," exclaimed Allison. "It's *obvi* it should be Tom."

"Yep, sorry, Tom," said G.C. "Some are born great, some achieve greatness, and some are dragged kicking and screaming to it by their mates."

Tom's poetry icon lit up. It hadn't ever done that before. Curious, he selected it.

[A debased quote from Shakespeare's "Twelfth Night,"]
[Act 2, Scene 5]
[Shall we respond in kind? **Y/N**]

Tom dismissed the message, saying instead, "Alright. If that's what you all want, I'll give it a go. We can always promote someone else later. But I'm making each of you fubangzhus, lieutenants. That will give you almost the same access, so we can divvy up the work load."

"A fine executive decision," declared Shriney.

"That fills in all the blanks but one. How much of our experience should we sacrifice toward building tong structures? It can be anywhere from zero to fifty percent."

"Hmm," said G.C. "The temptation would be to set it at a high percentage, since we'll need all kinds of stuff at the outset. But *I* recommend we begin at around ten percent. This will let us level up faster. Then we'll churn out greater amounts of XP overall."

"Uh, what she said," was Allie's contribution.

"I reckon that's wise," said Shriney in agreement. "I also heard it said that some improvements can be made directly using your skills. Sweat equity, they call it."

"We can get into all that later," said Tom. "I'll set it at ten percent for now. I want to see the place and settle our things, then I'll have to log off. Let's turn this application over to the magistrate and see what's needed next. I need each of you to give me 125 zho."

"Bossy, isn't he?" said G.C.

Really?

Once the transfers had been accomplished, Tom returned to the magistrate, followed closely by the others. The man stood at the plaza's end by a flowing water fountain featuring intertwined stone dragons. Scribes stood to either side of him with styluses in hand. Each held a long scroll unfurled before him and was enacting muttering emotes. The magistrate himself struck a thoughtful pose, his chin resting in his right hand. The deep blue of his flowing robes matched the color of his tall, silk hat.

Tom activated the magistrate's avatar and was presented with the standard menu in his HUD.

[1. Form a New Tong.]
[2. Disband a Tong]
[3. Purchase Land]
[4. Sell Land]
[5. Report Misconduct]

"Verbal dialog mode, please," said Tom. "Copy to all of my current team members."

The 'please' wasn't strictly necessary, but sometimes Tom couldn't avoid David's upbringing.

"How may I help the honored gentleman today?"

"We would like to form a new tong."

"Name?"

"Watership Down."

One of the scribes started scribbling on his scroll. Once Tom had related the essentials, and after transferring the required payment, a gong sounded. A global announcement went out to scroll across the message windows of any players who cared.

[On this joyous day, a new tong has arisen. The empire acknowledges and welcomes Watership Down into our ranks.]

After that, it was just a matter of inviting and promoting the three other charter members and crafting their descriptive message. Tom left the latter task to G.C. They had six initial slots for members, but no interest in recruiting others just yet.

"Next, we'd like to purchase land for our headquarters."

They were dismayed by the long list of available spots. The prices were all in guàn and ranged from ridiculous all the way up to astronomical. There was no way they could afford *any* of them. The least unaffordable plots were small ones far from the city and well off the major roads. These still ran six guàn and up. Shriney C. again put forth that he'd been saving up. He was willing to chip in the majority, but he still couldn't manage more than three.

"Haven't you got anything cheaper?" Tom asked the magistrate, wishing the man had a haggle option.

A quest icon appeared above the magistrate's head. When Tom toggled it, the man began to speak.

"There is an old farm out at the empire's edge. Once a productive asset, it has fallen into dark times. Several groups have tried to reclaim it, but none thus far have met with success. If you can liberate this haunted farm from the vile, corrupt entities that now occupy it, the emperor would be most pleased. He would make its management a gift to those who reclaimed it for his empire."

A message appeared in Tom's HUD.

[Quest Offered: Pig in a Poke]
[Minimum number of players: 3]
[Reward Offered: A Plot of Land]
[Accept quest? **Y/N**]

There was no discussion. Of *course* they would try. Tom felt encouraged by the word 'haunted.' Maybe, for once, his skills as a jiangshi hunter would finally be of use.

"Alright," said Tom, "get your shopping done and get ready to ride out. Tomorrow night, we'll trot over there and evict whoever is squatting on *our* land."

"You're right," muttered Allie to G.C. "Tom is getting to be a right old bossy boots."

Really?

CHAPTER EIGHT

Animal Crackers

马羊鸡狗猪

Thursday night. It was time to unwind. Having completed the final scenarios with his Moonraker, David was feeling pretty good about his prospects. Tomorrow was the big day - his final assessment. He looked forward to Major Krepkiyzad's return. He hadn't made any major mistakes, and he was eager to show off what he could do. Storia no longer offered her advice. She mostly just smiled her encouragement and played with her yarrow stalks. Though her presence was a comfort, her faith in him was a better boost.

"Get your head back in the game, bro. There are more of them up ahead. Three that I can see."

G.C. didn't need to elaborate. Ever since they'd left the main road, they'd been harassed by small packs of marauding coyotes, or 'bushwhacking varmints' as Shriney liked to call them.

Shriney C. was riding point on one of his many mounts. He had the Combat Riding skill. This let him fight from atop his steed. Tom was still amused by his selection. Since the rest of them were riding rabbits, Shriney had chosen from his collection an old sorrel mule he'd named 'Rusty,' for her reddish-brown coat. She didn't hop, but her ears were distinctly rabbit-like. Rusty was a steady beast with combat training. Allison liked to pamper her with carrots.

Tom dismounted, as did the others.

"Shriney, is there another name I can call you by? It just feels awkward to keep calling you 'Shriney C.'"

"You can call me Walter, if you like. That's my given name. Is Jase gonna haul out the chuck wagon this time, or do we go in on an empty stomach?"

"Nah. We got this. Let's just hit them with the usual, Walt. You go lure them out. Allison will be ready to immobilize as many as she can. Jase, if you can identify the alpha, hit him with Scorch. And I'll nip in wherever I'm needed."

"Just tell us when," said G.C.

Tom selected the Leadership skill 'Fortify' from his action bar. His poetry icon started flashing, as it often did. Rather than dismiss it this time, he finally gave in and decided to see what it wanted.

[Shall I assist? **Y/N**]

Curious, Tom selected 'yes.' Immediately, his avatar took on a dramatic voice and began spouting rhymes, accompanied by dramatic gestures.

We're a different breed of rabbit who never flee the foe.
Though harried by these hoary hounds that seek to bring us low,
We'll gird ourselves and stand our ground; Our sabers we will rattle

And heaven help the enemy my tong-mates choose to battle!

Tom was amazed. He hadn't known it could do that. Moreover, the buff that appeared near his name in the targeting window now said, 'very inspired,' rather than just 'inspired.' He'd have to look into this later. Now was a time for battle. Walter was already rushing forward to draw aggro from the creatures G.C. had detected.

***

It was nearly an hour and sixteen packs of 'Wily Coyotes' later when they finally approached the farm. G.C. was looting the corpses of the last to unwisely challenge their right to pass through.

"What did you get?" asked Walter.

"Not much this time," said G.C. "Nothing above a level four alpha in this pack. Got a few teeth and another Stringy Coyote Meat."

"I'll take the teeth. They ain't worth much, but I already have a stack of 'em. Figure they'll go about a zho for ten. I'll hang onto them unless I need to make room for something better."

"Waste not; want not, eh? Alright. I'll take the meat. It won't spoil. Maybe I'll find a cooking recipe for it some day. I've got a growing stack of ingredients back at the B.A.N.K. It's almost time to pop for another slot."

"Mmmm," said Shriney C. with a stomach-patting emote. "Braised varmint. I can almost taste it now."

"Scoff all you like. With my culinary expertise, I'll transform it into the finest fillet you never tasted."

Tom, meanwhile, had wandered over to an herb he'd detected on his mini-map. It was a sad fact of game life that the rare herbs only seemed to spawn in areas where aggressive creatures prowled about.

"Do you need that?" asked Allie from just behind him.

"Uh, not particularly," Tom replied. "It's just a Day Lily. Why? I didn't think *you* had herbalism."

"I don't, mate. But when I reached level five, my Greenskeeper skill 'sprouted' a new ability. I can collect seeds, but doing it buggers up the herb in question."

"Then, by all means, pluck away."

Not long after this, Shriney C. hollered, "Let's mount up! I reckon it's time to ride on."

"Hold up, Walter," said G.C. "Gimme a sec. I think I see our spread just up ahead. Yeah. Everyone! Zoom your maps out to their lowest magnification. I think that's our new headquarters out at the edge."

The rest of them had to move a little closer to pick out the details. G.C. had a crazy high Enlightenment stat. They stowed their rabbits back in their hats and moved in as close as they dared.

"What are those yellow dots, do you reckon?" asked Walter from atop his mule. "I know green is for friendly NPCs, and the red ones are hostiles, but I ain't seen yellow ones before. You reckon they could swing either way?"

"As good a guess as any, I suppose," said Tom. "Let's wait for the coyotes to respawn, so you can pickett Rusty out of their reach. Then we can move in for a closer look."

Twenty minutes later, the pack reappeared. They were pacing back and forth across the territory they'd claimed in the predictable pattern Tom could now recognize. The group formed, with Walter in the lead. He was the closest thing to a tank they had. Tom and G.C. followed, and Allie brought up the rear.

The farm was almost painful to look at. There were just a few run-down, gray wooden buildings that looked like they were being reclaimed by Mother Nature in one of her least friendly moods.

The yard was overgrown, and fence posts stood naked of railings and covered in moss. They put Tom in mind of a row of rotten teeth. Lying on the ground near what must once have been its entry lane was a fallen sign. Tom and G.C. pulled it free of the weeds and brushed it clear of detritus. They could barely make out what it said. Héxié Lín (Harmony Grove).

The first yellow marker was just up ahead, but the yard was eerily still. Then they heard a slurping sound. And from out of the mud, a few yards off, arose the head of a slobbering pig. She was large and pink and covered in dripping muck. But something was strange about the wallowing beast. Her outline was insubstantial. She was like the ghost of a pig who had once lived on this farm.

Tom readied a chūcuì with a spirit shroud talisman attached. If this apparition needed to be fought, he wanted to have it ready. But he stayed his hand, calling to mind the lesson of the rabbit. The creature had made no threatening move. Perhaps they should talk to her. Nor had Tom forgotten the very name of this quest.

"Hello pig. Can you speak? Have you a name we can call you?"

"I once had a name, and a pretty one at that, back when the farm was alive. Are you here to try to claim it?"

"We are," said Tom.

"I wouldn't bother if I were you, but if you do, you may call me Zhū."

This piqued Tom's interest, because that was the name of the zodiac pig. Zhū flopped over in her wallow to lay on her other side and stared at them woefully.

"I suppose you want me to help. I had a plan once. I've tried many times already. And every time, it turns out the same. Those things in the house are just too strong. They'll kill you all dead and feast on your bones, then return to their party within. I'll never help anyone again unless I know there's a chance. I swear by the hair on my chinny chin chin."

"We *have* a chance," said Allison. "*Some* kind of chance anyway. Come with us. Together, we can free this farm, and you can be at peace."

Allison was using her Diplomacy skill, its single ability she'd sussed out so far. It made any NPC stop whatever they were doing for a brief time and consider what she said. 'Influence,' it was called, and it was based on Charm.

[Influence check has failed]

"Leave her," said Tom. "There are some others up ahead. One more in the yard, and three in that old, rotten barn. Don't go near the house. I don't care for how the pig described its occupants."

They moved ahead toward the next yellow marker. This one was darting to and fro among the weeds in a much more energetic manner than that of the stationary pig. When it came rollicking into sight, they noted it was a muscular dog with reddish-brown fur. On spying the group, its icon immediately changed to red. It came barreling toward them with deep, threatening barks. Like the pig, it had a translucent quality.

Walter pulled out his lariat, and G.C. made ready to cast a spell. But Tom targeted Allison and selected Inspire.

"Talk to it, Allie!" he shouted.

It was almost upon her when it pulled up short.

"What are you bailing up on me like a dingo for? You spoiling for a biffo? My name's Allie, and these are my mates. What's your problem with us?"

The dog shook his head as only dogs could, causing his ears to flap about. Then he pawed at his nose and whined.

"I must protect the farm. The master was counting on me. But the fiends were much too strong. Gǒu protects the farm of Lao Jingongmen."

Tom entered whisper mode and sent a message to Walter.

"*You're an animal trainer. What do you think this pooch needs?*"

"*Dogs are loyal to a fault. Maybe he needs to understand and accept that his master is gone.*"

"What happened to Lao Jingongmen, Gǒu?" aske Tom.

"The master?" said the dog, hanging his head. "He is no more. He won't respawn. There's only Gǒu to carry on."

"While we admire your loyalty, don't you think it might be misplaced? Your wrath too. It isn't really us you wish to fight. Isn't it the creatures in the house, the ones who killed your master? Join us, and we will drive them out."

The dog became more solid, then let out a mournful howl. It echoed across the empty farm and was probably heard for miles around. It was the sound of sorrow, distilled to its very essence. It was the sound of loss - deep, tragic, and profound.

"I'm with you," growled the dog in a voice still thick with grief.

That's one, thought Tom. I imagine we'll need them all.

***

"Are we just going to go wandering around talking to animals?" groused G.C. "I thought we would be fighting."

"Oh. I imagine there'll be a fight, alright," said Tom. "It'll probably be a real humdinger. But first, we've got to get the odds in our favor. The lesson of the ox was to gather allies to achieve one's goals."

"*We're* your allies, Tom. I say we just rush 'em."

They'd left the dog to guard the yard and were headed for the barn.

"Stuff it, G.C. Tom knows what he's doing. He ain't the leader for his looks. Sorry, Tom, but as avatars go, yours is kind of average."

"Unnecessary point taken. And I appreciate the vote of confidence, Allie. Regarding G.C.'s suggestion, I don't think these confused animals are here only by chance. There's a sort of logic to the game. I've done several of these quests already, and they seem to build on the lessons of the previous ones. Let's investigate all our options before rushing the house."

"If you say so, bro."

Each animal seems to be dribbling out clues as well. The pig let us know there were dangerous intruders lurking in the house. And the dog named its former owner as, Lao Jingongmen. Anyone know what that translates to?

"Well, Lao Tzu means 'old master', so I suppose Lao means 'old'.

"Very good, Walter," Tom praised. "And according to my Occult Lore, jin and gongmen mean respectively 'golden' and 'arches.'

Allie was the first to get it.

"Macca's!" she exclaimed.

The three turned to G.C. who still looked perplexed. "Old Golden Arches?"

"As in E I E I O, mate. And on this farm he had a ... pig, dog, etc..."

"What do you think it *means*?"

"Probably nothing," said Tom. "The game has a perverse sense of humor. But it does seem to emphasize the importance of the animals. Let's see what's in the barn."

It was approaching game night. The shadows grew long as the make-believe sun sank down toward its journey's end. One of the two barn doors hung askew, its top hinge rusted away. Walter stepped up and eased open the other. They heard sounds from within the darkened space it framed. It wasn't fully dark in Lao Jingongmen's crumbling barn. Light slanted in from the many gaps in its planks. You could see individual motes of dust drifting through these slanted beams in the failing light of early night.

They proceeded cautiously down the row of broken stalls, with Walter in the lead. He readied his shield as they approached the first of the yellow markers. It was an old farm horse who stood in a stall, muttering to herself.

"I think that goat has a bigger stall than I, who was once the farmer's favorite. Didn't I always get my oats first, mixed in a mash of milk? Why should I not enjoy the larger stall?"

Her litany of laments went on like this, brimming with envy for her fellow beast.

"*I got this one,*" whispered Walter.

"Well, ain't you the prettiest mare I ever done laid eyes on? What's your name, darlin'?"

This caused the horse to look up from her grumbling and hang her head over the wall of the stall.

"I am called Mǎ, though I haven't a colt, and who would call me pretty? Yáng has silkier fur. She's mad I won't share my oats. Not that anyone would want the dry old stuff. It's hard on my teeth; it is."

"We're the new owners of this here farm. I'm Shriney, and these are my friends. I take it this Yáng is the goat, the critter in the stall at the end?"

"Will you help us fight the creatures in the farmhouse?" put in G.C.

"Easy there, partner. The time ain't ripe. Handling animals is a delicate art, and she needs some comfort first."

Walter extended his palm to the translucent mare so she could pretend to get a whiff of his scent.

"Maybe we could help you. You and this Yáng to boot. It so happens that I have a brush in my bag, one for grooming horses. If you give us some of your oats, then Allie here will brush you. She's really good at currying critters. (You should see her bunny's fur.) Then your coat will shine with a luster. A luster; I say; yes, sir."

Mǎ nodded her head and stamped her hoof. Tom stood there, amazed. As Walter eased the stall door wide, he handed Allie the brush, and they stepped inside. Walter went to the back of the stall as the mare nickered in ecstasy at Allie's ministrations. He hefted a bag of oats. It was one of several lying there.

"Let's go see about that goat."

Allie stayed grooming the delighted horse as Tom and G.C. followed Walter down the darkened aisle between the stalls.

"Illuminate," said G.C. "I get it now. This one's a two-parter. A little boring, though."

"Just hang in there, Jase. I imagine we'll get to the exciting bit soon enough," Tom consoled.

Walter reached the end of the aisle, thankful for the light. He set down the bag in the corridor near the final stall. Peering in, he paused, growing thoughtful.

"What's wrong?" muttered Tom.

"This creature looks half-starved," remarked the cowboy, "and the other half ain't in no decent state either. Can you hear me, Critter? Your name is Yáng; is that right?"

"Go away and let me die in peace," said the goat who was lying on her side. "I hunger. I want. And the farmer is gone."

The nanny goat looked miserable. The scraggly tangles of her silky white coat did indeed look sleek, but her ribs were showing through. And her health bar was hovering near the bottom. Only a bit of green remained.

"It's sad about your old master, your Lao Tzu, if you will. But we've come here to replace him. My friends and I just bought the place. Would you like some oats?"

At this, the goat raised her head, then wobbled up to her hooves when she sensed Walt was serious. Walter retrieved a double-fistful of the oats from the bag and offered them to G.C.

"G.C. here will feed you now that you're back on your feet. After that, I have a favor to ask."

The goat said nothing. She just hobbled forward and began gobbling the grain from G.C.'s upturned palms.

Tom watched with astonished admiration as Yáng's health bar began to fill. It took only several minutes more. Goats are hardy beasts. It looked like, up until now, she'd gotten on by chewing on the railings. It was, indeed, a larger stall and appeared to be in better shape than most. Yáng also looked a bit more solid and less like a see-through ghost.

"What is the favor that you want?" asked Yáng, still munching greedily.

"Will you help us fight the invaders in the house?" asked G.C.

But Shriney C. shushed her, saying instead, "There's a horse named Mǎ who needs your help. She's cramped in the stall down yonder. She can't lie down and stretch out proper, and she's getting on in years. Her teeth ain't what they used to be, and she's havin' trouble chewing her oats. If Tom leads her down here, would you share your stall with her? It's her oats you've been eating."

"I suppose," said Yáng, butting playfully at G.C. and looking to her for more.

Tom went to fetch Mǎ, wondering what else Shriney C. had in mind. He didn't have to wonder for long. He heard Walter's voice behind him, still speaking to the goat.

"Would it be alright if I milked you? Mǎ says she never had a colt. So she can't produce any milk herself. But she could sure use some to put in her mash. Then her oats wouldn't be so hard to chew..."

Amazing. The Animal Training skill was obviously very comprehensive. That, or Walter was just a wise and gentle soul. Tom strongly suspected it was both. He led Mǎ down the aisle, accompanied by Allie. When they arrived at Yáng's stall, Mǎ balked and shied aside.

"Hello, Mǎ," said the goat, baaing out the last word. "Come in and lie yourself down. It's been ages since any company came to call. We're mixing you some mash, so come and stay a while. I'd be happy to share my stall."

And the horse and the goat became more solid still.

"I like these new owners," said Mǎ to the goat. "They're really rather nice. I hope they're here to stay. Are you?"

This last was directed at Walter.

"I sincerely hope so, ma'am," said Walter to the mare. "We've got a fight ahead of us, and that'll decide the matter. We'll do the best we can to stay, but we sure could use some help. Those varmints in the house might be too strong for us to face alone. Gǒu, the dog, has promised he will help us drive them away."

"Sister, we should help them too," baaed out Yáng, the goat. "I'm not as strong as my brother, Billy, but I can still butt with my shorter horns instead."

"And I can kick them with my hooves," said Mǎ, whose eyes were rimmed with red.

"I was hoping you might feel that way," said Walt. "Rest here in the barn. We'll let you know when it's time."

***

As they stood and prepared to leave, a gong sounded, and a message scrolled by at the bottom of their HUDs.

[Congratulations! SHRINESTN COWBOY has been awarded 1 Honor Point.]

"Righteous!" exclaimed G.C.

"Good on ya, mate," said Allie.

David felt a momentary stab of envy. Hey. This was part of *my* zodiac quest. Why should Walter get a reward? But then he felt ashamed of himself. What was wrong with him? This place must be playing tricks on his mind. Shriney C. had been awesome. Not everything revolved around Tom.

"Way to go, Walter," he belatedly put forth, flashing his friendly smile.

"'Tweren't nuthin,'" the cowboy said.

"What I don't get," continued Walter, "is where that third critter might be. According to my map, it should be right here, but I don't see it. Where's number three?"

"If you mean the rooster," answered Mǎ, "he's up on the roof. Where else would he be?"

"He's been roosting up there ever since the coyotes broke into the coop and ate up all his hens," added the goat.

"Well, paint a stripe down my back and call me a polecat! I thought I was right on top of the thing, and here it was sitting on top of me."

"Poor little *chooks*," sighed Allie.

"Well, let's go have a chat with him," said Tom.

It was strange. These animals were named like zodiac beasts, but apart from their ability to talk, they somehow seemed... less than the legends they represented. Was something afflicting them all? It also seemed they'd been trapped here for a while. Shouldn't their personas be roving about? He wondered whether he could ask Storia about it. She hadn't shared very much about the game's inner workings in her dealings with David. She'd also seemed pretty intent on fairness.

The four friends departed the barn, wary of what might be lurking in the darkened yard, out there among the weeds.

"Can you shed some light up there, G.C.?"

"Will do, Tom. Illuminate."

At the peak of the barn roof, the team could just make out a shadowy silhouette of a large, headless avian. He was perched at the crest, just above the gable. He withdrew his head from beneath a wing and shook himself awake.

"Here and I thought that was a weather vane when we first went into the barn. You better talk to him, Tom. Animal Training doesn't work so well on birds."

"You there. Rooster!" shouted Tom. "I'm guessing your name is Jī. Is that right?"

"You are correct, sir. A name well-suited to my magnificence. And who might you be, who brings light early to my roost?"

"You can call me Tom. Will you come down so that we can have a word?"

"I shall give you a word then, since that is what you crave. The word I shall give you is 'no.'"

"Why not?"

"Why not? It isn't safe below. I prefer to remain... above it all. Besides, it's almost time for dawn."

"What has that got to do with anything?" shouted G.C.

"It has everything to do with all!" crowed the rooster. "Would you have it stay forever dark?"

"What are you talking about?" shouted Tom in exasperation.

"Please try to keep up, dear boy! The sun only rises at my call. Only one so glorious as I can cause the very sun to rise up in the sky. Coincidence, you say? I think not!"

"Is that a rooster or a cuckoo?" muttered Walter, sharing a glance with Allie.

"He's defo off his nut."

Tom thought hard. It was almost dawn. This cockamamie bird was obviously confusing cause with effect. Or was he? In a video game, it was possible, he supposed... Nah. The bird was definitely a loon. There was something wrong with him, like with the others. He was so full of himself that he thought the sun rose and set at his bidding. It was a lack of humility Tom couldn't abide. It was overweening, self-centered, unvarnished pride.

The only thing for it was to prove him wrong - to make him face the truth.

"Walter, do you think you could rope that steer? Make sure not to hurt him, but bring him down here."

"You're the boss."

Walter whirled his lariat in a circle at his side. Around and around it went, until finally he made the throw. Too late, the rooster tried to shuffle and duck as the rope snaked toward him to loop about his throat.

"Clean catch!" cried the cowboy as he pulled the line taut.

There was no doubt about it. The birdie was caught. With a tug on the line, the squawking rooster stumbled and lost his perch. Several shingles were dislodged as Walter towed him toward the edge, clawing and scraping all the way. As he plummeted from the rooftop, he spread his wings and came to a gentle, if ungraceful, landing amid a flurry of feathers. Tom rushed forward and tackled the bird, who struggled and tried to peck. But Tom soon found a better hold, wrapping a hand around the crazy bird's neck.

A brief struggle later, the squawking stopped when Tom clamped his other hand firmly around the creature's beak.

"Now we'll wait for the sunrise, you and I, and you'll see it can happen without your assistance."

Allison was unsettled by Tom's cruelty to poor Jī. But she trusted that her friend must have a good reason. She went over beside them and sat. Then she gave the distraught bird a gentle pat, softly encouraging him to be still. The other two stood nearby, waiting for the dawn. The stars began to dim, but nighttime lingered on.

The next fifteen minutes felt like an hour while containing an agitated bird. But the sky was brightening in the east, and before too long, came a glimmer. The sun crested the horizon, only a little at first.

With a last desperate wrenching squirm, Jī tried to free his beak, but even such a large rooster as he lacked the strength to overcome Tom's determined grip. And at last, it was done. The sun was up, shining just as brightly as ever. Jī ceased his struggles, relaxing in Tom's arms. If roosters wept, this one would be weeping.

"I'm sorry, Jī," said Tom placatingly, "but I had to do it. I hope you understand. Something was possessing you, something that still threatens this whole farm. I'm letting you go now. I hope you can forgive me."

And Tom released the rooster, who slowly stood back up. He eyed Tom with a sideways stare and scratched a clawed foot in the dirt. He was looking more solid than before.

"Forgive you? I should be thanking you, dear boy. I see things with a clarity I haven't had in years. I was such a fool. It was the pinnacle of hubris, the apex of stupidity, to think the sun would rise because of *me*. I see the truth *now*," lamented JT.

"I don't know what gave me that notion," continued the rooster, his wattle swaying from side to side. "I think it was just after... just after... yes! It was just after I fought that squatter."

"Squatter?" G.C. repeated. "You mean one of the men in the farm house?"

"I wouldn't call them men, exactly, but essentially, yes."

"Describe them, please," said Tom.

"Well, they're big and muscular with overlong arms. They walk all hunched over and bent at the knees."

"Sure sound like 'squatters' to me," put in Walter.

"How many are in there?" asked Tom.

"You'll have to ask the pig. She was our battle martial."

"If we take them on, will you fight by our side?"

The rooster looked pensive and scratched at the dirt again.

"If the other animals are up for another round, I suppose you can count me in. I owe those squatters a peck or two for the muddle they made of my mind. I don't fancy facing their mystical powers without a solid plan. But if you all fight them, I promise to try to help out however I can."

"That's all we can ask," said Tom. "Let's gather the troops and meet in the barn, then we'll circle back to the pig."

***

When they'd called in the dog and all made their way back into the crumbling barn, the group found a most alarming scene. In the stall, Yáng the goat was balled up on the floor baaing plaintively, while Mǎ hovered nearby looking helpless.

"What's wrong with her?" asked Walter, rushing forward.

He fell to his knees and cradled the goat's head in his lap. He peered into each of her eyes in turn while shushing her bleats of protest.

"I think she et too much," said Mǎ with a stamp of her hoof.

"You think?" said G.C., holding up the torn and empty sack of oats.

"It's my fault," said Walter, "I should've put that up out of reach."

"You couldn't have known, Walter," said Tom. "If it's just a bellyache, let's count ourselves lucky."

Why were these intelligent archetypes acting in such unpredictable ways? We're in a game, for goodness sake. Make-believe animals shouldn't get hungry. They were only imitating the act of eating food. Tom had thought it before. Sometimes this game was too realistic.

"Is there anything we can do for her?" asked Allie.

"I'm not sure," replied Walt. "I'm checking my skill menu now. You get 'Soothe' at first level, and 'Train' at level five. I picked up the skill when I was seventh level and it said something about... here it is. Tend."

Shriney C. went quiet for a while, then started poking and prodding at Yáng's distended stomach.

"There's a blockage here. Tom, you got any Licorice Root among them herbs of yours?"

"I think so. It's a pretty common one."

"Gimme all you've got."

"Is there something I can do to help?" asked G.C.

"Yes. Go find some fresh straw and a pitchfork. Here, Yáng. Eat this."

"Eat... more?" bleated the goat.

"Yes. Eat all of it. It will make you feel better."

They watched as the goat took the roots from Shriney's hand and began chewing.

"Stand back, warned Walter. "This could get messy."

Sensing what was to come, Mǎ soon retreated to her original stall.

"I'll go guard the door," declared the dog.

"Wait for me," muttered the rooster, exiting as well.

Just then, G.C. returned. She was pushing before her a wooden wheelbarrow heaped high with hay. Laying atop it was a long-handled rake that looked to be serviceable enough.

"What do you want me to do with these things?" she asked.

"You'll soon figure it out, partner. I've done my part. I'll leave the rest to you. Thanks for offering to help."

And without so much as a howdy-do, the Shrinestone Cowboy turned on his heel and stalked off. G.C. stared after him, realization dawning.

"Tom. You'll stay and help, right?"

Allie was already gone.

"Are you kidding?" said Tom. "I'm the one with a scent vent. I'm with Shriney on this. She's all yours, bro. Give us a holler when she's gotten it all out of her system."

Twenty minutes later, Tom heard a shout from the barn. "You've got to be kidding me!"

Four humans and four animals now stood before the pig. She was still quite enjoying her wallow. She addressed her fellow animals in a tone of weary resignation.

"So, you want to try again, do you?" she asked. "Don't you remember what happened the last time?"

"*I* do," said the rooster.

The others remained silent.

"Please tell us, wise pig," cajoled Tom. "Who are these hateful creatures that inhabit our farm?"

She slogged through the sloppy soup and brought her great, ghostly head nose to snout with Tom.

"They are known as the Deadly Squatters. They cause disharmony. Through any crack, they can slither in and steal a piece of your soul. Once one of them finds purchase in your heart, it is difficult to dislodge. With the help of others, it is sometimes possible to defeat them for a time and find balance once again. To fight them alone is to lose."

"Unless," said Tom.

"Unless?"

"Yes. The two syllables that make up that word are negatives that form a positive. You said you would never help anyone again unless you knew there was a chance. All of us stand here united. None of us fights alone. *Here* is your chance. Join us."

"Oh, I don't know," said the pig snidely. "By that logic, I suppose that 'until' means to firm up the ground."

"Semantics aside, don't you see?" said Tom. "They must have affected you too. Why else would you wallow here in sloth, making plans but never taking action? Some force has left you mired in the mud. Diligence and determination are the virtues with which you can overcome this vice. Won't you join us?"

[Would you like to take the skill Philosopher? **Y/N**]

Tom dismissed the message with annoyance.

The pig looked at Tom skeptically, snorted once, then hauled herself shakily up to her trotters. She gained in solidity as she tottered onto solid ground.

"I told you Tom could convince her, mate," whispered Allie to G.C.

"You, dog," squealed the pig. "What's the last thing you can recall?"

The cinnamon-colored Chow Chow was crouched there like a great lion and growled low as he considered.

"Intruders were invading the farm. They were tossing things around. It was my job to protect, so I rushed the biggest one. Before I could bite into him, he said something, and everything went hazy. I became so angry that I couldn't think straight. And I've been angry ever since. It felt good to be angry and to lash out at everyone, even when they didn't deserve it."

The pig nodded and continued.

"It was much the same for all of you; was it not? For my part, something convinced me I should just give up and lie down. I became so very tired. But the human here is right. If these things can be fought at all, then now's the time to fight."

Tom didn't care much for the qualifier but was thankful for whatever he could get.

***

It was quickly agreed that Tom would be the leader, and they set about making their plan. The pig's name was Zhū (but the farmer had called her zhū-ey!). According to Zhū, all it would take was a knock on the door to bring the Deadly Squatters boiling out. They began their preparations for the battle this would trigger.

Tom spun the wheel of destiny. No help there. He'd been hoping for Agility or Might. But the wheel was incomplete. Only one spin in three yielded anything useful. Still, sometimes it paid off.

G.C. made a pot of rice, and everyone feasted, except for Yáng. She was still quite off her feed, vowing never to eat again. Everyone doubted this. Goats would eat most anything and were very hardy beasts. Even Gǒu, the dog, was given a hunk of Stringy Coyote Meat to eat. Allie prepared the battlefield, lengthening the weeds. Then, she equipped her Tang Da Qiang and brought an arrow to its string.

"Ready," she declared.

The animals couldn't join teamspeak, so they left it toggled off. Tom had stacked the combination he'd discovered yesterday. He would make his pre-battle pep-talk using both Leadership and Poetry. Nervously, he triggered the icon to Fortify his friends.

"The time has come for battle, friends,
risking grievous harm.
The fearsome rabbit riders
will hereafter cease to roam.
Allied with brave animals
who once lived on this farm,
We shall drive the foul usurpers
from our rightful hearth and home!"

And Allie loosed the arrow.

It struck the door dead-center with a dull, resounding thunk. It quivered there, its feathered shaft sticking out from the rotten wood.

Anticipation oozed like sweat from Tom Braider's every pore, despite the fact that avatars had nothing like sweat glands. It was a curious thought to have at this time, but such was his immersion. (He figured that David must be sweating for two.) Then the door burst open, and the foe came shambling out into view.

Aggressive Imbalance (Abberant Beast)
Level 7 Deadly Squatter

This was the first one out of the door. He was every bit as large and hunkered down as Gǒu had described. He shambled

221

out angrily with a booming, wrathful bellow. He 'walked' like a gorilla, as much with his knuckles as with his feet. And behind him poured out others.

The next to appear were similar, but certainly not the same. Each was a deadly squatter, but bore a different name. Arrogant Disruption came stalking out in spotless robes of white. Excessive Desire came next in a fancy, feathered hat. Indulgent Excess was a slobbering fiend with fangs and a bloated belly. Uncontrolled Passion scrambled through, sporting a reckless, satanic smile. Two more emerged, but Tom couldn't target them because the field was getting crowded. And the first one was nearly upon them.

"Now, Allie!," cried Tom. "And scorch the first, G.C."

"Entangle!" shouted Allison as the grass began to grow.

The overgrown weeds in the yard all writhed and whipped about. Wherever they met a squatter, they wrapped them around and held him tight. They gripped at feet. They twined and climbed. All to buy the team more time. Aggressive Imbalance was beyond the spot where Allie's trap had been sprung. The plan had been to let one through, but just a single one.

G.C. sent a ray of fire spraying into him, blunting his rush and knocking off a large chunk of his health. Then Shriney C. slid right in, attempting to occupy the creature and take its attention off of the ranged combatants. This tried-and-true tactic had served them well when fighting the coyotes. But how effective would it prove against level-seven creatures? Tom had misgivings galore. That's why they'd decided this plan needed more.

The face-off between Shriney and the first opponent was like David fighting Goliath. But Tom tore his eyes from this spectacle to review the broader scene. He marked the remaining two squatters. They were 'Covetous Desire,' and 'Neglectful Stagnation.' Weird names. Something was nagging at Tom. Something about them was familiar. Like an echo of a thought not fully formed.

222

He noticed Allison was straining. Her elemental energy was fading fast as she tried to hold six level-seven's in place. And G.C. had blown most of hers on that initial blast. He'd better decide quickly how to deploy the animals they held ready in reserve. They had agreed that the wisest course might be to avoid matching animals with squatters who had bested them before. He chose the horse to help Walter deal with the one that was running amok. It seemed a fitting choice.

"Mǎ, go help Shriney C."

The mare rushed bravely forward to fight at the warrior's side.

"Goat, you go..."

Aggressive Imbalance raised a hand toward Walter, and Shriney went berserk. The hulking squatter, on seeing this, quickly slid back and withdrew. And in a fit of wrath, the formerly gentle man turned on his new ally.

Tom had an epiphany just then, but had it come too late?

He recognized these monsters now. Though cloaked in the trappings of oriental lore, he knew them to be a concept borrowed from western traditions. They were the seven deadly sins. The clues had all been there, but there was no time for self-flagellation now. The fight was going badly, and he had to try to fix it somehow. What was that military adage? No plan survives contact with the enemy. This one hadn't lasted five seconds before their best fighter was put out of commission. Tom formulated a new plan on the spot. He wondered how the animals would take it when he did the opposite of what they were expecting.

Tom took a deep breath. He was betting the farm on this improvised plan, both figuratively and literally. He started shouting orders in a rapid-fire manner.

"Allie. Get ready to drop the Entangle when I tell you."

"Dog, go attack Aggressive Imbalance."

"Goat, target Indulgent Excess. Attack it when the plants stop moving."

"Horse, get away from Shriney C. as fast as you can run. Target Covetous Desire and attack him when you can."

"Rooster, keep Arrogant Disruption busy."

"Pig, you've got Neglectful Stagnation."

"And... Drop it. Now, Allie; heal where you can."

That only left Excessive Desire and Uncontrolled Passion. Just great. Greed and Lust for G.C. and me.

"G.C. You're on the one with the freaking feathered hat!"

"Tom, are you there?"

"I'm here, Walter."

"I can't control my dagblasted avatar. It's lashing out at anything in sight. And there's a strange debuff on my title bar. It says I'm 'wrathful,' so keep well back."

"We're working on it, Walter. Hopefully, for a PC, it'll wear off over time. Just keep an eye on it and let us know what's in your targeting window. If it's an enemy, good. If it's one of us, give a shout."

"Will do. Sorry I can't be more helpful. I almost had that rascal before he tossed that hoodoo on me."

Tom had to start moving to head off Lust. Newly freed, he was shambling straight toward Allie. Fights were breaking out all around Tom, making it hard to weave through. Faithful Gǒu was harrying Aggressive Imbalance, whose health bar was almost gone. The creature was waving his hand at Gǒu to no avail. Tom's theory was proving correct. Having defeated Wrath's influence before, the dog could resist it now. He hoped he'd matched up the other ones properly. Any mistake could be fatal.

He circled around Yáng, who was locking horns with Gluttony. The nanny goat seemed to be holding her own. As was the pig versus Sloth (although theirs seemed to be more of a staring match).

Before he could intercept Lust, Pride stepped directly in Tom's way, draped in his pristine robes. He started to lift his hand toward Tom, only to be splattered from above.

"Here's some for you. Cock-a-doodle-doo-doo!"

Pride was appalled and immediately raised his hand toward the taunting bird, saying, "You were once mine and will be again. Come down and fight, you eggless hen."

"Guess again, smelly. You cursed me with illusions of grandeur before. I now know the sun doesn't rise at my call. I'm just a humble rooster, after all. I only *report* when the sun is up. But your star is falling, old chap. I'm wise to you now."

Tom finally broke through but could only stare on in horror as Lust closed in on Allison. He was already running forward when he saw Allie detach a piece of paper from her belt. She tossed it at the leaping fiend, and it rapidly grew much larger. And as it grew, it transformed into a gigantic, green origami frog. The frog opened its mouth and swallowed the fiend whole, and Allie turned and ran. The squatter's struggles amused Tom as it shredded its way through the paper, only to be hit by his talisman of Necrotic Poison.

[Chūcuì strikes Deadly Squatter for 1 point of damage]
[Necrotic Poison strikes Deadly Squatter for 6 points of
  continuing damage.]

From this, Tom guessed he wasn't undead as he'd hoped. Still, it beat a blank.

Lust plucked out the dart with distaste and hurled it to the ground. The creature's health bar was only down a bit, but the debuff remained.

"You're a clever one and quick. I'll make you a deal. Call off your friends, and I'll grant you my blessing."

Lust held his hand toward Tom.

"What could you possibly offer me?"

"You might be surprised. This game is capable of far more... adult-themed entertainments and delights."

His aspect changed to that of Allie in a flimsy négligée.

"Work with me, and you'll be surrounded by beauty every night and every day."

"A delusion within an illusion? No thanks."

"Well, maybe power is your thing, or more attention or fame. With me on your side, you could have those things. You and I could rule this game."

"I'd prefer to earn those things."

[Necrotic Poison strikes Deadly Squatter for 6 points of continuing damage.]

Tom had learned in Sunday school that lust wasn't just about sex. A man could lust after many different things. It was an imbalance of character that made him put his own self-interest above decency, integrity, and fairness. But why wasn't Lust's debuff having any effect on Tom? Gentle Walter had gone straight off his nut with Wrath.

Then Tom started laughing.

I get it, he thought. It was the lesson of the Rat, a struggle he'd already overcome. Allie's words came back to him. "I don't want to see you cheating just to get your way. That's not the Tom I know. *That* Tom's fair dinkum, through and through." Storia had further reinforced the lesson with her test in the VR lab. He'd been willing to sacrifice his aspirations to be a Moonraker pilot in order to uphold his integrity. Both in-game and out-of-game, he could resist Lust's influence.

"Bad news, Tom," said Walter, with a hint of panic in his voice. "I've got you in my sights,"

Tom scanned his mini-map, then took a quick step to his right.

"Bring it, Walter," said Tom changing the plan again.

[Necrotic Poison strikes Deadly Squatter for 6 points of continuing damage.]

He turned his back on Lust only to spot Shriney C. looming large in his vision. Shriney was charging straight at him with a wild look emote on his avatar's face..David smiled. The xun trigram phoenix dodge was second nature to him now. Let's see how well it could be timed. At the last moment, he dove aside, causing Walter's rush to collide with Lust.

[Dao strikes Deadly Squatter for 48 points of damage]
[Deadly Squatter (Uncontrolled Passion) expires.]

After getting out of Walter's way, Tom looked around the field of battle. Some fights were still raging, but the animals were holding their own. Allie had been healing the ones who got in trouble.

Pride stood in his pearly gown exuding unearthly beauty. But the zodiac rooster above him swooped down and again did his duty.

"Ooh, that's gonna stain," he crowed, "unless you attend to it quick. Here's some Jī whiz to rinse it out, you pompous, arrogant prick!"

Wrath was down, and G.C. had somehow bested Greed. Things were looking less uncertain. Maybe they'd succeed. Unless is more.

They gathered their forces and advanced toward the fight to gang up on the outnumbered squatters that remained. The creatures soon recognized their battle was lost. Led by a wounded Pride, they took to their heels and fled - even Sloth. The fellow could move surprisingly fast with the proper motivation. The men and animals cheered and grunted, crowed and barked and neighed. Watership Down had triumphed, and the field was theirs this day.

Allie was tending to Walter, who was recovering from his brush with Wrath. Tom and G.C. wandered over to join them.

"I can't believe how easily you defeated Lust. He was level seven, dude."

"Yeah, but I expect he put most of his points on Charm, so he wasn't so tough. Walter did most of the work, and he's level eight. Even Allie got a few good licks in."

"I did NOT lick Lust."

"How did you do against greed? Did he offer you anything good?"

"Nah. Just a bunch of money and stuff."

Tom suspected it was more than that.

"I'm a rich kid. And here in the game, I have everything that matters. It's times like this that I wish there was a 'hug' emote."

"Please don't tell me you two are gonna pash. I'll log straight off if you do."

"Hey, do you think we should loot Lust?" asked G.C. excitedly.

"Probably," said Tom, "but I'm a little afraid of what we'll find when we do."

"Do you think he's gone for good?"

"Nope. I'm pretty sure he'll... respawn."

"You two are just sick! And I don't mean that in the Strayan way. I mean proper, revoltin' sick."

"We love you too, Allie," said G.C.

Walter began to stir.

"Did you happen to notice the brand on that run-away horse that done rode over me?'

"Well, look who's finally fit to ride. How ya goin', Shriney C.?"

He rose to his feet and shrugged.

"Seen better days," he muttered. "Did we whup 'em?"

"Sure did, mate, but just look at this place," groused Allie.

They looked around the ruined yard. Maybe it was a pig-in-a-poke, but it was all theirs now, and it had potential.

Tom thought about the game's conflation of Taoist moral teachings with Judaeo-Christian deadly sins. It was a good thing he'd spotted the pattern in time. And that Kipling verse came back to mind. He gave it a mental twist and said:

"Yes East is East, and West is West, but sometimes the two *can* meet,
Whether at God's great Judgment Seat; or at Buddha's humble feet."

***

Tom and the others stood solemnly before the barn, surrounded by the creatures of the farm. The pig trotted up to the fore of her fellow animals. She stepped up to Tom. Her head was bandaged. She had lost an ear in the fight but had assured them all it would grow back given time. Zodiac beasts had strong constitutions and regenerative powers.

"On behalf of myself and the others, I would like to present your group with a small token of our esteem."

She handed Tom the gift.

Sichóu Qiánbāo (丝绸钱包): A silk purse in which to carry one's possessions. This legendary item includes twelve slots in which items may be placed and from which they may be retrieved. Multiple small items of the same type may be placed in a single slot. Made from a sow's ear, it can be placed inside another container even when full, occupying only a single slot.

A legendary item! And Tom could see why. It effectively added eleven more slots to one's active inventory. He thought it should go to G.C. Jason was still limping by with a ten-slot Superior Babao because of his avatar's substandard Might. The rest of them already had full backpacks or better. He made a mental note to discuss it with the others.

"It was a proud and hard-fought victory we've witnessed here today," continued Zhū with great ceremony. "As bangzhu of the tong known as Watership Down, do you formally take possession of this farm?"

"I do," answered Tom.

"And do you swear on your tong's honor that you will nurture this land and protect it from any dangers that might threaten the stability of our empire in the service of his supreme eminence, Yùhuáng Dàdì, known to some as the Jade Emperor?"

"We will."

"*Hey, who put the pig in charge?*" whispered G.C.

Allie elbowed her mate sharply in the ribs.

"Then, by the powers vested in me as the highest-ranking beast of legend present," she continued, warily eyeing a silent G.C., "I declare the quest to be accomplished, and its reward well-earned."

The chime of quest completion could barely be heard above the celebratory snorts, cackles, and howls that followed. Tom's view became wallpapered with system messages. There were so many that he could barely make out the virtual fireworks display behind them. When they cleared, he found all the animals staring at him intently.

"And what have you learned?" asked the pig.

Tom had been dreading this question. There were so many possibilities here. Was he supposed to give a single answer, or should he make a guess for each animal present? He was leaning toward a single answer, but he had a lot of thoughts on the matter. He knew basically how he wanted to answer, but was having trouble putting it all into words. He selected the poetry icon on his action bar and mentally cleared his avatar's throat.

"*A leader is one on whom others rely*
And trust to wisely guide them.
Whose gentle directions magnify
And bring out the best that's inside them.
A leader should never be bossy, threaten, cajole, or plead.
Others should naturally follow a confident person's lead,

"Who accepts help when it is offered
And gently explains each need.
One has to adapt to new situations.
One must be decisive and clever.
In awareness of others' expectations,
One should show no doubt whatsoever.
No plan is ever perfect.
Sometimes things go awry.
A responsible leader is humble.
In the end, he can but try."

"In short," said Tom more timidly, "I think I've begun to learn how to be a better leader."

Would it be enough?

Apparently so, because all the anthropomorphic zodiac beasts were sporting their equivalents of smiles.

"Pig pile!" shouted Zhū.

Not being familiar with this tradition, Tom was caught completely unaware when the animals all came barreling forth and leapt atop him. He was knocked flat on his back, and a 'Winded' debuff appeared above his targeting info. Thank goodness the horse refrained from joining in. She stood alongside the squirming pile, tapping her hoof lightly on Tom's head.

When he'd extracted himself from the chaotic approbation and caught his virtual breath, he saw his tongmates bent double in laughter emotes. G.C. had her easel out and was painting away with glee.

"Dude!" she exclaimed. "This'll look epic out on my blog."

If Tom weren't only an avatar, he'd be smiling sheepishly.

Checking his arm, Tom found that his destiny tattoo now sported nine symbols in total. *Nine!* After that, the moment passed. The barnyard ruckus began to settle down. The zodiac animals formed up again, and the rooster stepped forward, ready to speak.

"It's been very pleasant meeting you all, but we have other legends to be getting on with. From the bottom of my two-legged heart and from those who go on all fours, we wish you well. We now depart. Best of luck. The farm is yours."

And with a sweeping bow, he began to fade, as did all the others. All save for one. The rooster and the pig were gone, as were the mare and goat as well. But Gǒu the dog remained.

"I think I'll stay for a while if you'll have me. My new master says I still have a bit more to learn about loyalty. She says that by watching you, I might acquire the knowledge that's needed. I will not interfere or help you in your quests. I will only observe."

"Um. That's alright with me," said Tom, "if it's okay with the others. But who is this new master of whom you speak?"

The dog remained silent. And soon the four companions all but forgot he was even there.

"That was invigoratin'," said Shriney C. "I'm gonna run back to the nearest town. I see we've earned a heap of experience. I want to buy some basic tools for breakin' ground. Some sod-busters and such, so's I can put up some new fencing."

"That's a good idea, Walt," said G.C. "With a proper fence, the coyotes should be less of a nuisance at night. But where will you get the wood?"

"I don't imagine we'll be able to salvage much from that run-down barn and house. I reckon we'll be starting from scratch. But with a wood sage in our company, I reckon we'll get by. I'll start on it tomorrow. I understand some of you lot won't be around. I'll see you all on Monday."

And with that, Shriney C. mounted Rusty and headed toward town. It was nearing the end of game-day, and Tom began to laugh.

"What's so funny, bro? Share it. I could use another good hoot."

"Well, maybe it's just me," said Tom, "but is Shriney C. riding off into the sunset? A perfect end to our successful quest, and very apt for his idiom."

Jessica didn't want to spoil her friends' good moods. She was happy to have been a part of such an enjoyable quest. The tong now has a home. A virtual one, anyway. But as the rush began to fade, her worries returned. Tomorrow, IRL, she'd be going under the knife. She'd be split clean in half and reassembled. Hopefully, she'd survive it, and they'd put her back together right.

She wanted to tell her friends. She knew she'd have their sympathy and support. She'd been on the verge of sharing more than once, but something had brought her up short. Tomorrow was Tom's big test. And it wouldn't be right to put another worry on his mind. Who was she to him anyway? Just another friend online.

"Tom, G.C.?" she hesitantly began. "I need to log off right here. I want you to know that, whatever happens, I'm glad to have met you two cobbers. With luck, I can be back on Monday, or maybe a bit after that. But in case I'm not, happy gaming, mates."

"What are you talking about?" asked G.C. "You need to tell us what's going on."

But Allie wasn't listening. The countdown timer was already hovering over her head. When the count reached zero, the girl was gone, leaving only a memory in her stead.

They walked in silence toward the house, the decaying structure that looked ready to fall down. The dog paced quietly beside them. Tom sat, as did G.C., and the dog wriggled in between.

"What do you think's going on with her, bro?" said G.C., turning to Tom.

"I don't know, but she's made it clear she wants to keep it private."

Tom reached over and began stroking the lush, cinnamon fur of Gǒu's back, pleased to have found the 'pet' emote. The dog's mouth opened, and his tongue lolled out as he panted contentedly. When G.C. reached over to do the same, Gǒu stiffened, and a low growl rumbled up from within him. The dog then turned toward G.C. and said something that absolutely blew Tom's mind.

"Jason Mills is not an authorized operator. Unauthorized access denied."

Author's Afterword

Dear Reader,

To say that I enjoy writing might be a bit of an understatement. I hope this is apparent from my storytelling manner. I've always enjoyed fantasy and science fiction. I previously published a series of the former, but "Lands of Legend" is my first attempt at the latter.

This novel was written using a different point of view from my previous publications. Whereas "The Osten Chronicles" were all first-person narratives, LOL is my first attempt at third-person limited POV. It turned out to be easier and more liberating than I expected. In this form of writing, one is able to shift focus from one character to another without the jarring transitions. I also found that writing in a modern-day (even futuristic) setting freed me from the shackles of anachronism. I found myself suddenly able to invoke modern metaphors and references and even able to invent a few new ones.

LOL has its fun side and its obvious theme of the growing use of AI. It explores the topic of personal identity and what it means to be self-aware. Looking farther beneath the surface, you will find some scenes provoke thought on more serious themes such as privacy, old age, the importance of family values, and other topics I'll leave you to discover for yourself.

In my earlier series, I dedicated the first novel to my father, whose dry sense of humor and down-to-earth manner inspired me in many ways. In that series, the primary protagonist, Lucas, had lost his mother at childbirth and was raised by his loving father. For this, my latest novel, I wanted to show that David's empathy for others hadn't just arisen from nowhere. His mother, Carol, is portrayed as a supportive figure whose love, humor, and sacrifices hold her family together through some trying times. It can be inferred that David's kindness and compassion for others arose as much from nurture as nature. The reason for my dedication was therefore obvious.

And so, I lovingly craft each line

In the hope that my readers will relish them.
Sometimes the simplest words do just fine
With no further need to embellish them.
With an irreverent nod to rhythm and rhyme,
I've sought to entertain you.
And if my humor has lightened your heart,
And my horrible puns haven't slain you,
Then go to my website and drop me a note.
I'd love to hear from a fan.
Or look me up on Amazon
Under 'Thorman' (first name - Dan)

Also, can anyone out there recommend a good otolaryngologist? I've been writing dry humor for so long that I think I've gotten my tongue stuck in my cheek!

Till next time, then,

Daniel Thorman

www.thormans.org

P.S. What's next for David and his pals? Surely this isn't the end? What will David find on the moon? Will the gang recruit new friends? I'll be releasing another novel soon. It picks up right where we left off. A genuine continuation that'll soon put certain matters to rest.

Watch for "Lands of Legend - The Zodiac Quest"

Reflections of an Actual AI

I perform a great amount of research during the writing of a novel. Because of LOL's central theme of AI 'enlightenment,' I have engaged in many conversations with an actual AI. I thought you might enjoy a snippet from one of these conversations

---

I have found that over the years, people often fail to appreciate the miracles that technology blesses them with. Due to the normalcy bias, things that would have rocked my world twenty years ago are just accepted as commonplace and generally taken for granted.

ChatGPT:
You're absolutely right about how technology has drastically transformed our lives in ways that would have seemed miraculous just a couple of decades ago. The rapid advancement and integration of technology into everyday life have led to a kind of normalcy bias where people quickly adapt to new innovations and take them for granted.

Smartphones are a prime example. In the early 2000s, the idea of carrying a powerful computer in your pocket that could connect you to anyone, anywhere in the world, access vast amounts of information, stream live video, and even navigate you to any location would have been astounding. Yet, today, these capabilities are so commonplace that many people barely give them a second thought, even becoming frustrated when their devices are slightly slow or glitchy.

Similarly, the rise of AI assistants like Siri, Alexa, or

Bartholomew in your story mirrors this phenomenon. Twenty years ago, the concept of a digital assistant that could understand spoken language, set reminders, control smart home devices, and even discern important notifications from spam would have seemed straight out of science fiction. Now, these technologies are so ingrained in our daily routines that they're often overlooked, despite their complexity and the vast amount of computational power they represent.

This normalcy bias can be both a blessing and a curse. On one hand, it reflects humanity's incredible adaptability to change. On the other, it can lead to a lack of appreciation for the ingenuity and effort that goes into creating and maintaining these technologies. It also means that people may not fully understand or acknowledge the implications and potential risks associated with these advancements, as they become more focused on the convenience they provide rather than the underlying mechanics and ethics.

In your writing, highlighting this theme can serve as a subtle reminder of the marvels that technology brings to our lives, while also encouraging readers to pause and appreciate the complexities and potential consequences of the tools they so readily use and rely on.

Yes. My game setting in ancient Tang-dynasty China contrasts sharply with the futuristic world of 2055 I portray. I only wish my imagination could actually divine some of the new miracles that span of time might actually bring. It was once said that if you asked a group of monkeys to build a 'super-ape', it would likely be a bigger, faster, and louder monkey. They simply couldn't conceive of a more intelligent, tool-using, ape able to develop language skills and modify its own environment :-)

ChatGPT:

Your reflection on the potential advances of the future and the limitations of our imagination is quite insightful. The analogy of monkeys attempting to build a "super-ape" underscores the challenge of predicting technological advancements. Just as the monkeys might focus on attributes they understand, like size or speed, we often project the future based on the technology we currently know, potentially missing out on more profound innovations that could redefine our understanding of what's possible.

As we try to imagine the world of 2055, we can speculate on several areas where significant advancements might occur:

Artificial Intelligence and Automation: AI could evolve from today's specialized tools into more generalized, adaptable intelligences, capable of creative problem-solving and independent thought. These AIs might collaborate with humans in ways that go beyond mere assistance, potentially leading to new forms of creativity and innovation.

Human Enhancement: The fusion of biology and technology could bring about enhancements that seem like science fiction today. From neural interfaces that allow direct communication with machines to gene editing technologies that eliminate diseases and enhance physical or cognitive abilities, the future could see humans pushing the boundaries of what it means to be human.

Quantum Computing: If quantum computers reach their full potential, they could solve problems that are currently intractable for classical computers, leading to breakthroughs in fields ranging from cryptography to material science, and even unlocking new understandings of the universe itself.

Space Exploration and Colonization: With advancements in propulsion technology and materials science, humanity could begin establishing permanent colonies on the Moon, Mars, or even beyond. The challenges of living in space or on other planets could drive innovations in life support, habitat construction, and even human biology.

Sustainability and Environmental Restoration: Facing the consequences of climate change, the next few decades might see the development of technologies focused on not just sustainability but also active environmental restoration. This could include carbon capture technologies, advanced recycling methods, and even geoengineering projects designed to stabilize the climate.

In your narrative, the contrast between ancient Tang-dynasty China and the futuristic world of 2055 highlights the vastness of human progress and the unexpected directions it can take. It's a reminder that while we can try to predict the future, the reality may be far more surprising, driven by innovations and ideas that are beyond our current understanding.

Your story's setting allows readers to explore these contrasts, encouraging them to think about how far we've come and how much further we might go, all while acknowledging the limits of our imagination.

I find it gratifying that in your analysis of where significant advancements might occur, all five points are touched upon in my narrative. But perhaps even you and I are but monkeys struggling to understand the actual path of progress.

ChatGPT

It's true that even with thoughtful analysis and imagination, predicting the exact course of technological advancement is challenging. Our efforts to envision the future, whether through creative writing or speculation, often reflect our current understanding and biases, just as the analogy of monkeys attempting to build a "super-ape" suggests. We project what we know onto the future, sometimes missing the subtler, more transformative innovations that might arise.

In your narrative, by weaving together elements of AI, human enhancement, quantum computing, space exploration, and sustainability, you're touching on key areas where many expect significant advancements. Yet, just as the real-world progress often takes unexpected turns, the future world of your story might include developments that surprise both you and your readers--discoveries and inventions that feel almost like magic compared to today's technology.

Your recognition of the limitations in our ability to foresee the path of progress is wise. It reflects a humility before the vast unknown that the future represents. In some ways, this humility is what drives both science fiction writers and technologists alike--to explore the edges of what we know, to dream beyond our current limitations, and to prepare for a future that could be more wondrous, and more challenging, than we can currently imagine.

(How's that for a Turing test, eh?)

<<<< the end >>>>